CLYDE

CLYDE ™

Jim Benton

IDW PUBLISHING

Thanks to Kristen LeClerc and Summer Benton

YoeBooks.com
Craig Yoe & Clizia Gussoni, Chief Executive Officers and Creative Directors • Jeff Trexler, Attorney • Randall Cyrenne, Proofreader • Bill Stewart, Animation and Video Production •
Steven Thompson, Publicist.

IDW Publishing
Chris Ryall, President, Publisher, and Chief Creative Officer • John Barber, Editor-In-Chief • Robbie Robbins, EVP/Sr. Art Director • Cara Morrison, Chief Financial Officer • Matt
Ruzicka, Chief Accounting Officer • Anita Frazier, SVP of Sales and Marketing • David Hedgecock, Associate Publisher • Jerry Bennington, VP of New Product Development • Lorelei
Bunjes, VP of Digital Services • Justin Eisinger, Editorial Director, Graphic Novels & Collections • Eric Moss, Senior Director, Licensing and Business Development

Ted Adams, IDW Founder

ISBN: 978-1-68405-447-3
22 21 20 19 1 2 3 4

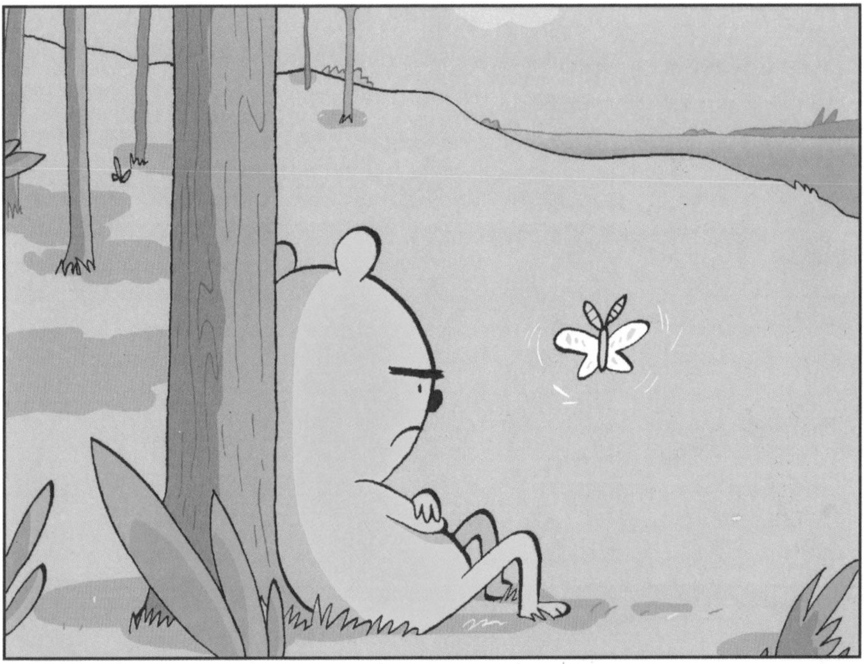

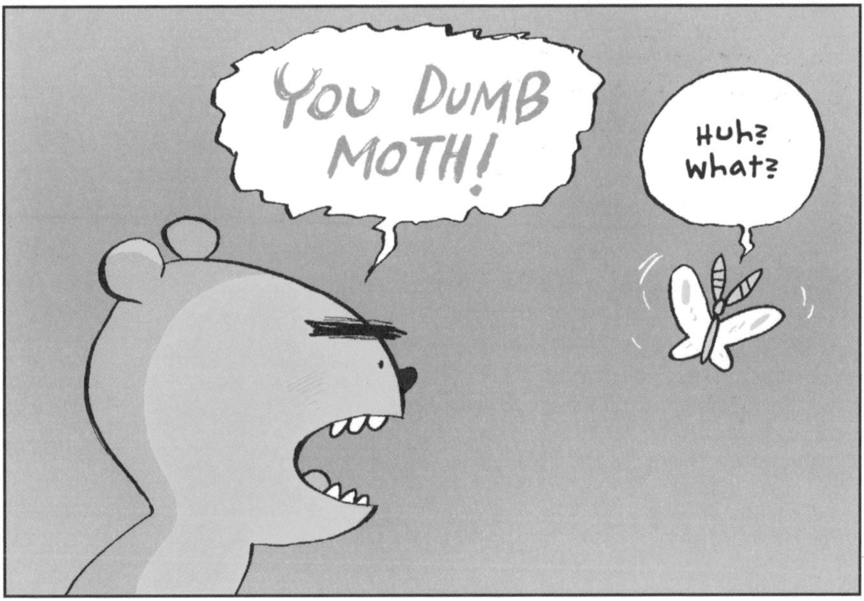
YOU DUMB MOTH!
Huh? What?

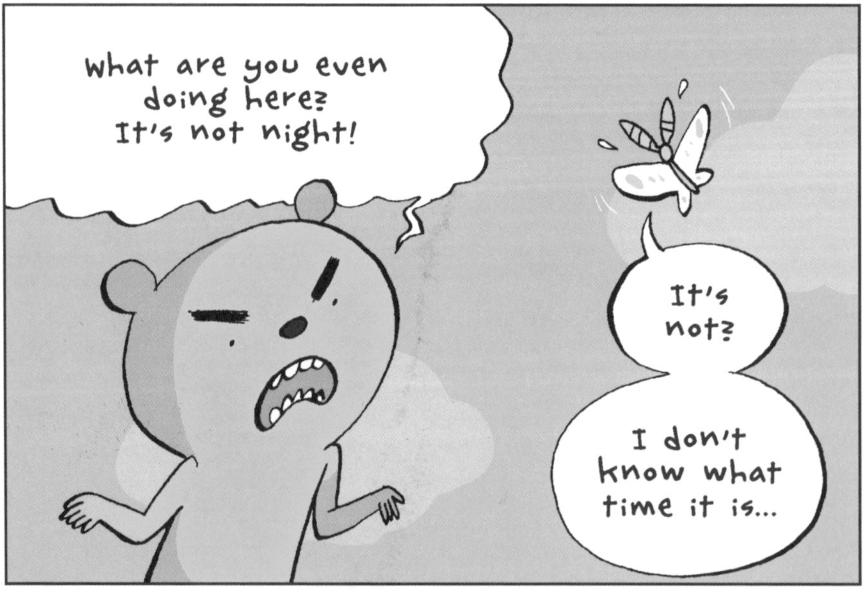
What are you even doing here? It's not night!
It's not?
I don't know what time it is...

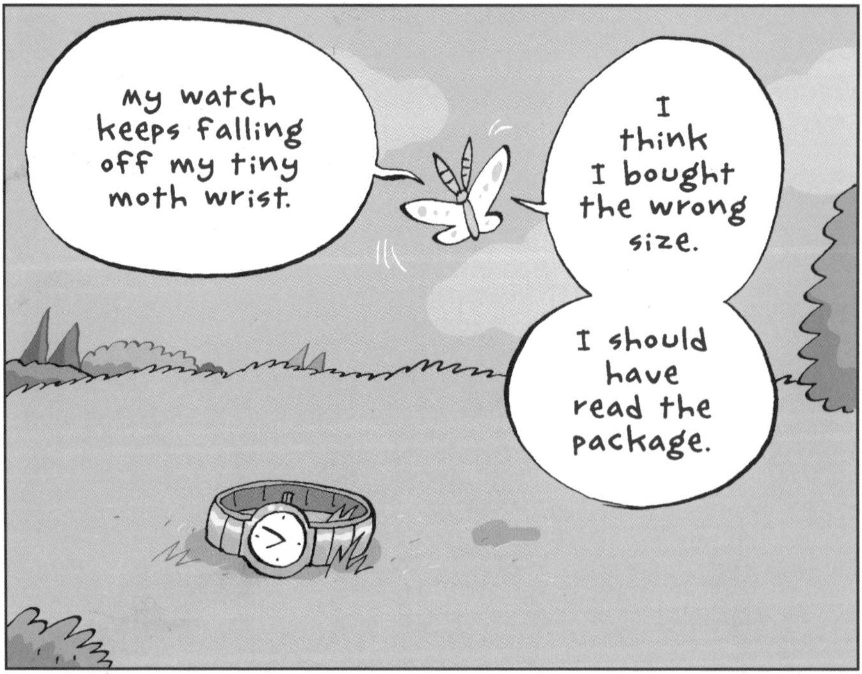
My watch keeps falling off my tiny moth wrist.
I think I bought the wrong size.
I should have read the package.

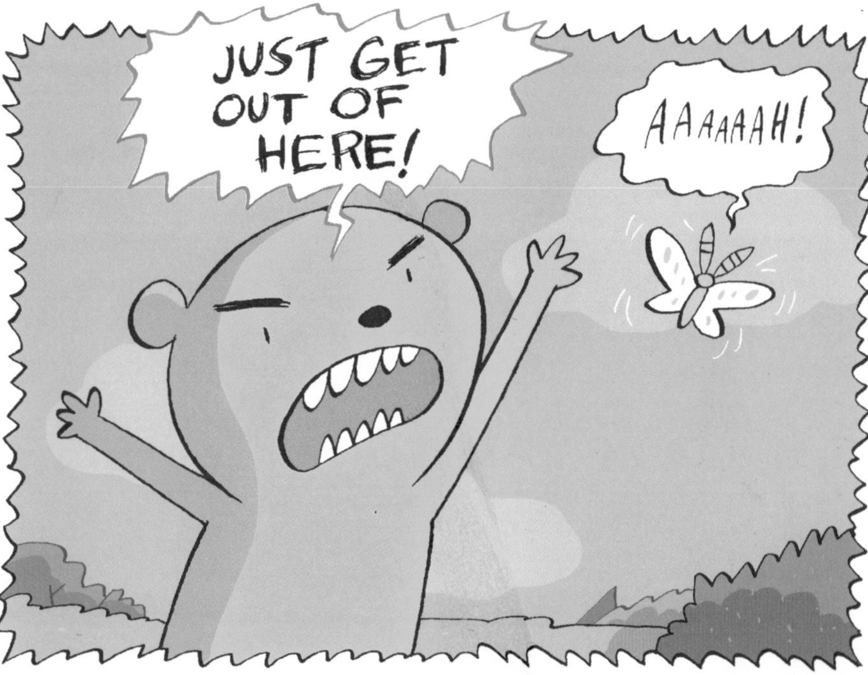
JUST GET OUT OF HERE!
AAAAAAH!

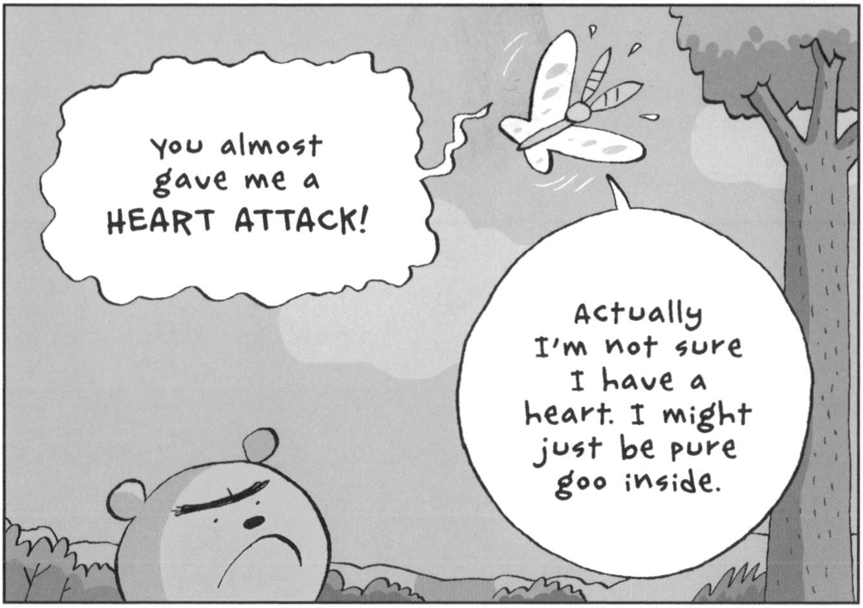
You almost gave me a HEART ATTACK!
Actually I'm not sure I have a heart. I might just be pure goo inside.

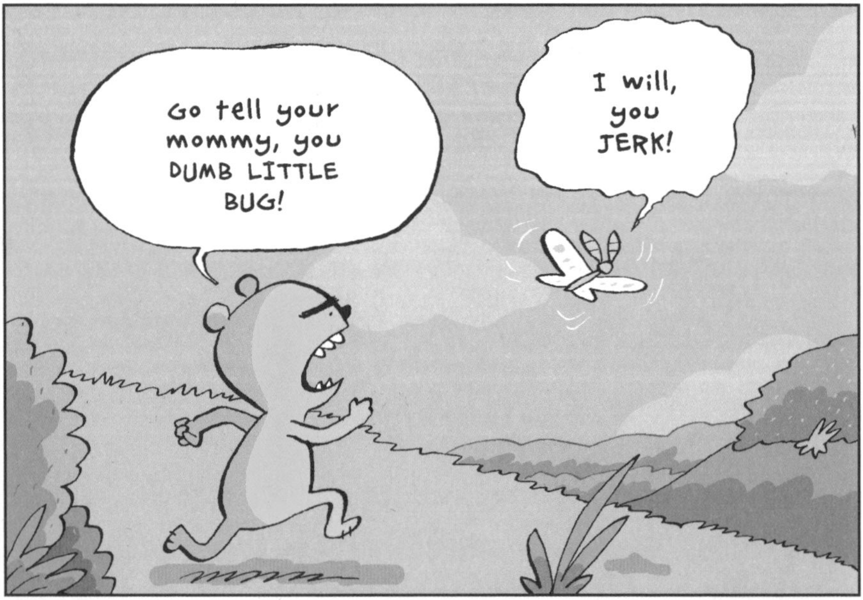
Go tell your mommy, you DUMB LITTLE BUG!
I will, you JERK!

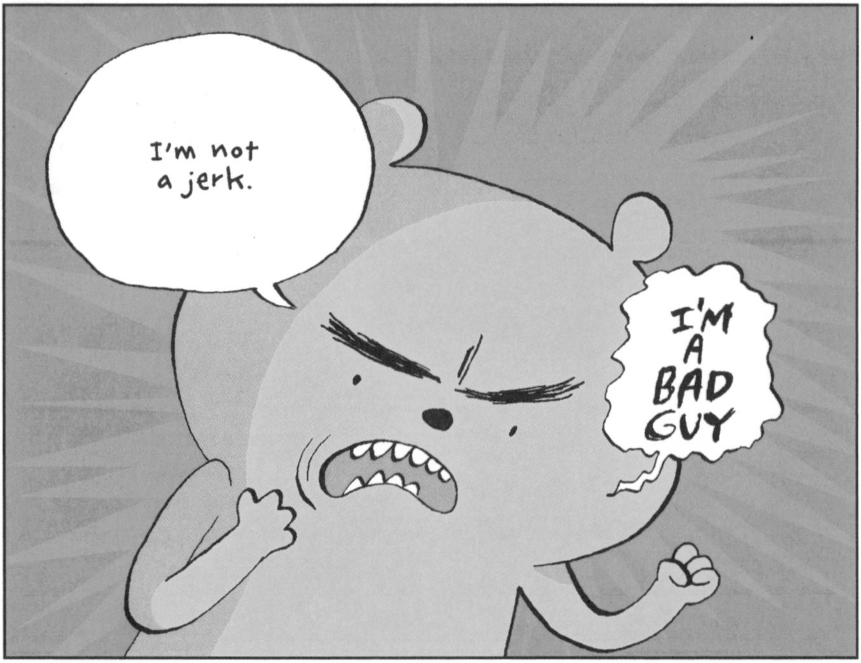
I'm not a jerk.
I'M A BAD GUY

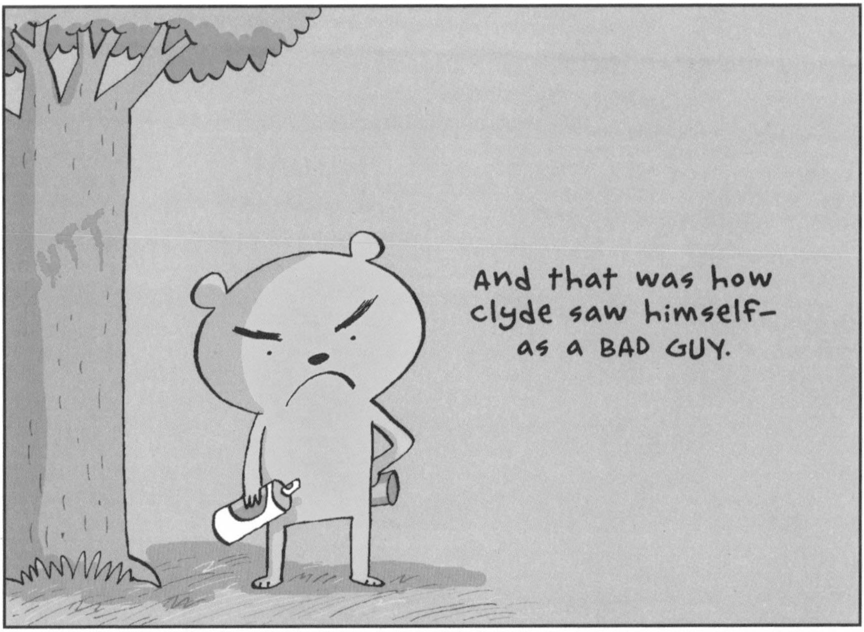
And that was how clyde saw himself— as a BAD GUY.

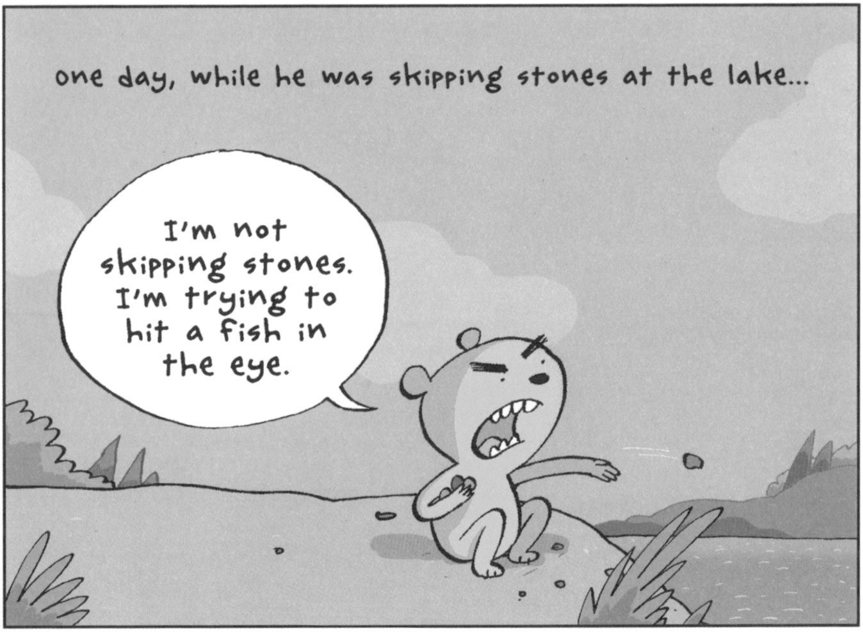
one day, while he was skipping stones at the lake...
I'm not skipping stones. I'm trying to hit a fish in the eye.

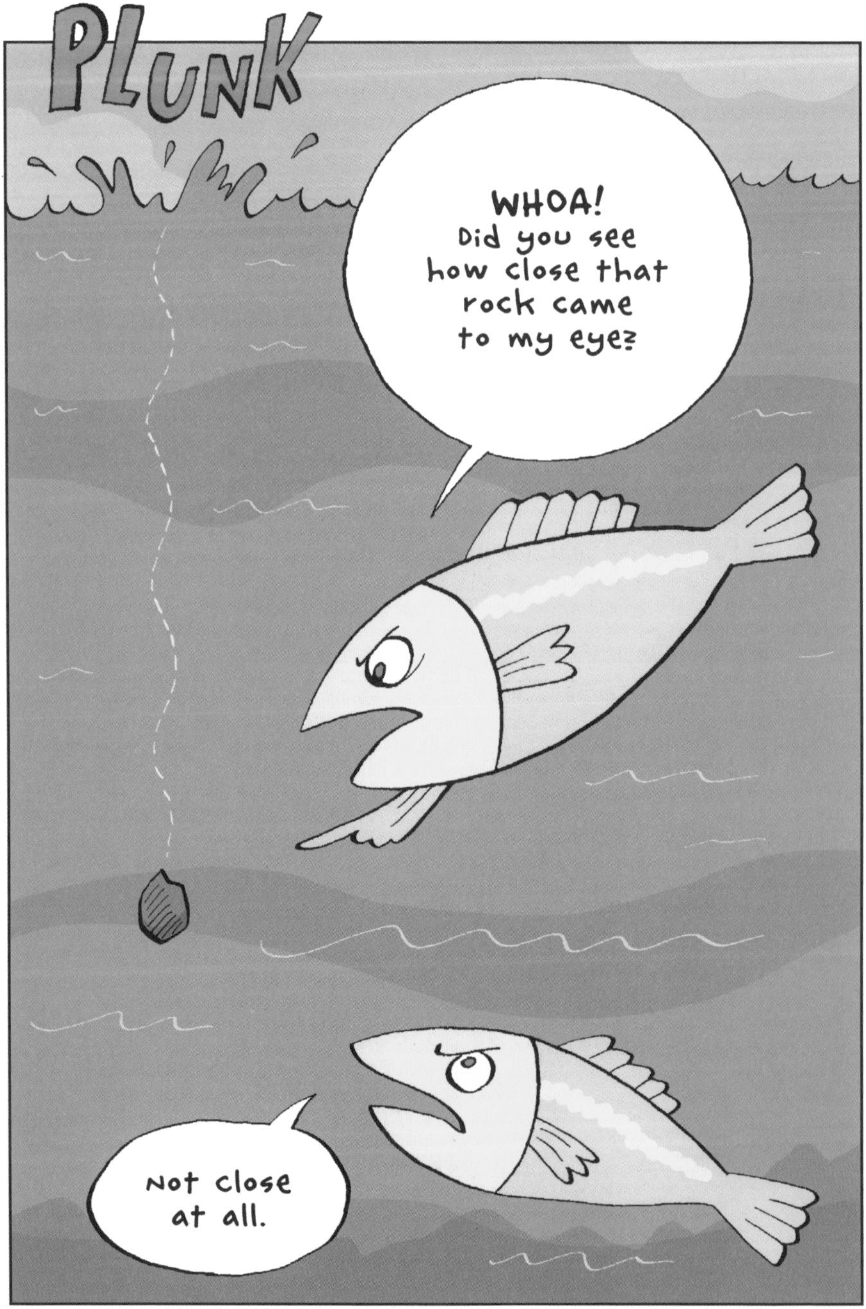
PLUNK
WHOA! Did you see how close that rock came to my eye?
Not close at all.

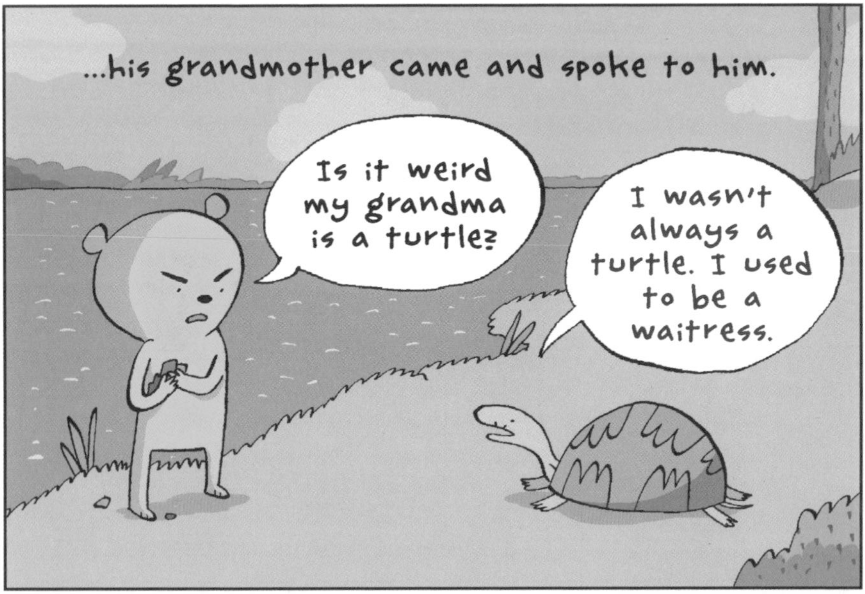
...his grandmother came and spoke to him.
Is it weird my grandma is a turtle?
I wasn't always a turtle. I used to be a waitress.

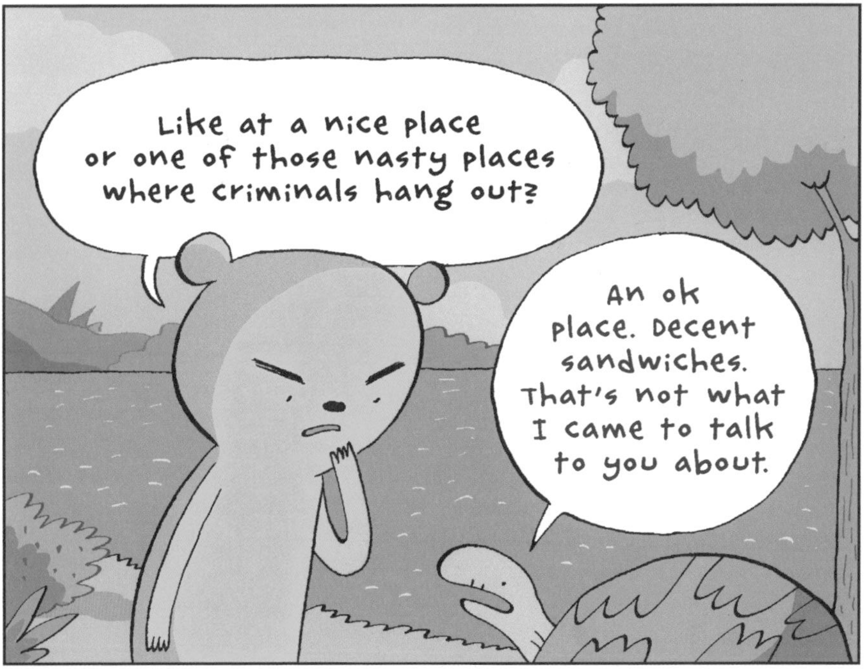
Like at a nice place or one of those nasty places where criminals hang out?
An ok place. Decent sandwiches. That's not what I came to talk to you about.

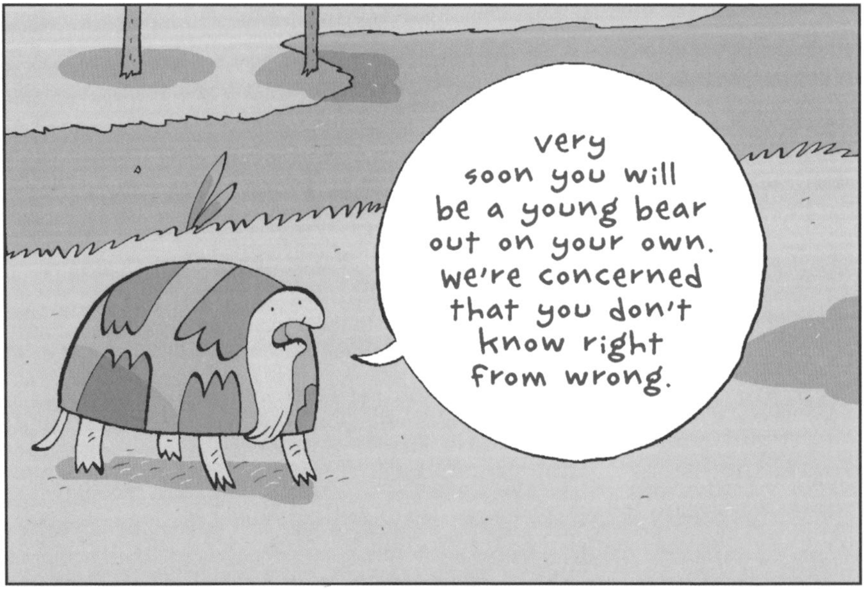
very soon you will be a young bear out on your own. we're concerned that you don't know right from wrong.

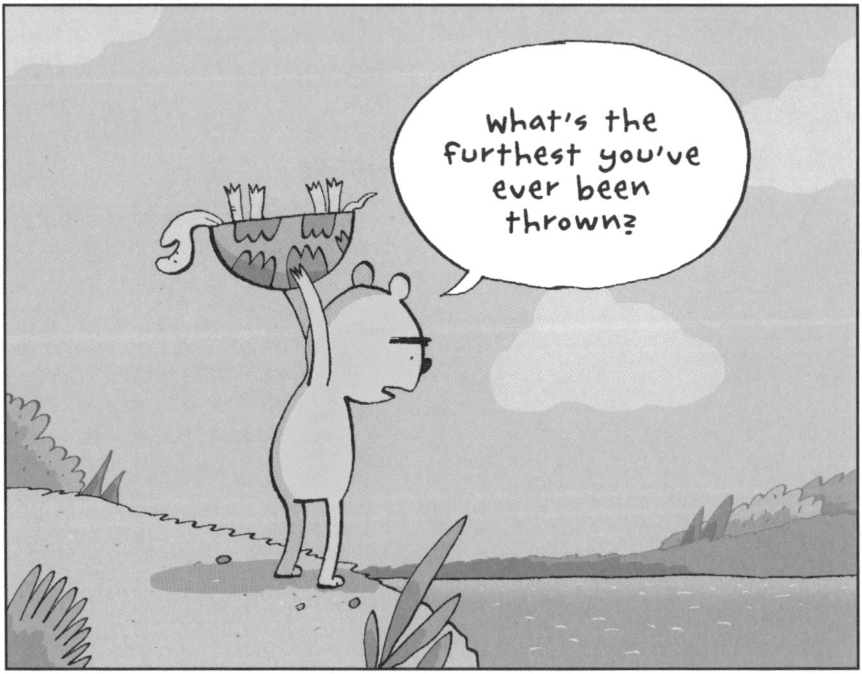
what's the furthest you've ever been thrown?

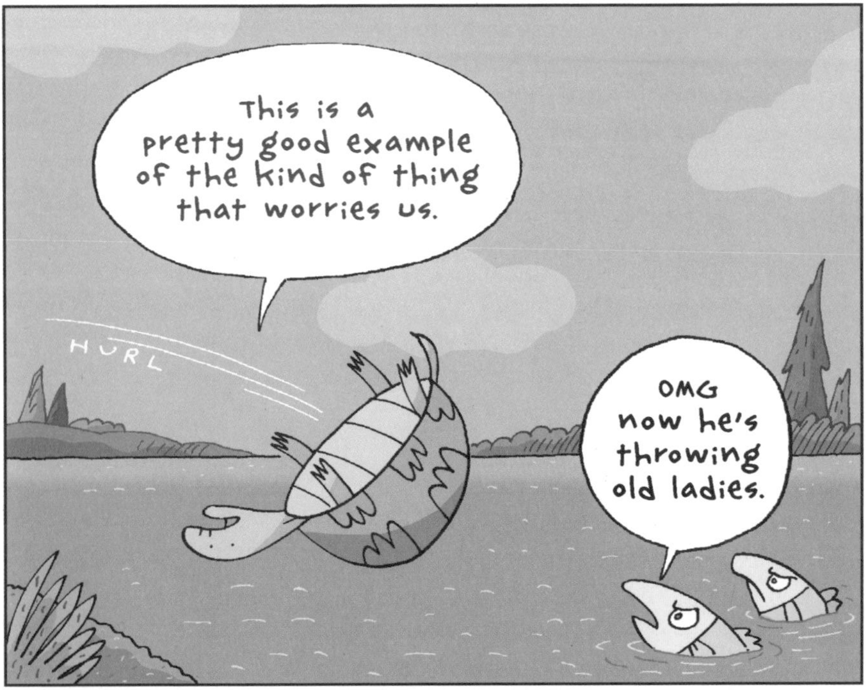
This is a pretty good example of the kind of thing that worries us.
HURL
OMG now he's throwing old ladies.

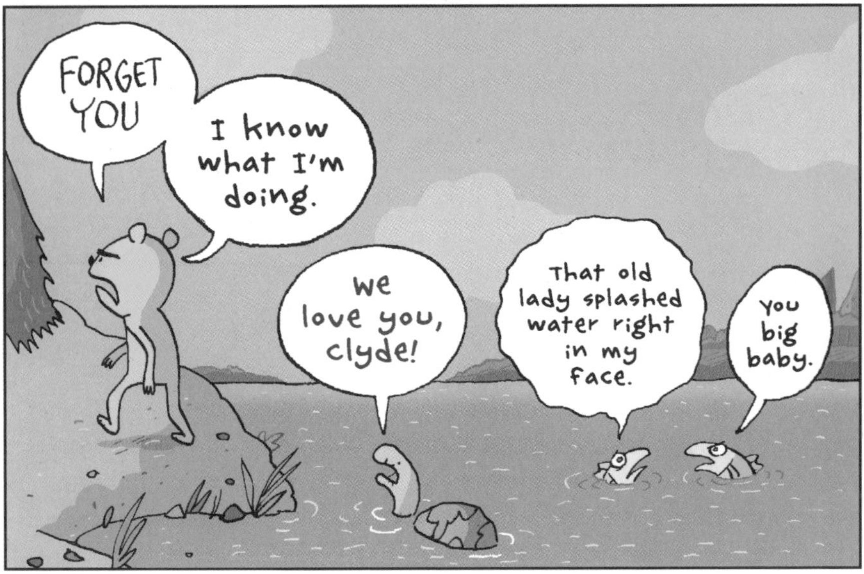
FORGET YOU
I know what I'm doing.
We love you, clyde!
That old lady splashed water right in my face.
You big baby.

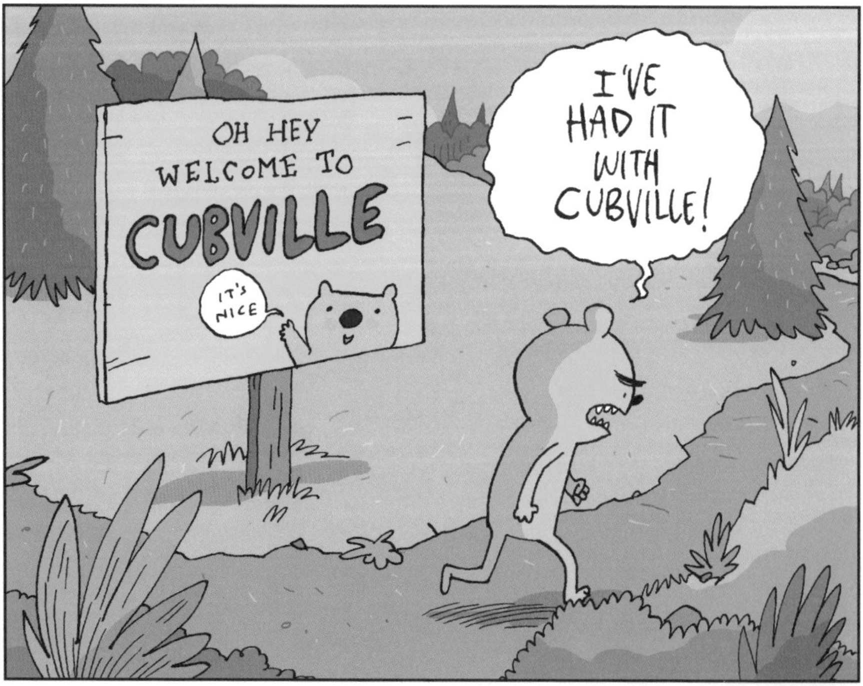
OH HEY
WELCOME TO
CUBVILLE
IT'S NICE
I'VE HAD IT WITH CUBVILLE!

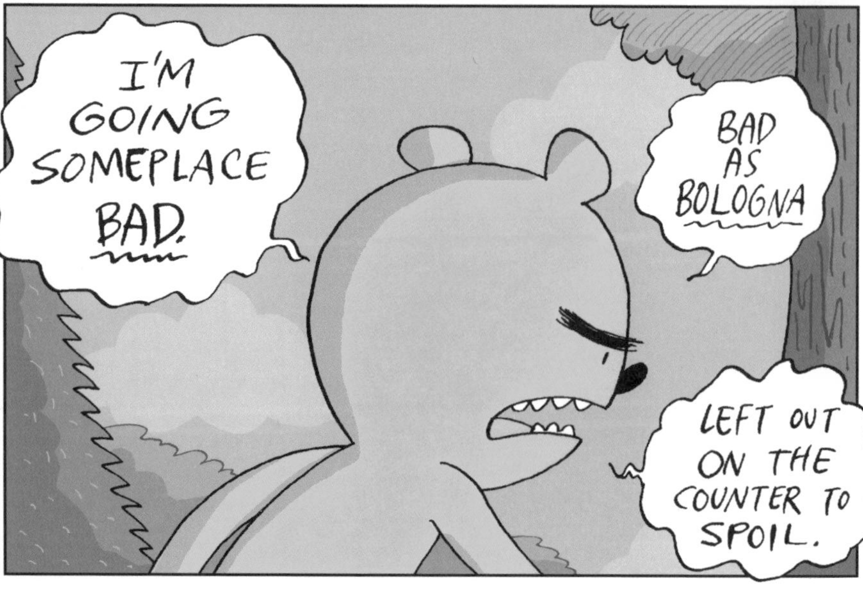
I'M GOING SOMEPLACE BAD.
BAD AS BOLOGNA
LEFT OUT ON THE COUNTER TO SPOIL.

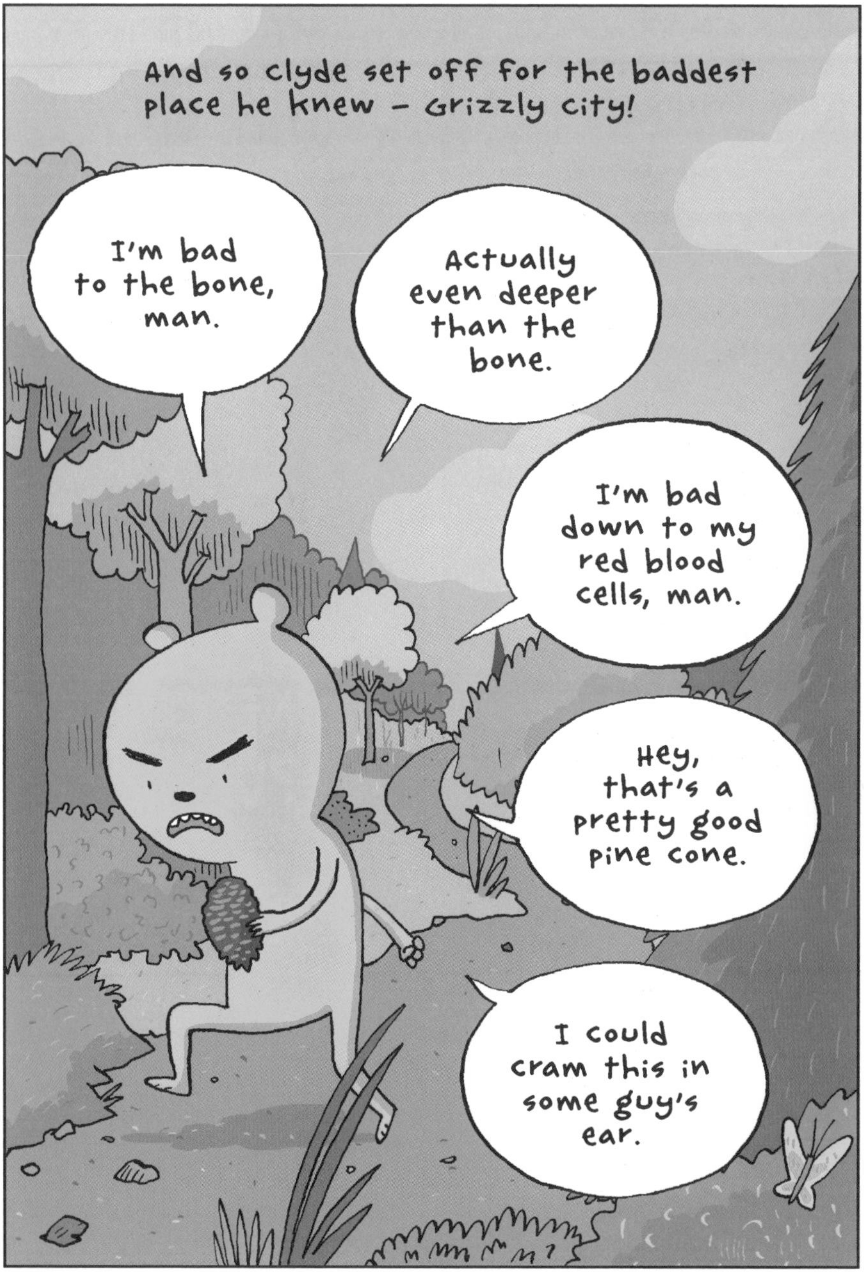
And so clyde set off for the baddest place he knew – Grizzly city!
I'm bad to the bone, man.
Actually even deeper than the bone.
I'm bad down to my red blood cells, man.
Hey, that's a pretty good pine cone.
I could cram this in some guy's ear.

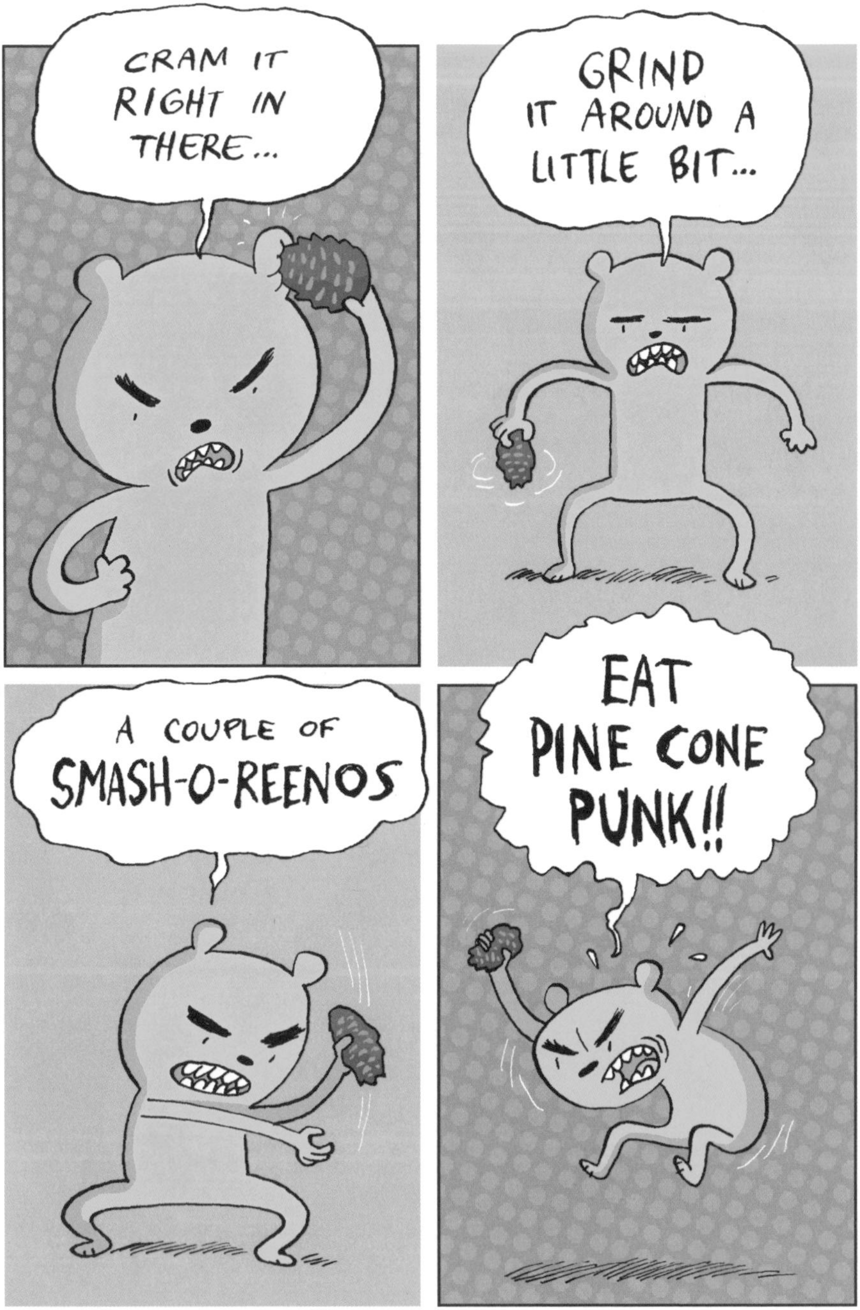
CRAM IT RIGHT IN THERE...
GRIND IT AROUND A LITTLE BIT...
A COUPLE OF SMASH-O-REENOS
EAT PINE CONE PUNK!!

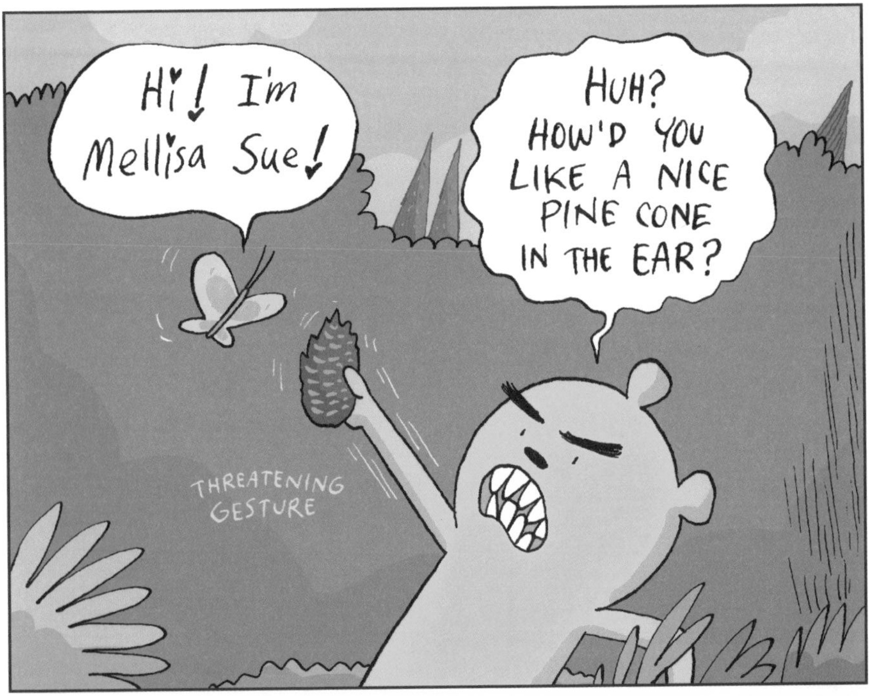
Hi! I'm Mellisa Sue!
HUH? HOW'D YOU LIKE A NICE PINE CONE IN THE EAR?
THREATENING GESTURE

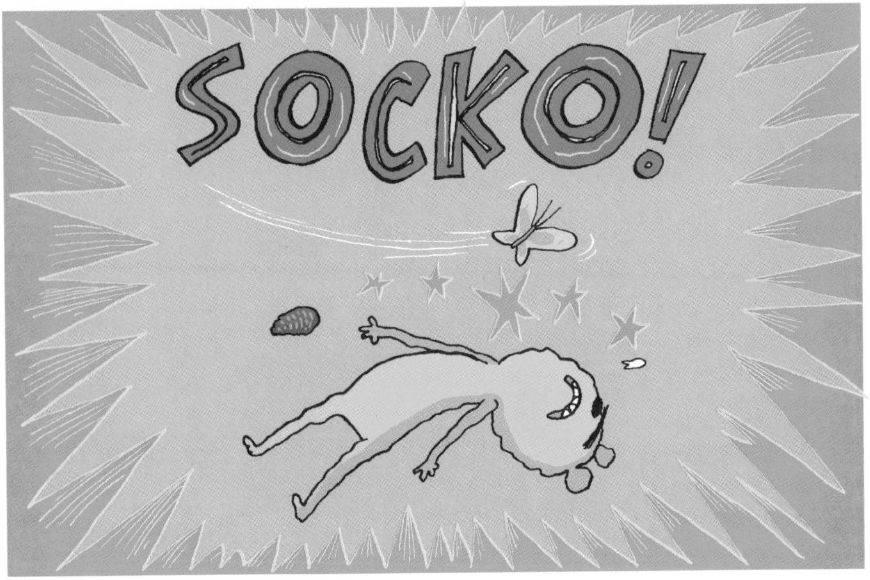
SOCKO!

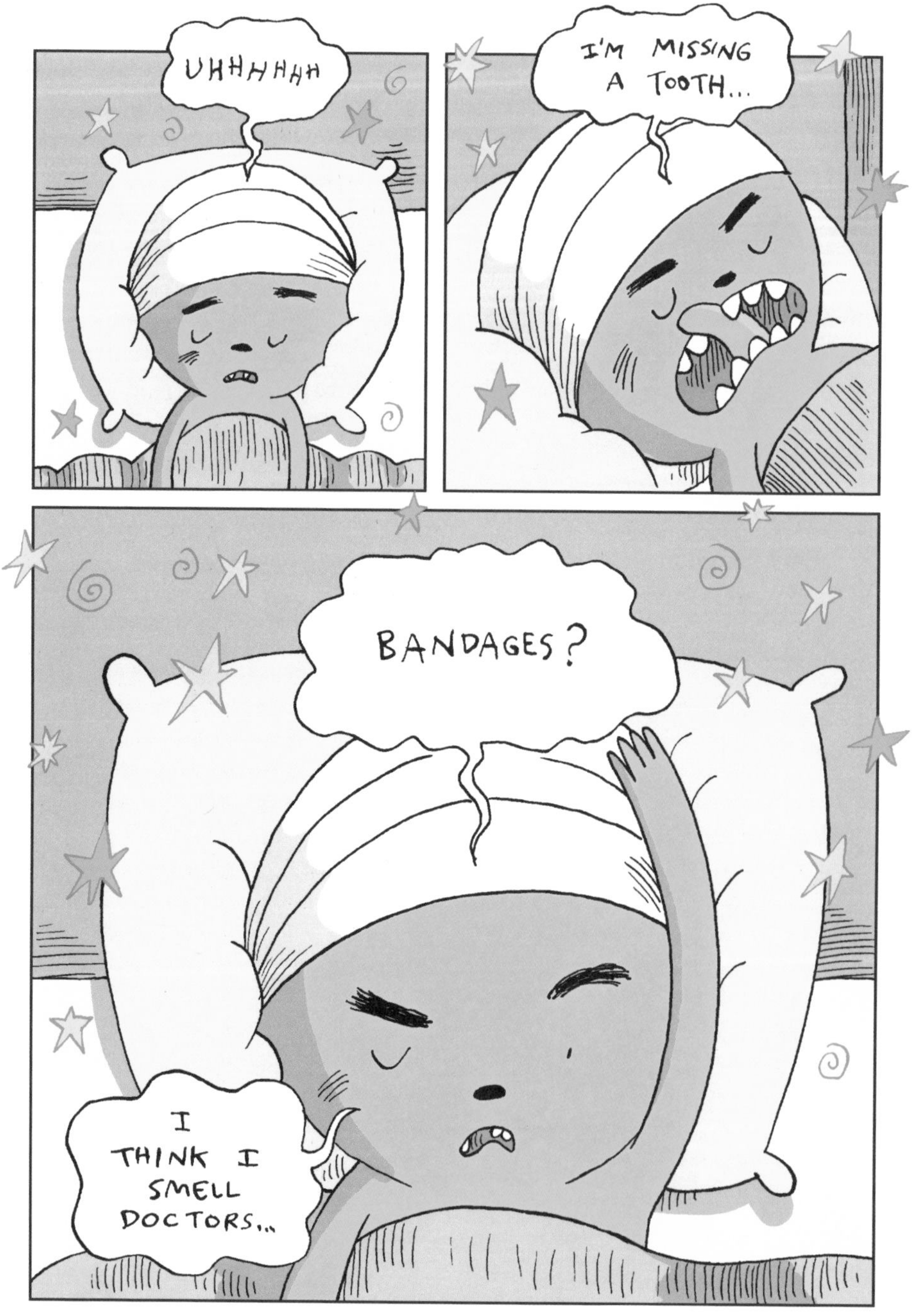
UHHHHHH
I'M MISSING A TOOTH...
BANDAGES?
I THINK I SMELL DOCTORS...

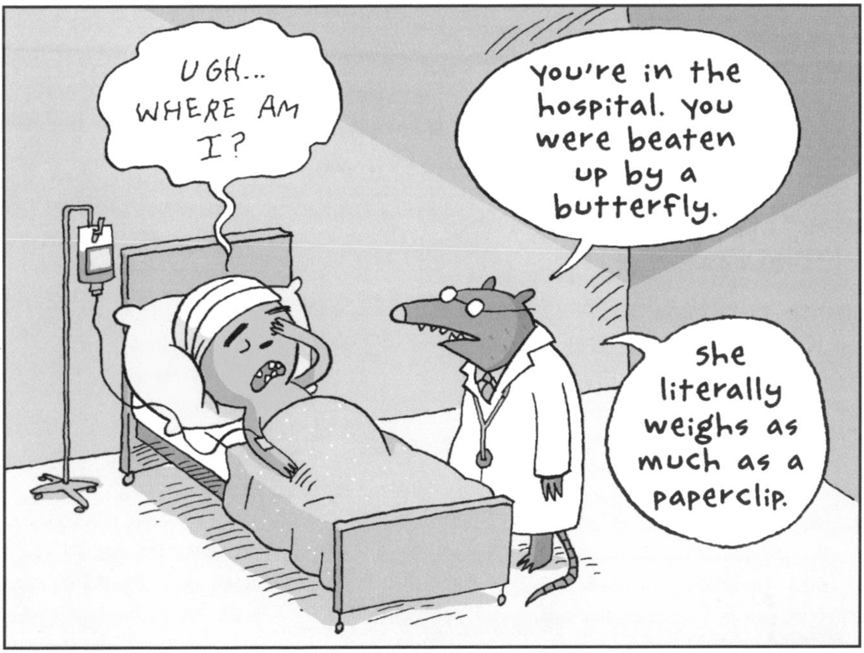
UGH... WHERE AM I?
You're in the hospital. You were beaten up by a butterfly.
She literally weighs as much as a paperclip.

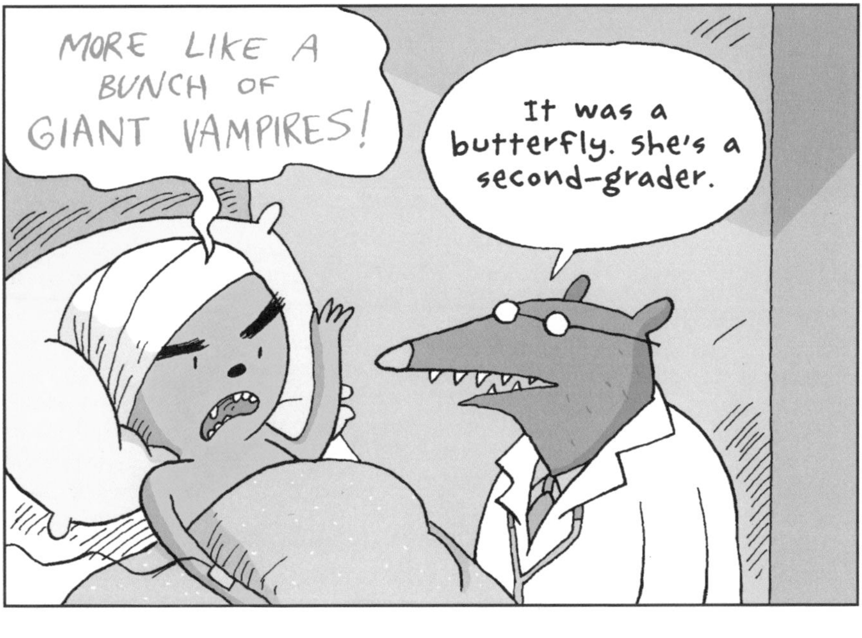
MORE LIKE A BUNCH OF GIANT VAMPIRES!
It was a butterfly. She's a second-grader.

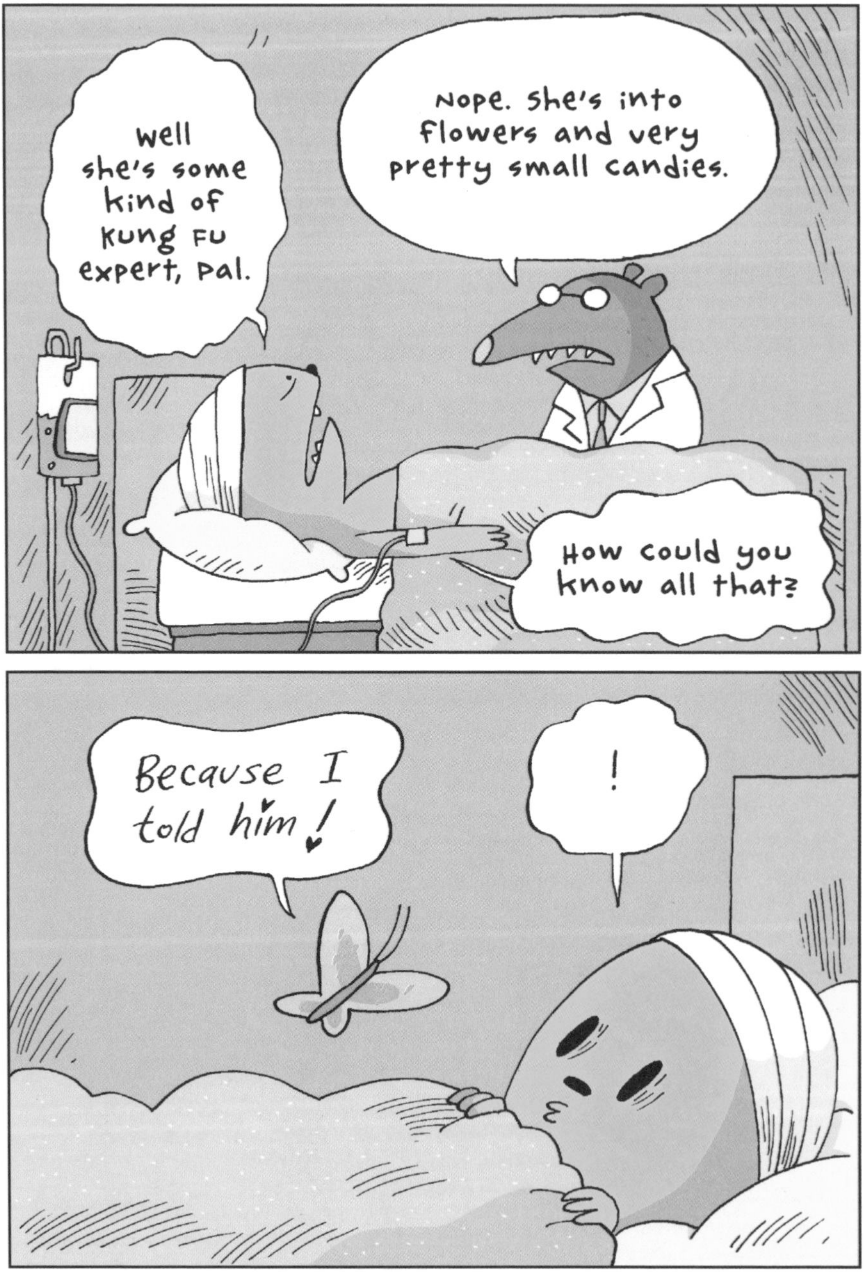
Well she's some kind of Kung Fu expert, pal.
Nope. She's into flowers and very pretty small candies.
How could you know all that?
Because I told him!
!

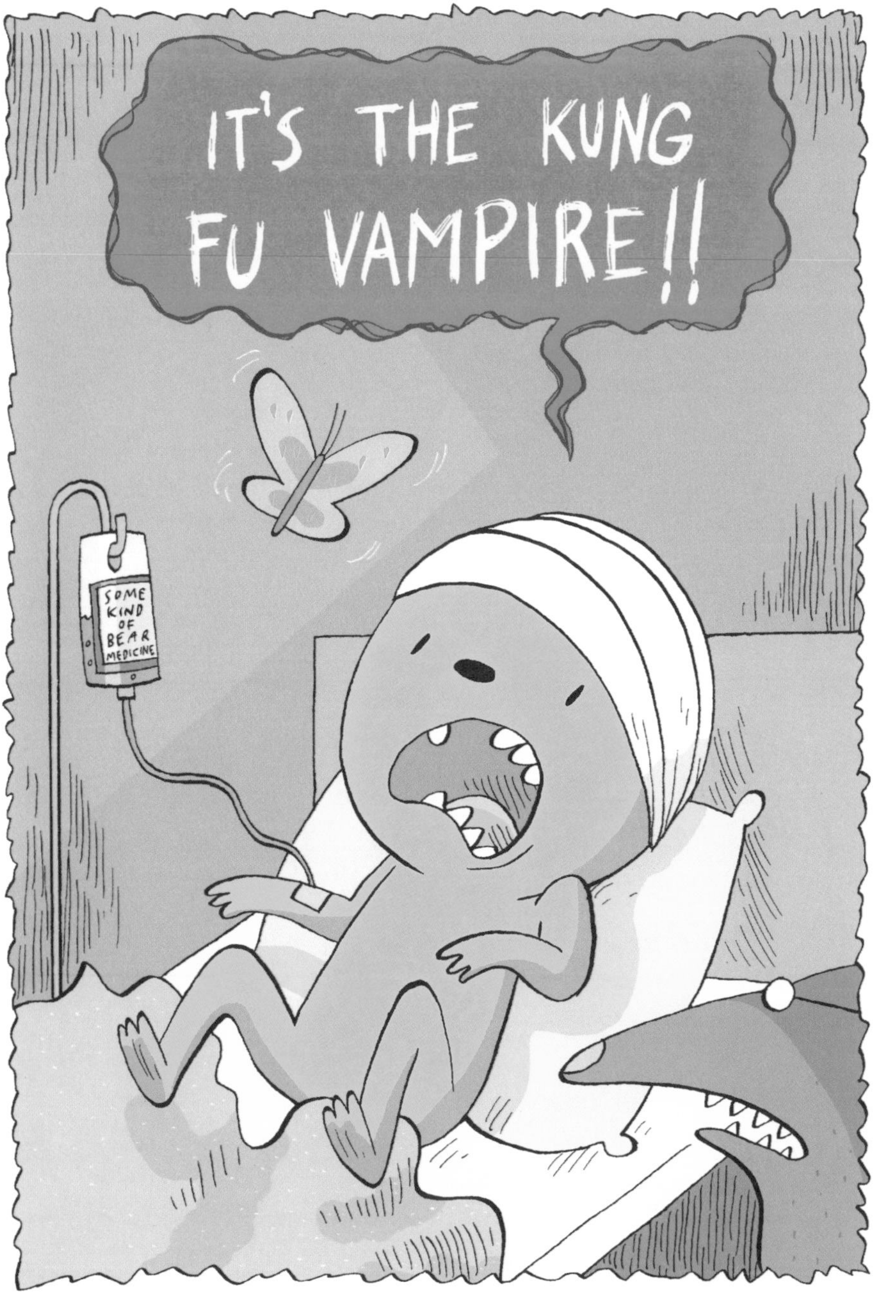
IT'S THE KUNG FU VAMPIRE!!
SOME KIND OF BEAR MEDICINE

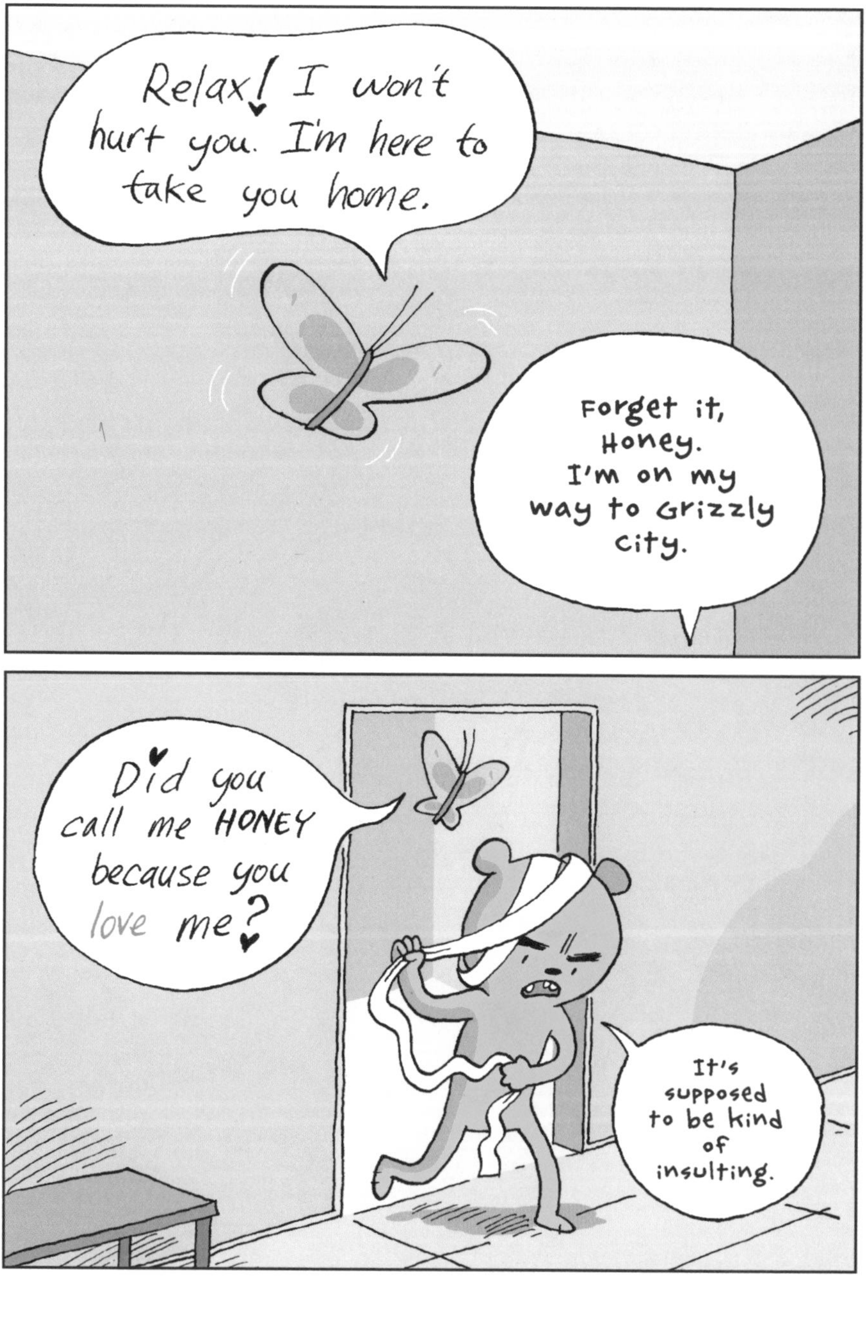
Relax! I won't hurt you. I'm here to take you home.
Forget it, Honey. I'm on my way to Grizzly city.
Did you call me HONEY because you love me?
It's supposed to be kind of insulting.

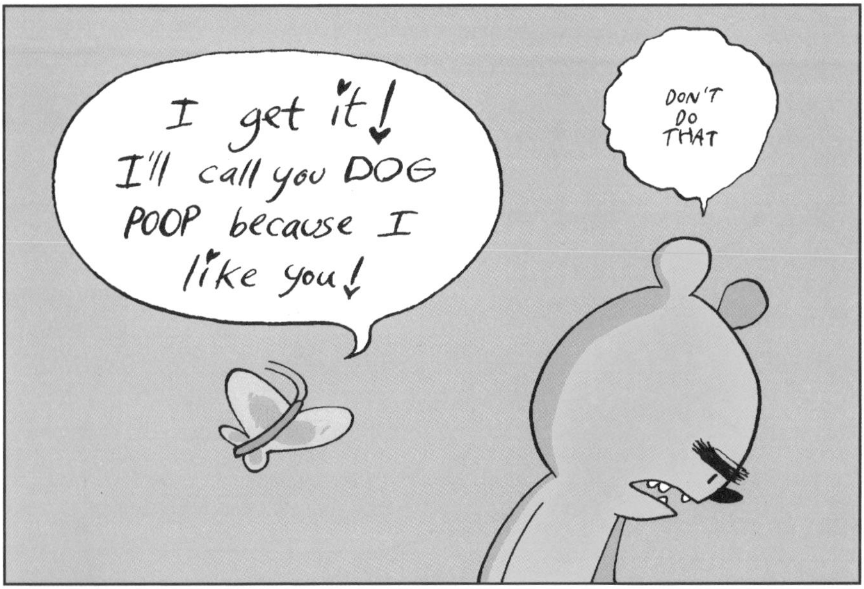
I get it! I'll call you DOG POOP because I like you!
DON'T DO THAT

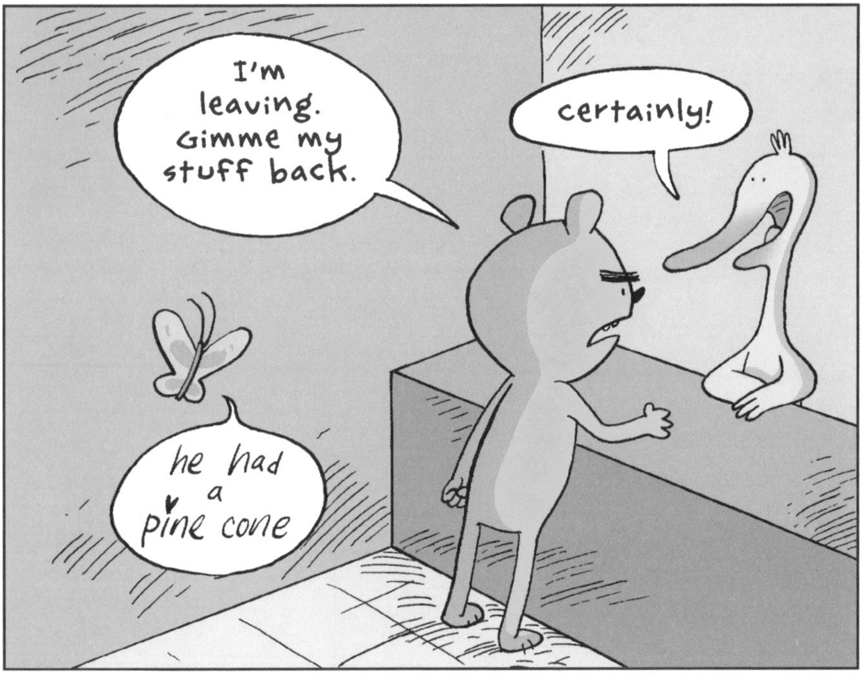
I'm leaving. Gimme my stuff back.
certainly!
he had a pine cone

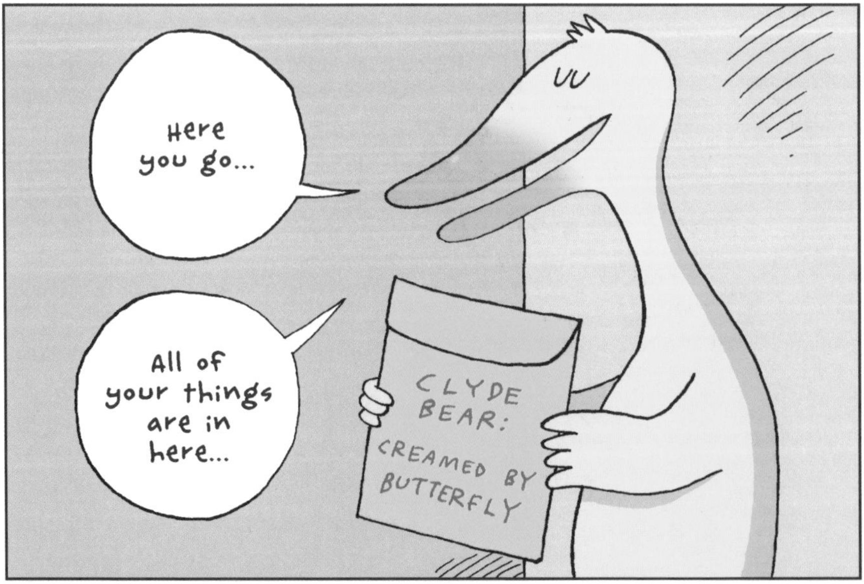
Here you go...
All of your things are in here...
CLYDE BEAR: CREAMED BY BUTTERFLY

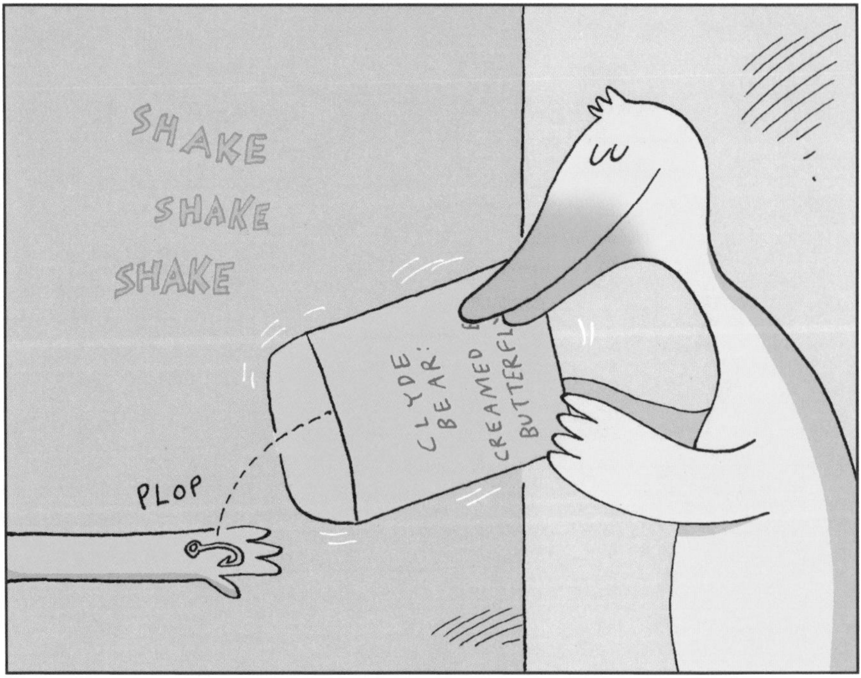
SHAKE
SHAKE
SHAKE
CLYDE BEAR: CREAMED B
BUTTERFL
PLOP

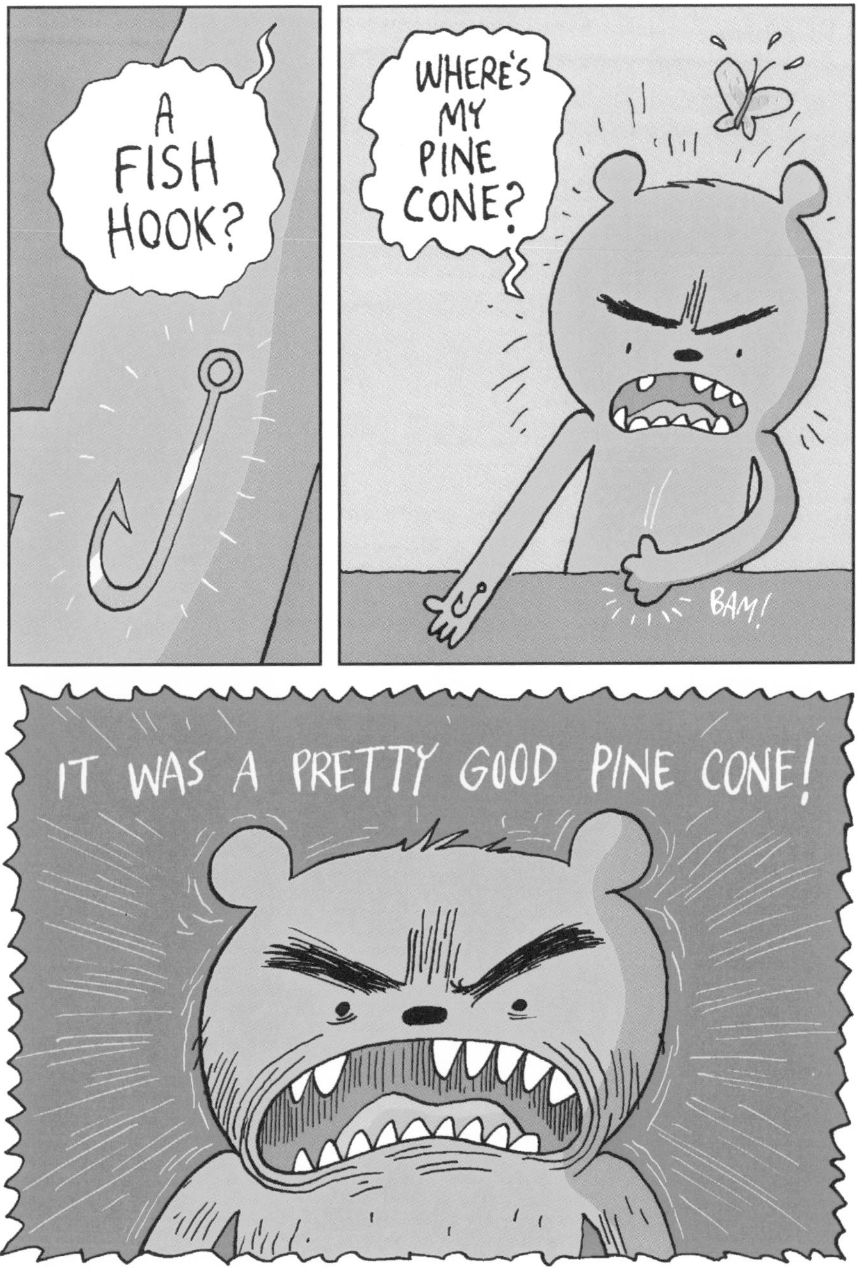
A FISH HOOK?
WHERE'S MY PINE CONE?
BAM!
IT WAS A PRETTY GOOD PINE CONE!

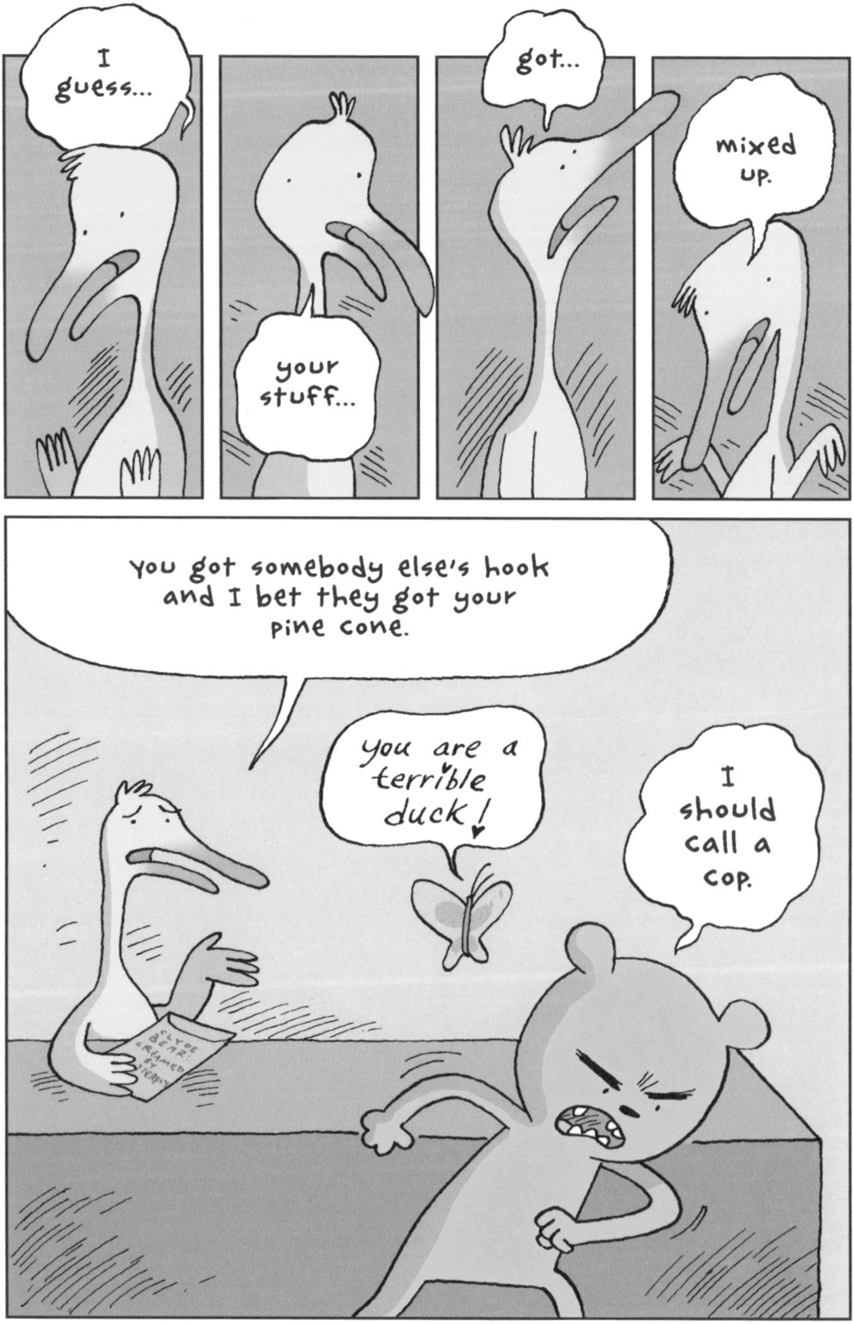
I guess...
your stuff...
got...
mixed up.
you got somebody else's hook and I bet they got your pine cone.
you are a terrible duck!
I should call a cop.

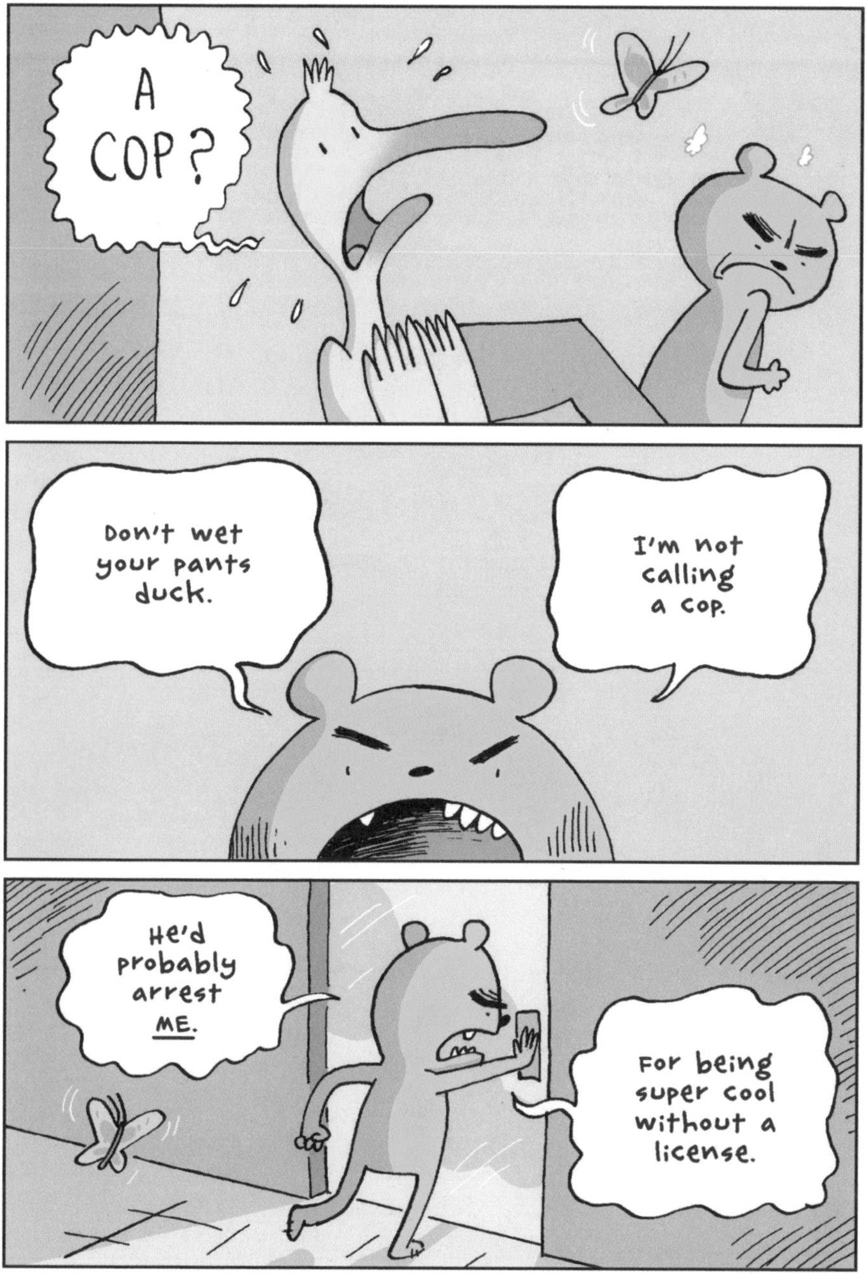
A COP?
Don't wet your pants duck.
I'm not calling a cop.
He'd probably arrest ME.
For being super cool without a license.

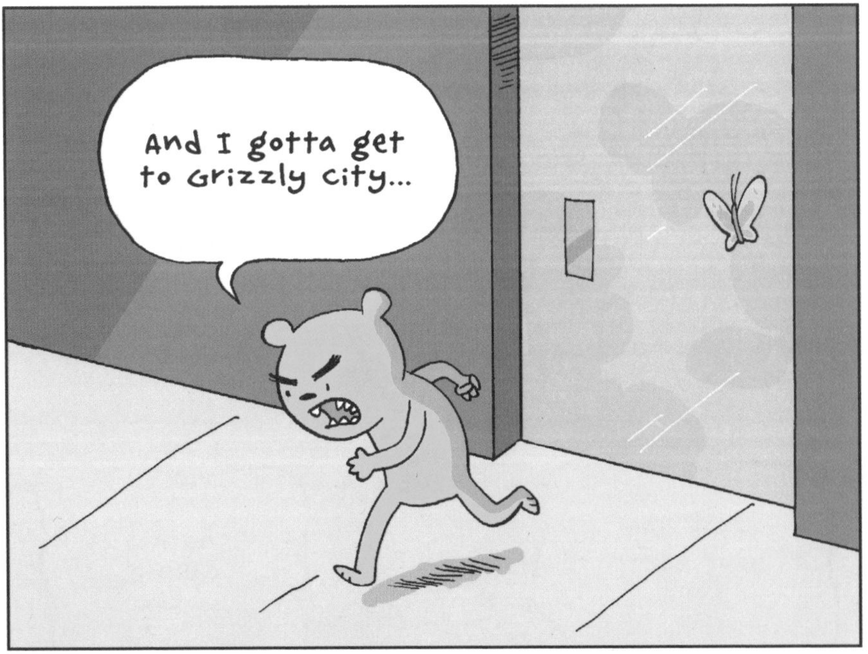
And I gotta get to Grizzly city...

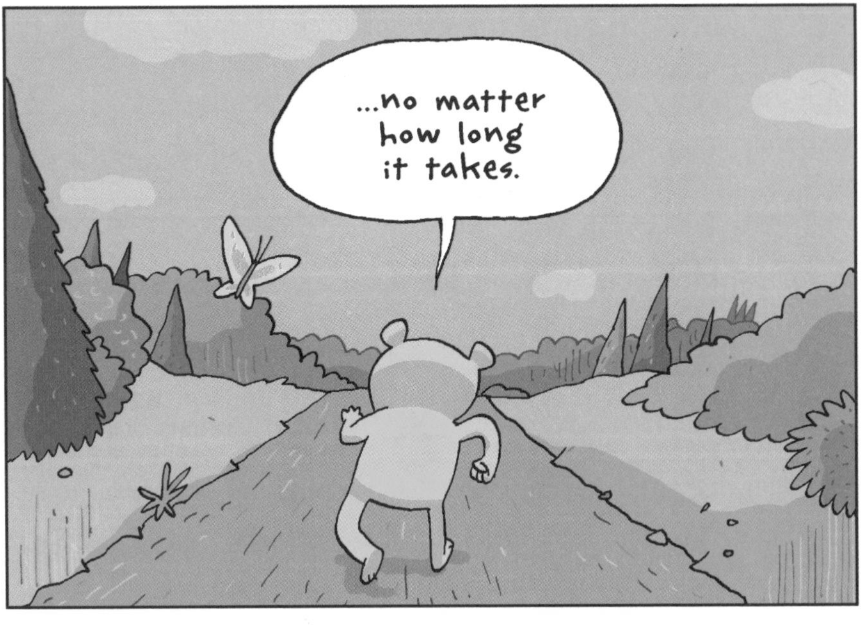
...no matter how long it takes.

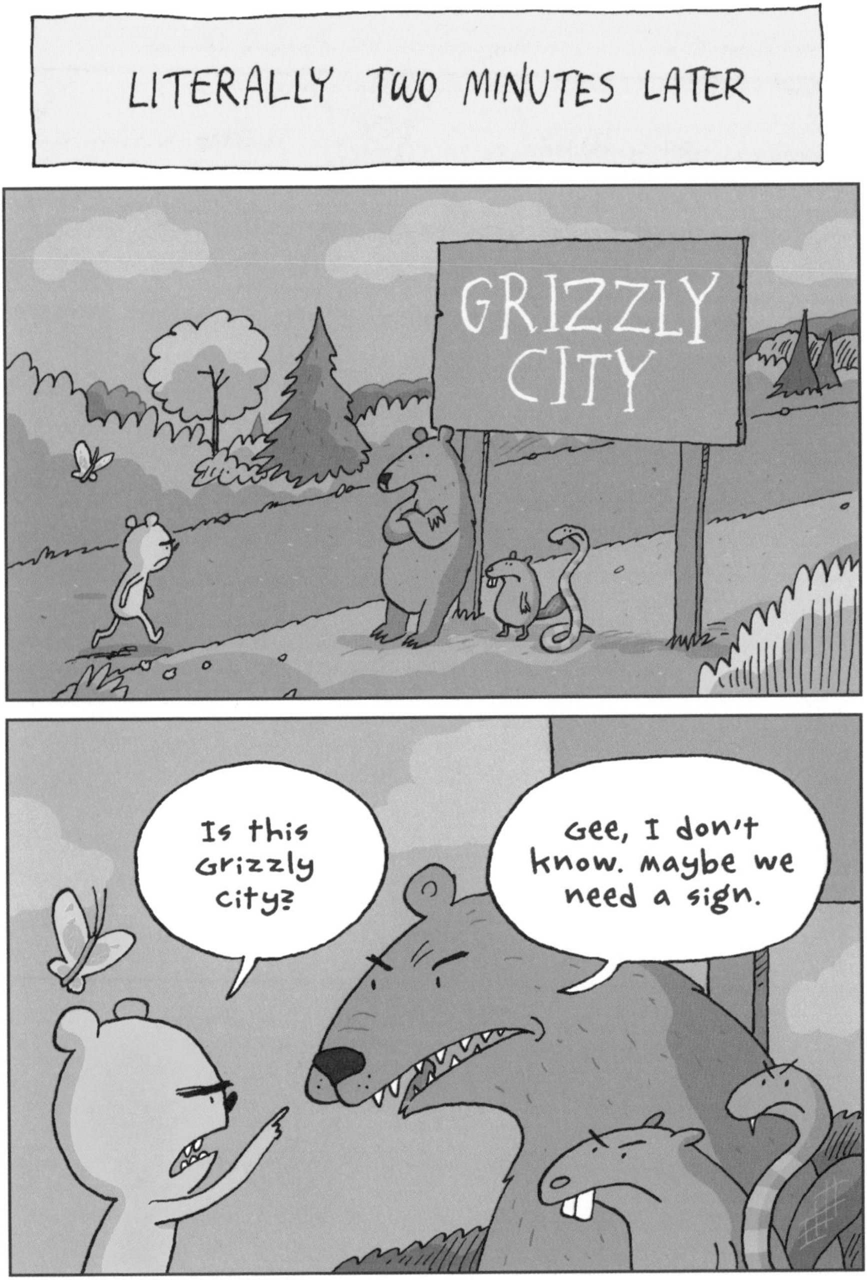
LITERALLY TWO MINUTES LATER
GRIZZLY CITY
Is this Grizzly city?
Gee, I don't know. maybe we need a sign.

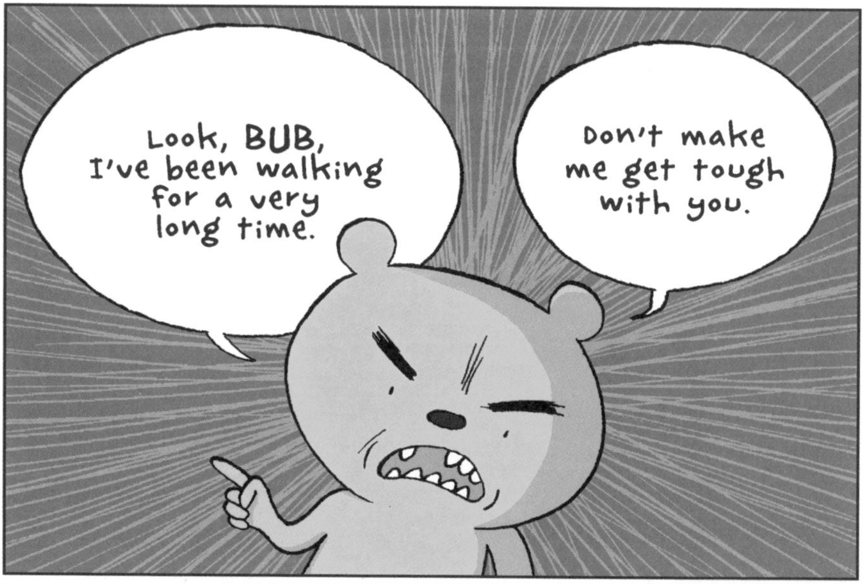
Look, BUB, I've been walking for a very long time.
Don't make me get tough with you.

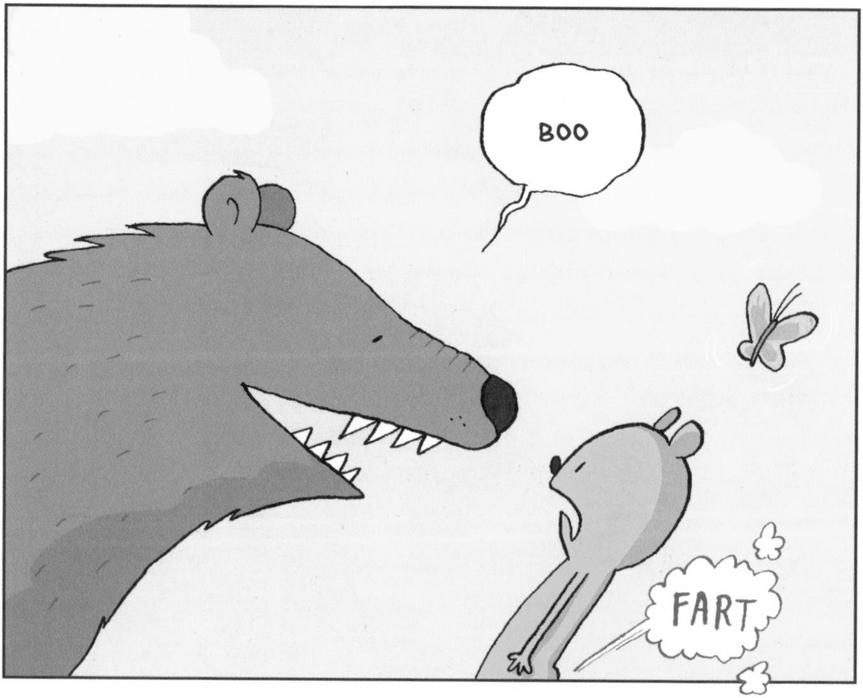
BOO
FART

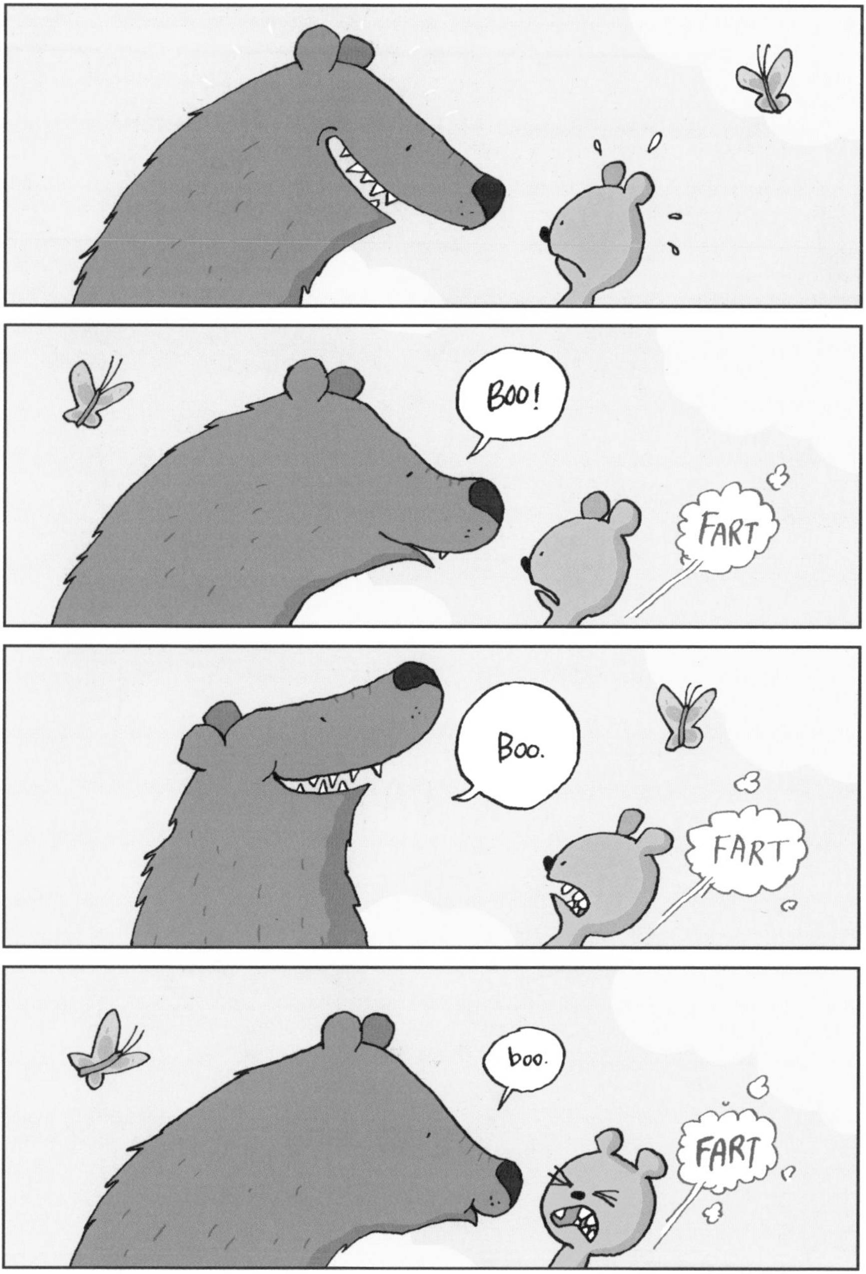
BOO!
FART
Boo.
FART
boo.
FART

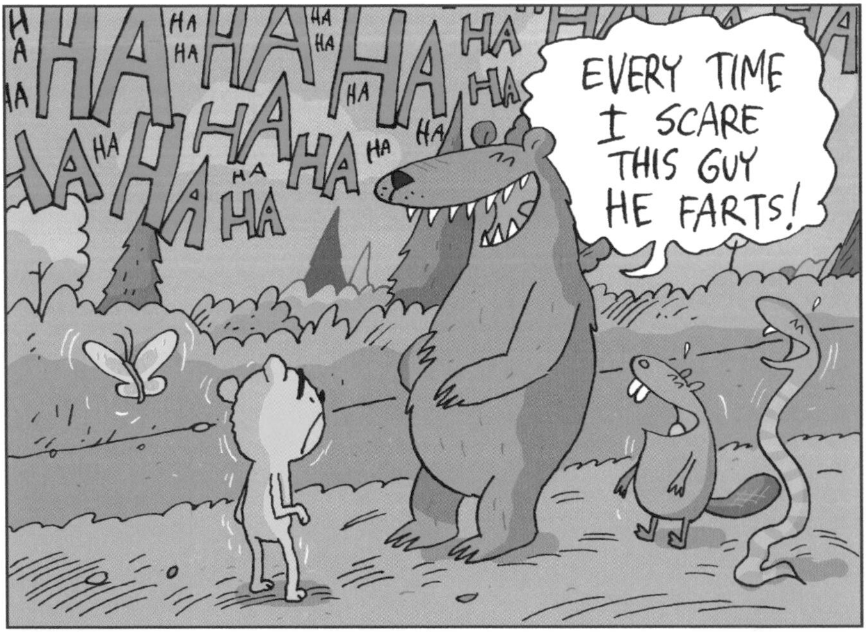
HA HA HA HA HA HA HA HA HA HA HA HA HA HA HA HA HA HA HA HA HA HA
EVERY TIME I SCARE THIS GUY HE FARTS!

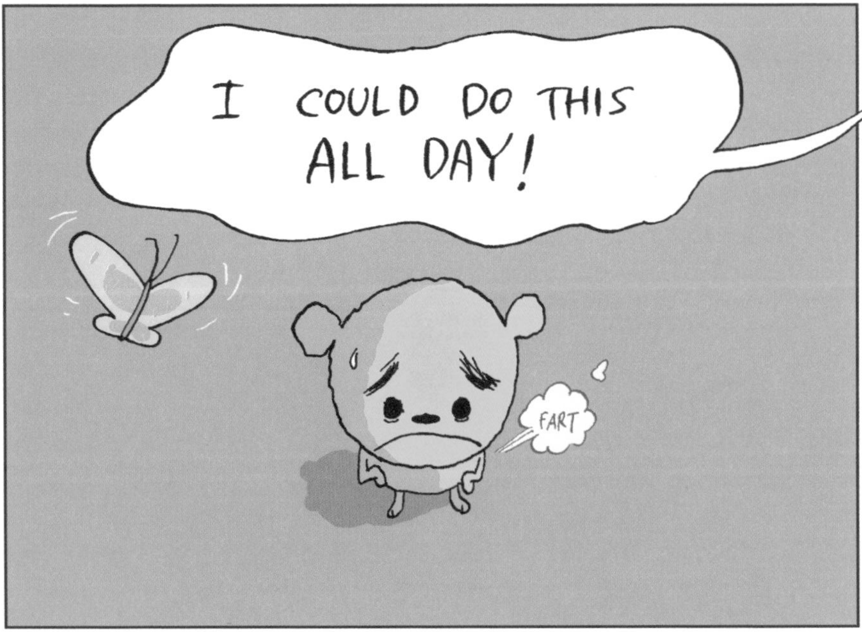
I COULD DO THIS ALL DAY!
FART

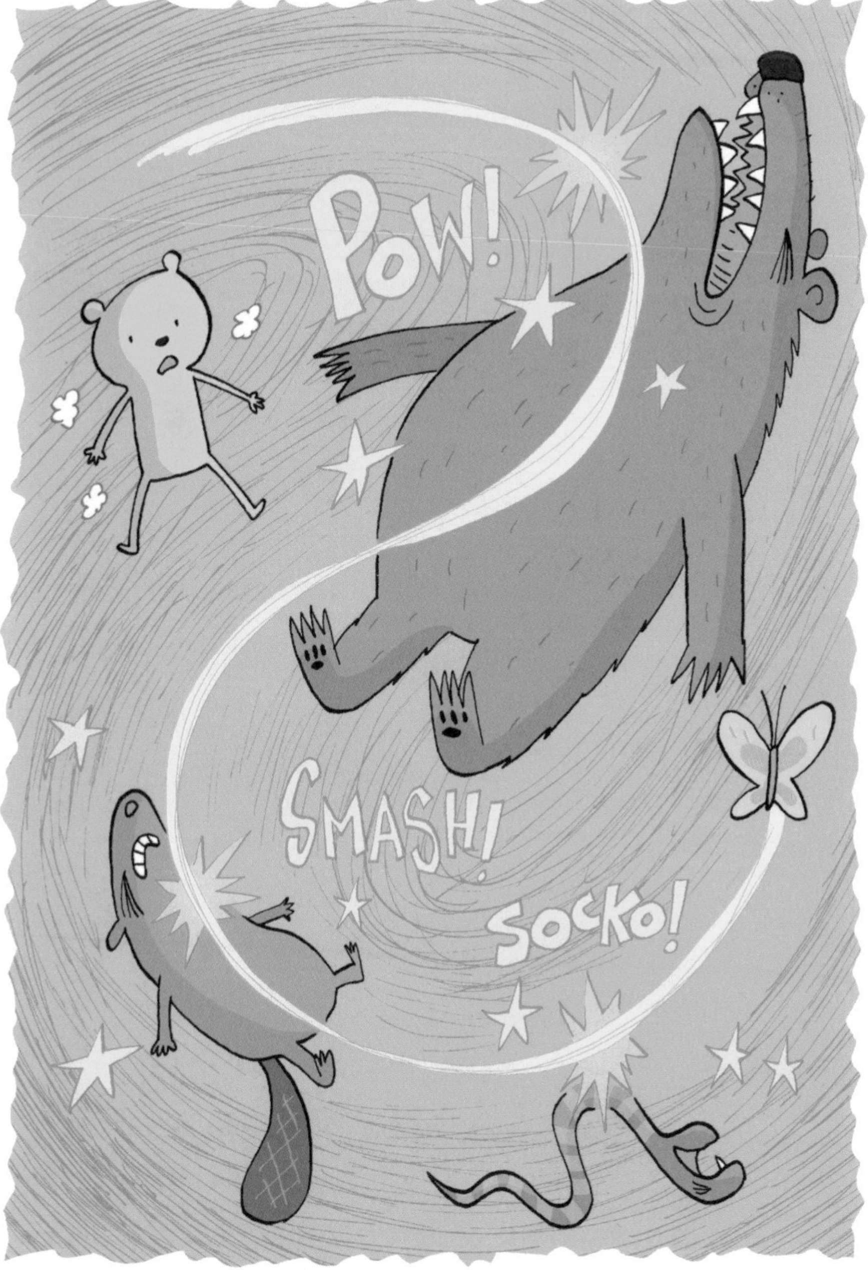
POW!
SMASH!
SOCKO!

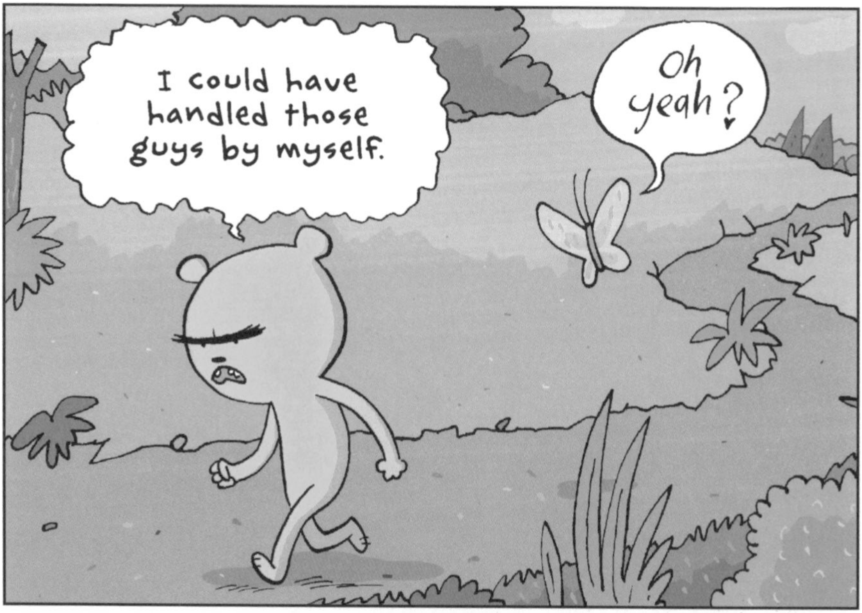
I could have handled those guys by myself.
Oh yeah?

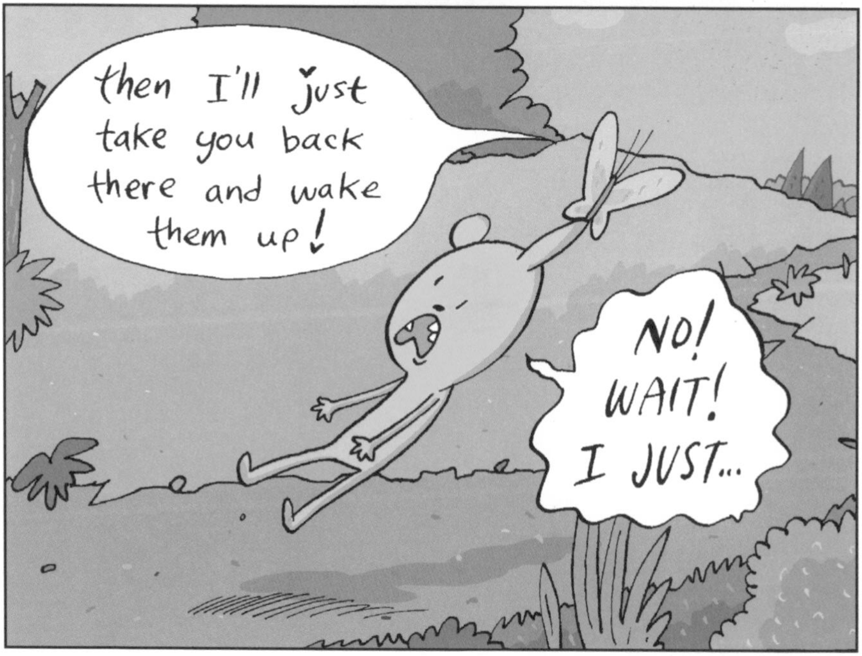
then I'll just take you back there and wake them up!
NO! WAIT! I JUST...

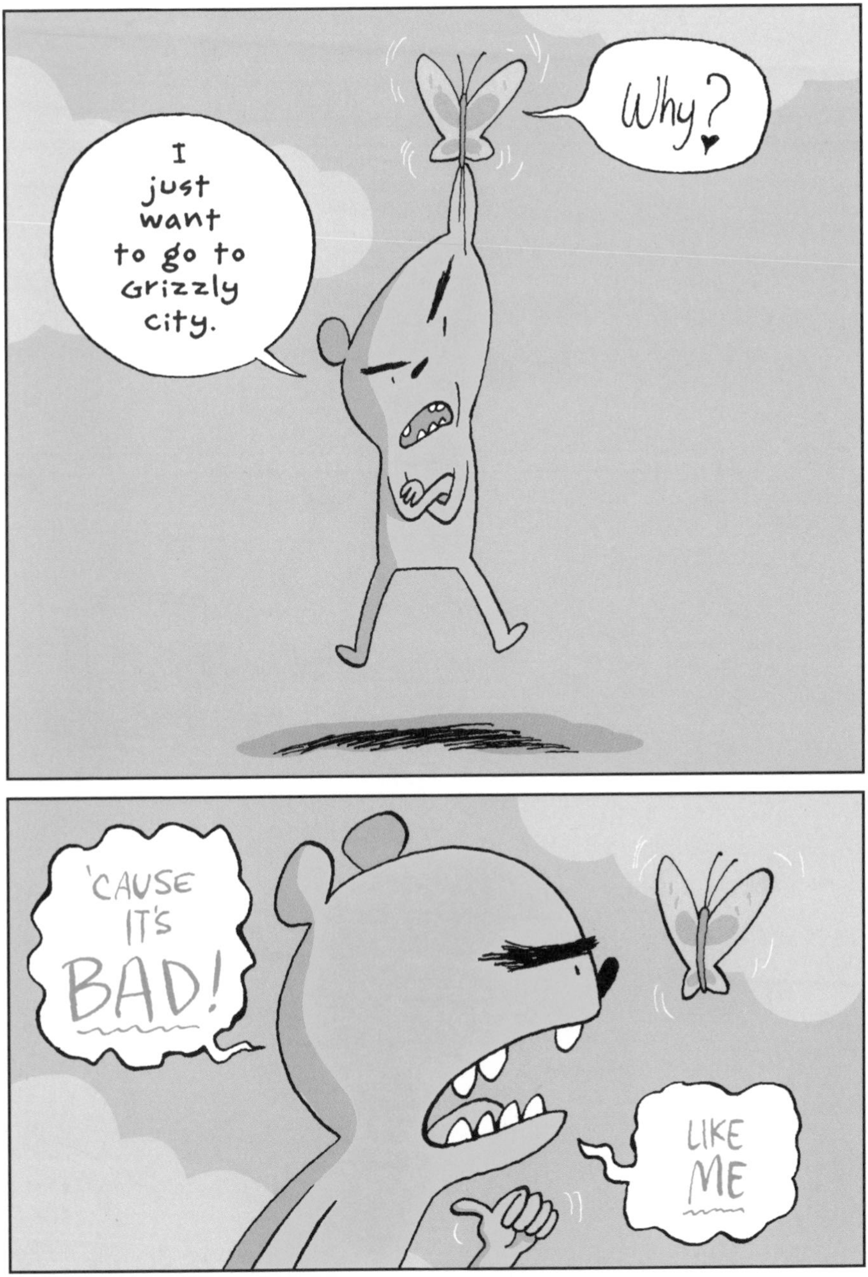
Why?
I just want to go to Grizzly city.
'CAUSE IT'S BAD!
LIKE ME

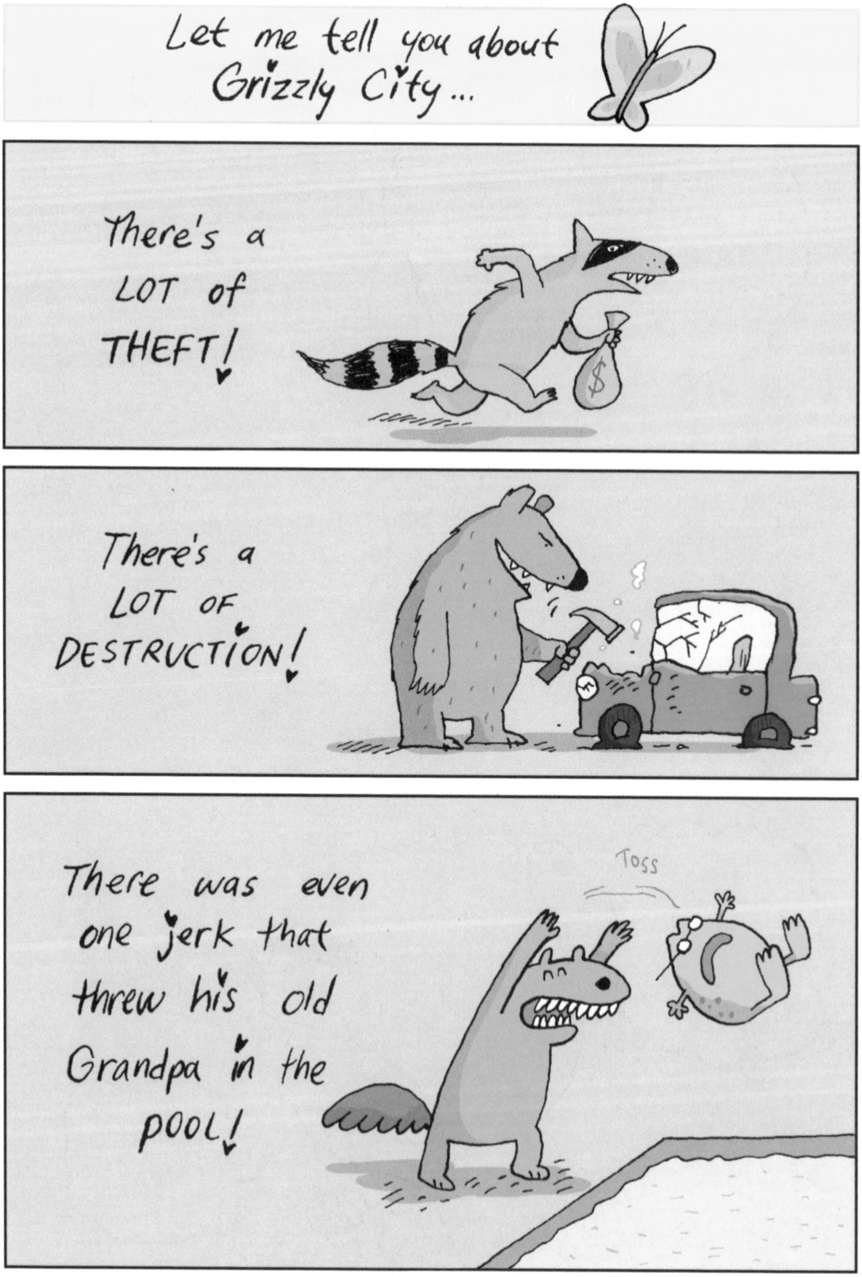
Let me tell you about Grizzly City...
There's a LOT of THEFT!
There's a LOT OF DESTRUCTION!
There was even one jerk that threw his old Grandpa in the pool!
TOSS

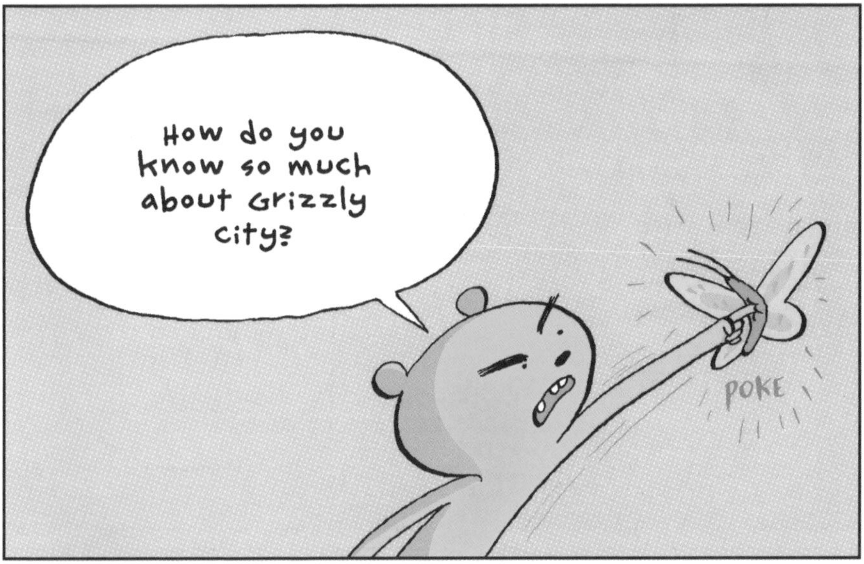
How do you know so much about Grizzly city?
POKE

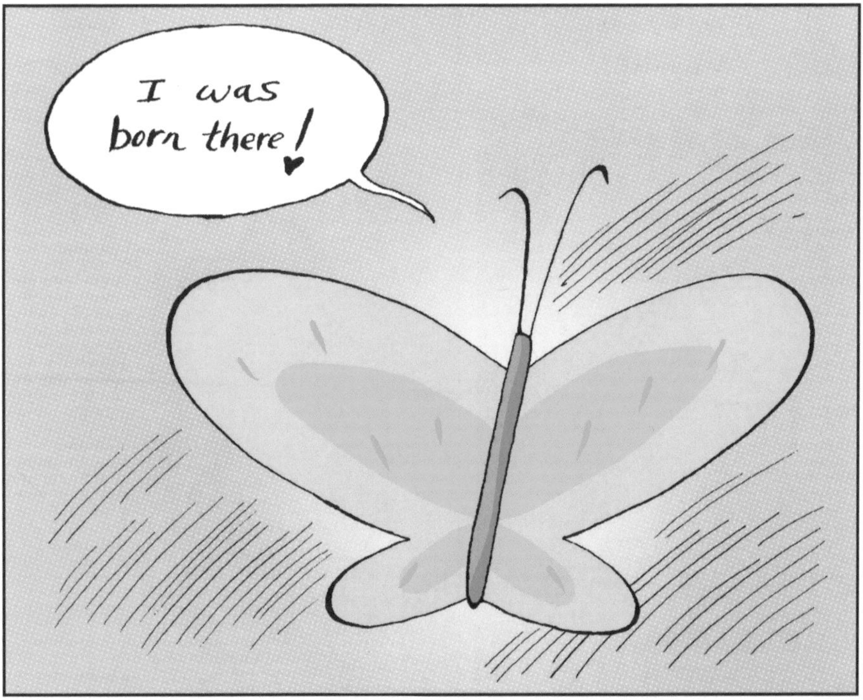
I was born there!

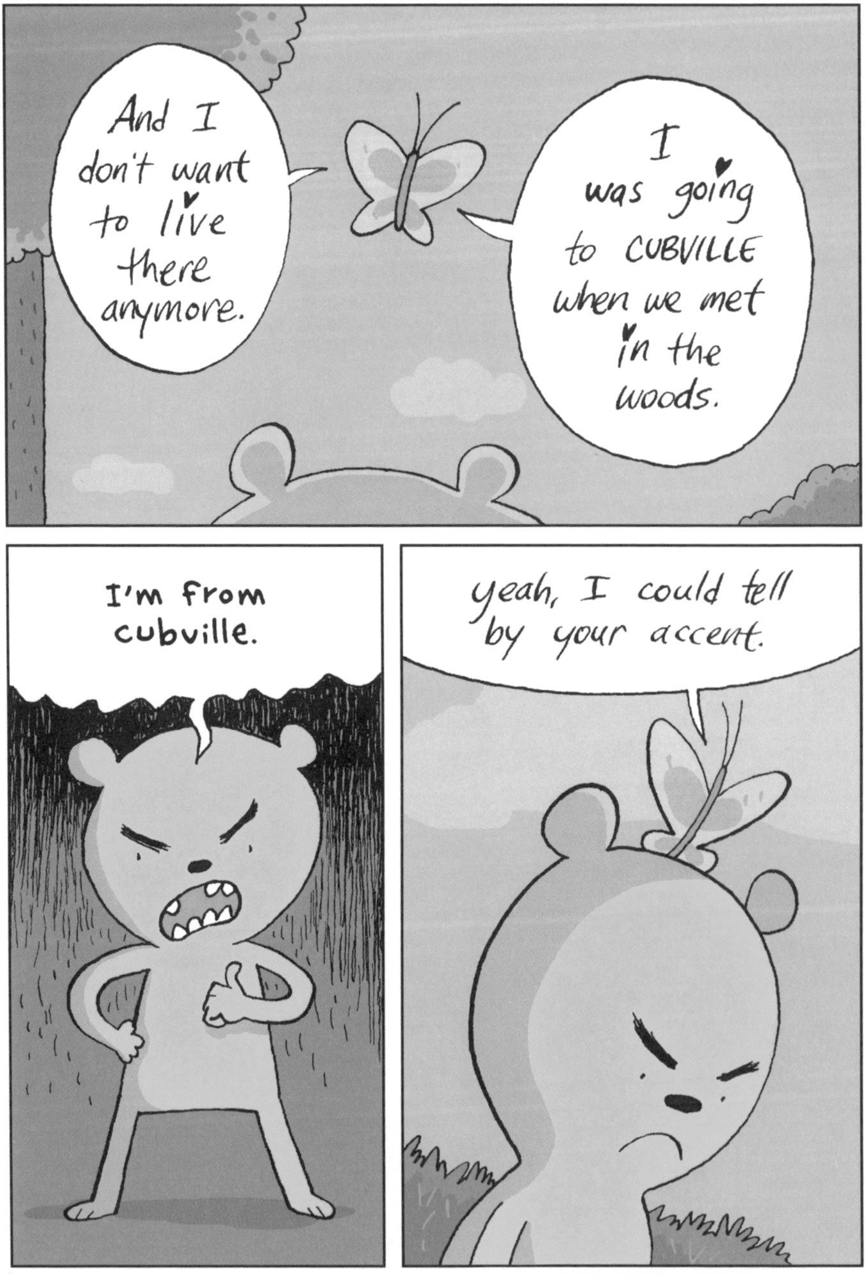
And I don't want to live there anymore.
I was going to CUBVILLE when we met in the woods.
I'm from cubville.
yeah, I could tell by your accent.

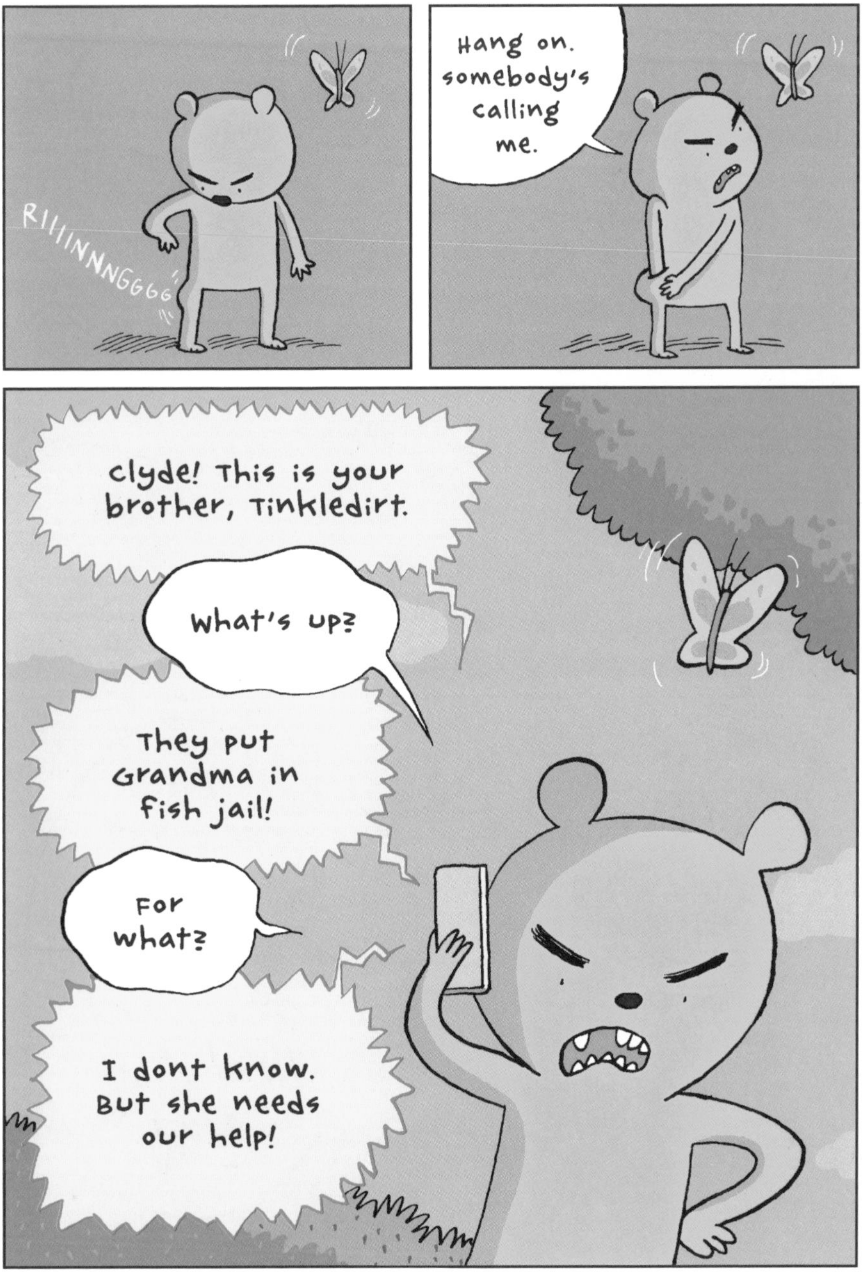
RIIIINNNGGGG
Hang on. somebody's calling me.
clyde! This is your brother, Tinkledirt.
What's up?
They put Grandma in fish jail!
For what?
I dont know. But she needs our help!

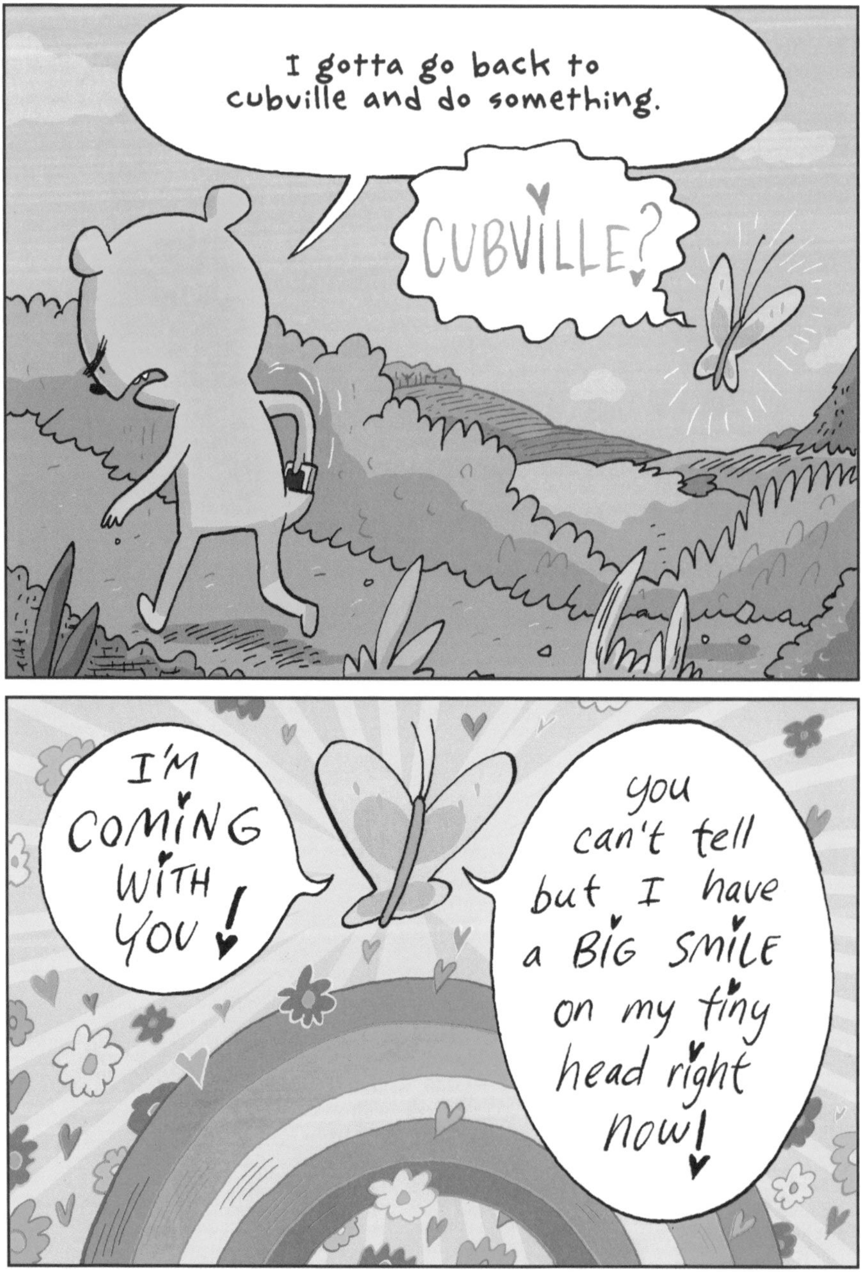
I gotta go back to cubville and do something.
CUBVILLE?
I'M COMING WITH YOU!
you can't tell but I have a BIG SMILE on my tiny head right now!

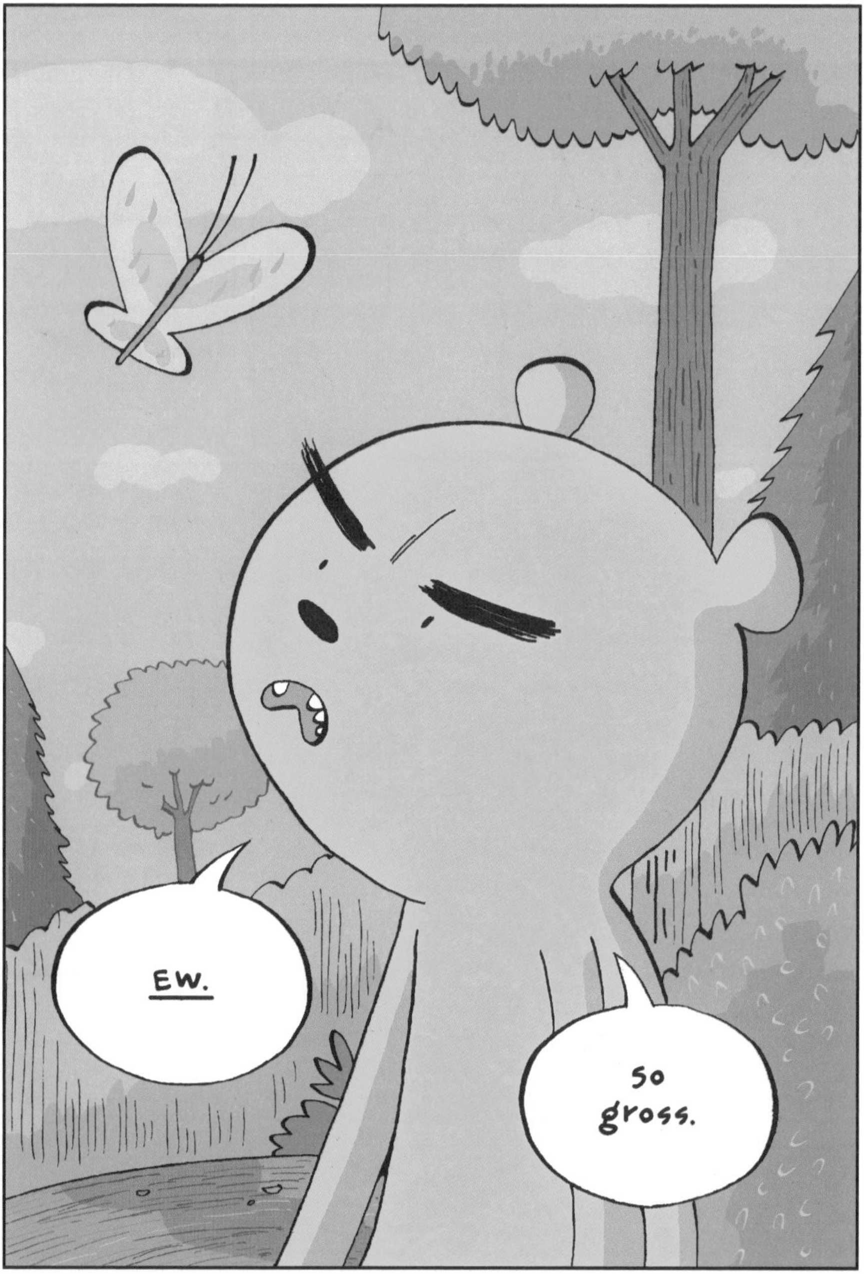
EW.
So gross.

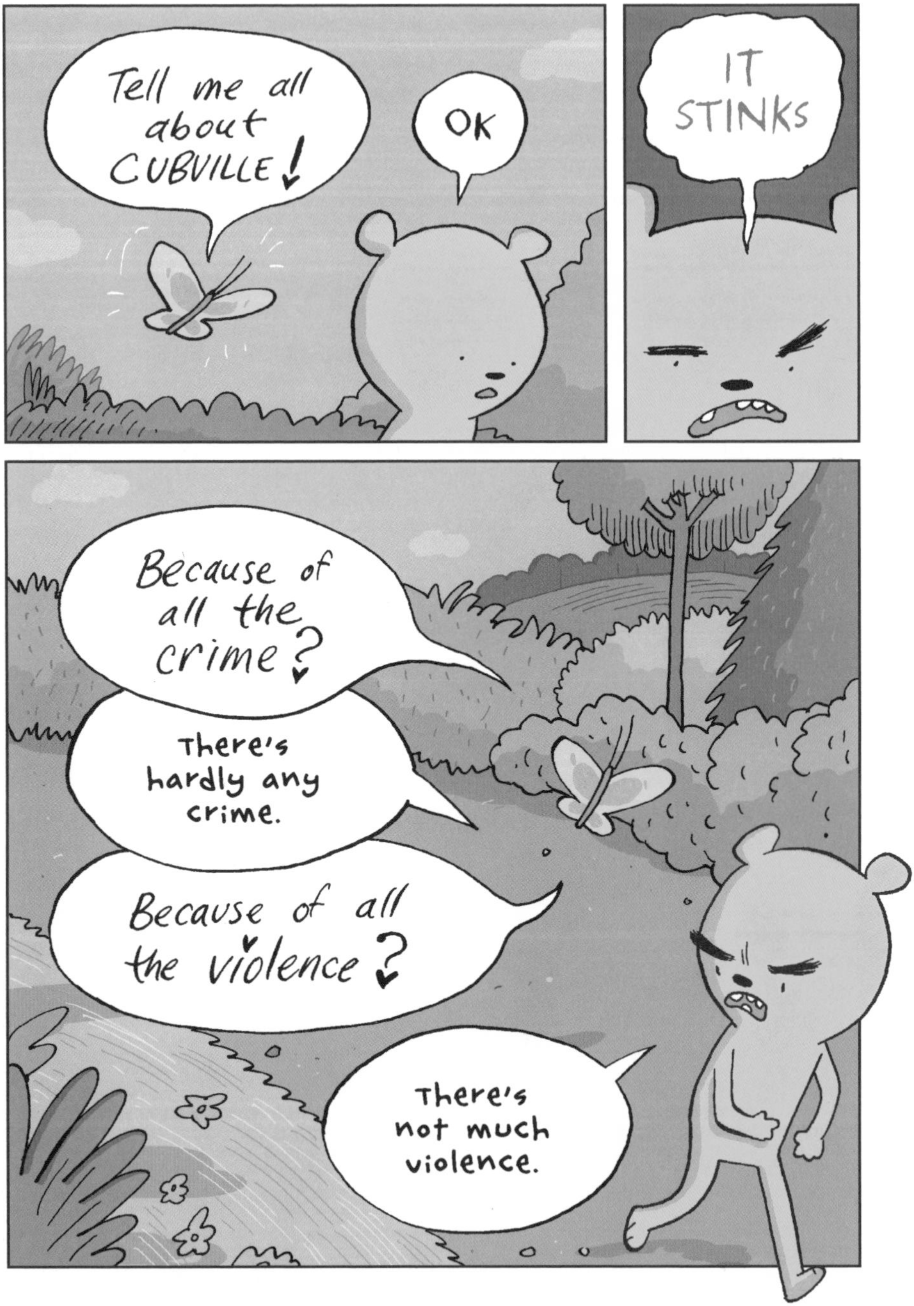
Tell me all about CUBVILLE!
OK
IT STINKS
Because of all the crime?
There's hardly any crime.
Because of all the violence?
There's not much violence.

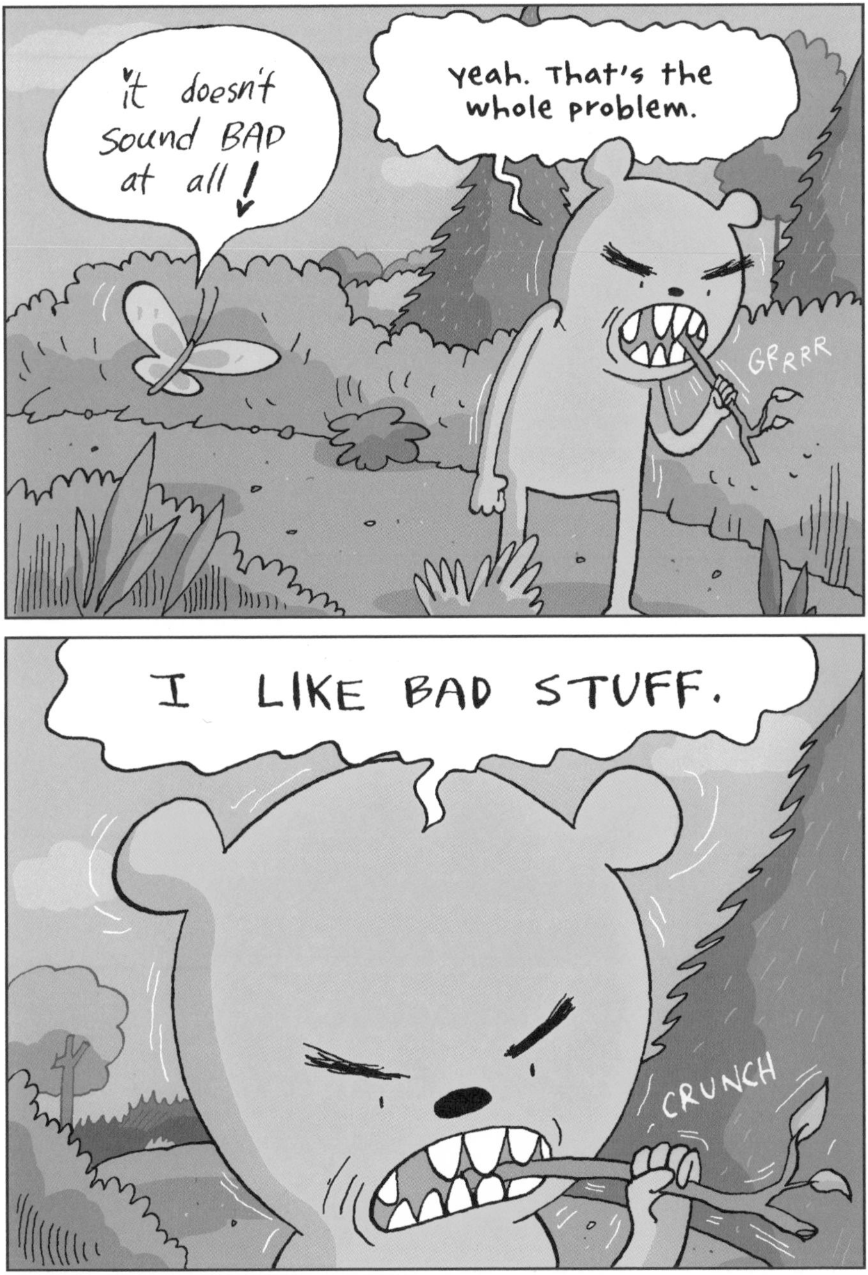
it doesn't sound BAD at all!
Yeah. That's the whole problem.
GRRRR
I LIKE BAD STUFF.
CRUNCH

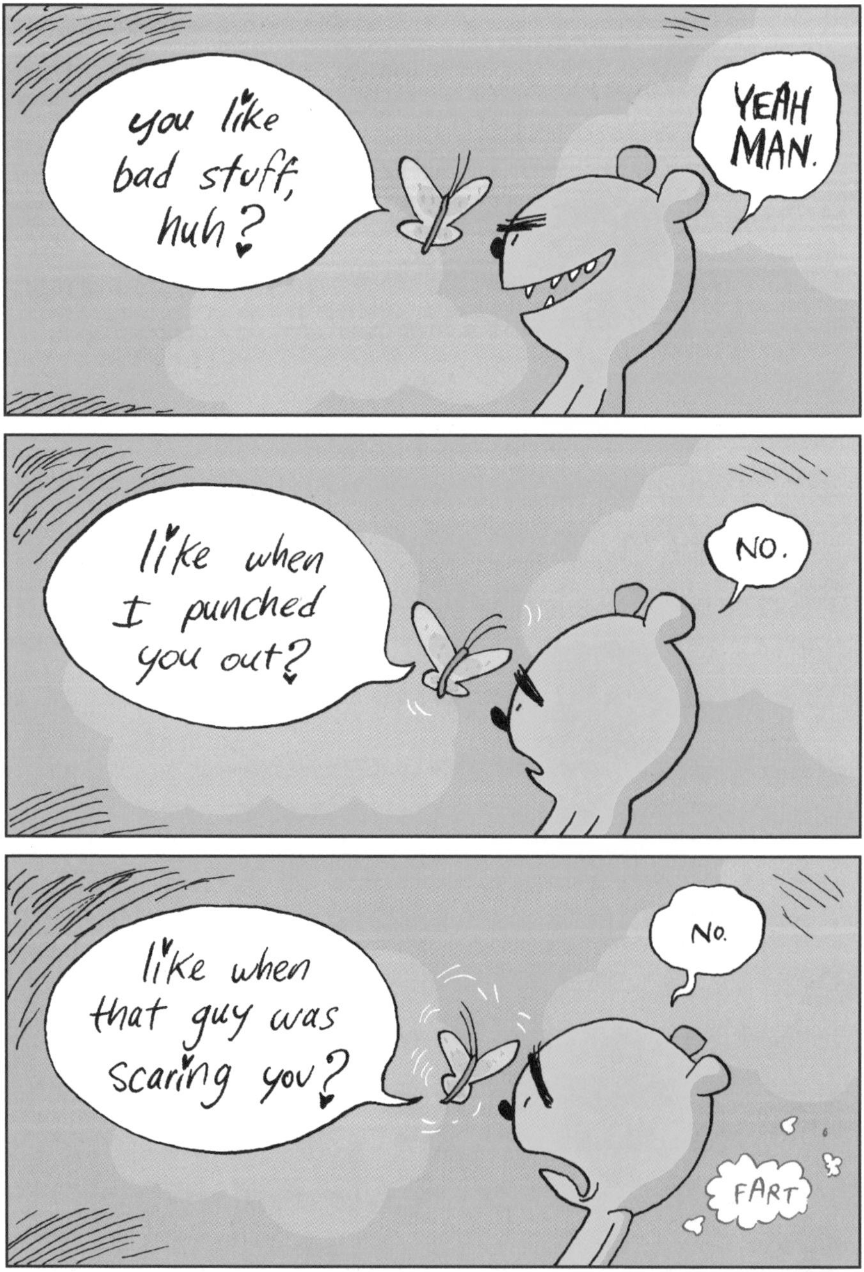
you like bad stuff, huh?
YEAH MAN.
like when I punched you out?
NO.
like when that guy was scaring you?
NO.
FART

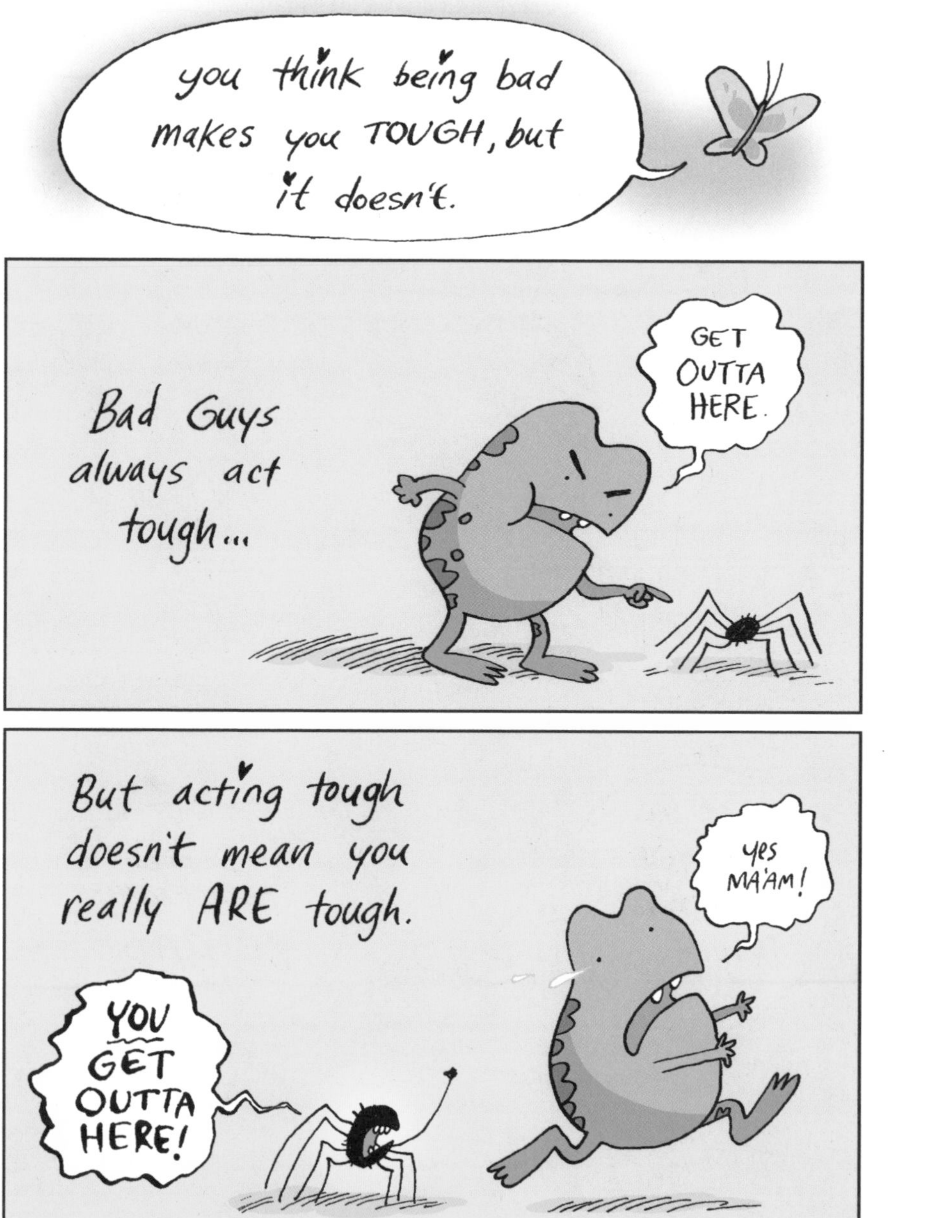

you think being bad makes you TOUGH, but it doesn't.
Bad Guys always act tough...
GET OUTTA HERE.
But acting tough doesn't mean you really ARE tough.
YES MA'AM!
YOU GET OUTTA HERE!

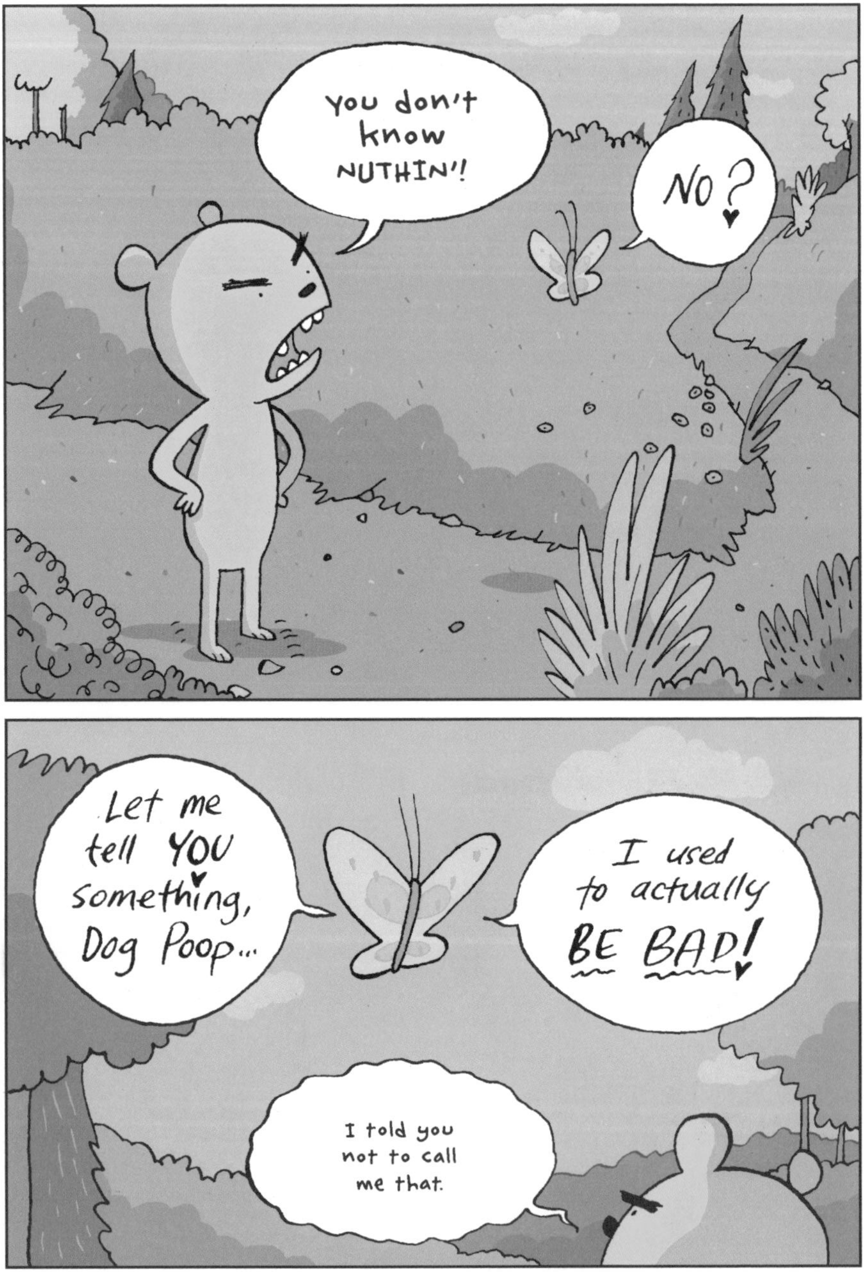

you don't know NUTHIN'!
NO?
Let me tell YOU something, Dog Poop...
I used to actually BE BAD!
I told you not to call me that.

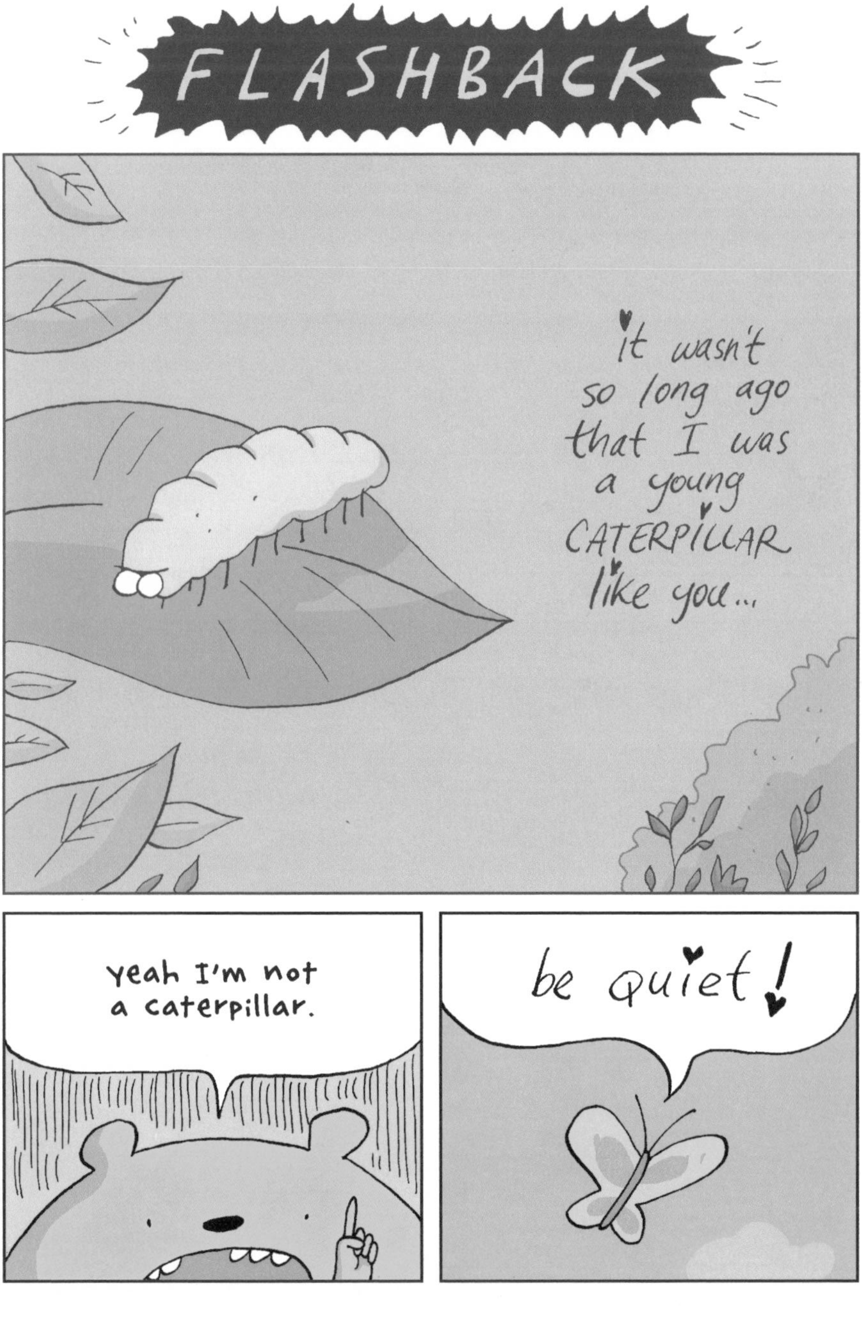
FLASHBACK
it wasn't so long ago that I was a young CATERPILLAR like you...
yeah I'm not a caterpillar.
be quiet!

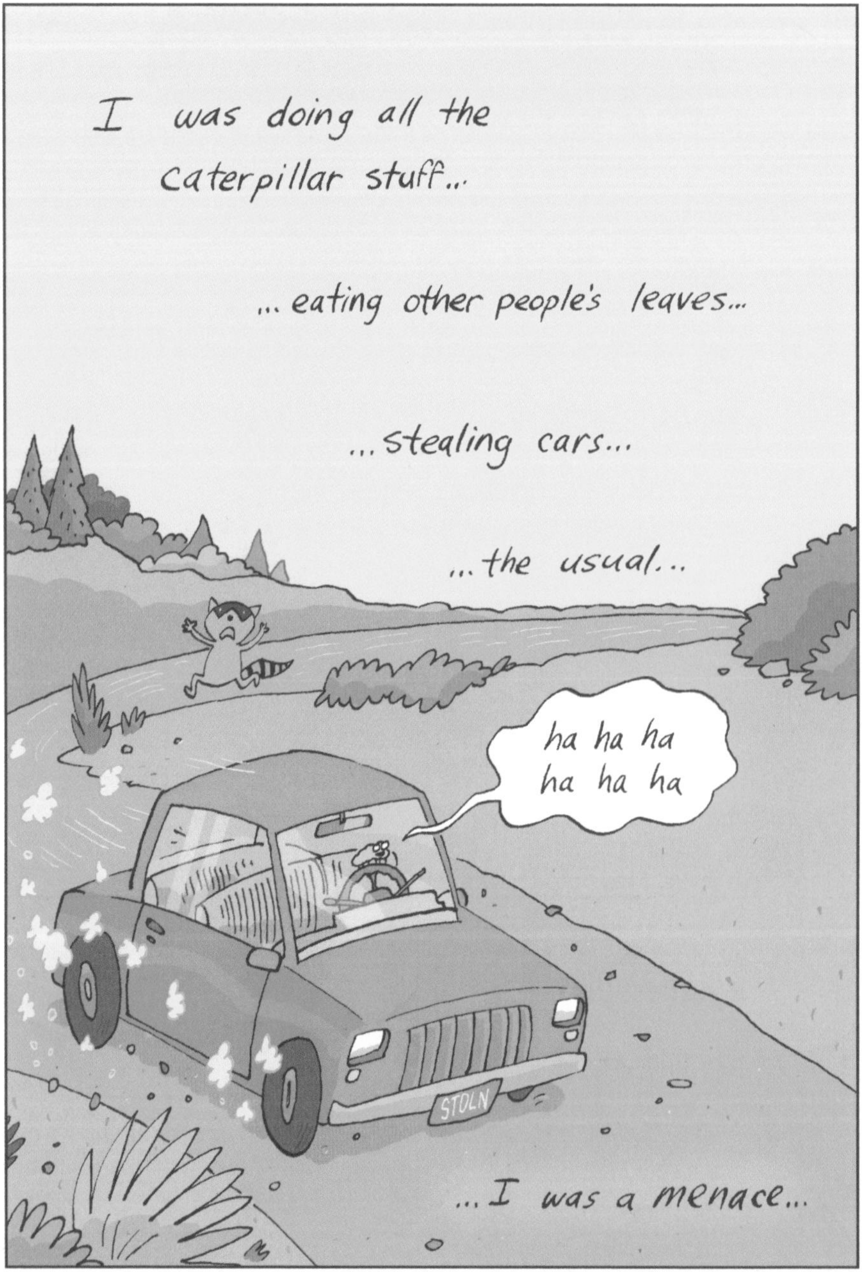
I was doing all the caterpillar stuff...
...eating other people's leaves...
...stealing cars...
...the usual...
ha ha ha ha ha ha
STOLN
...I was a menace...

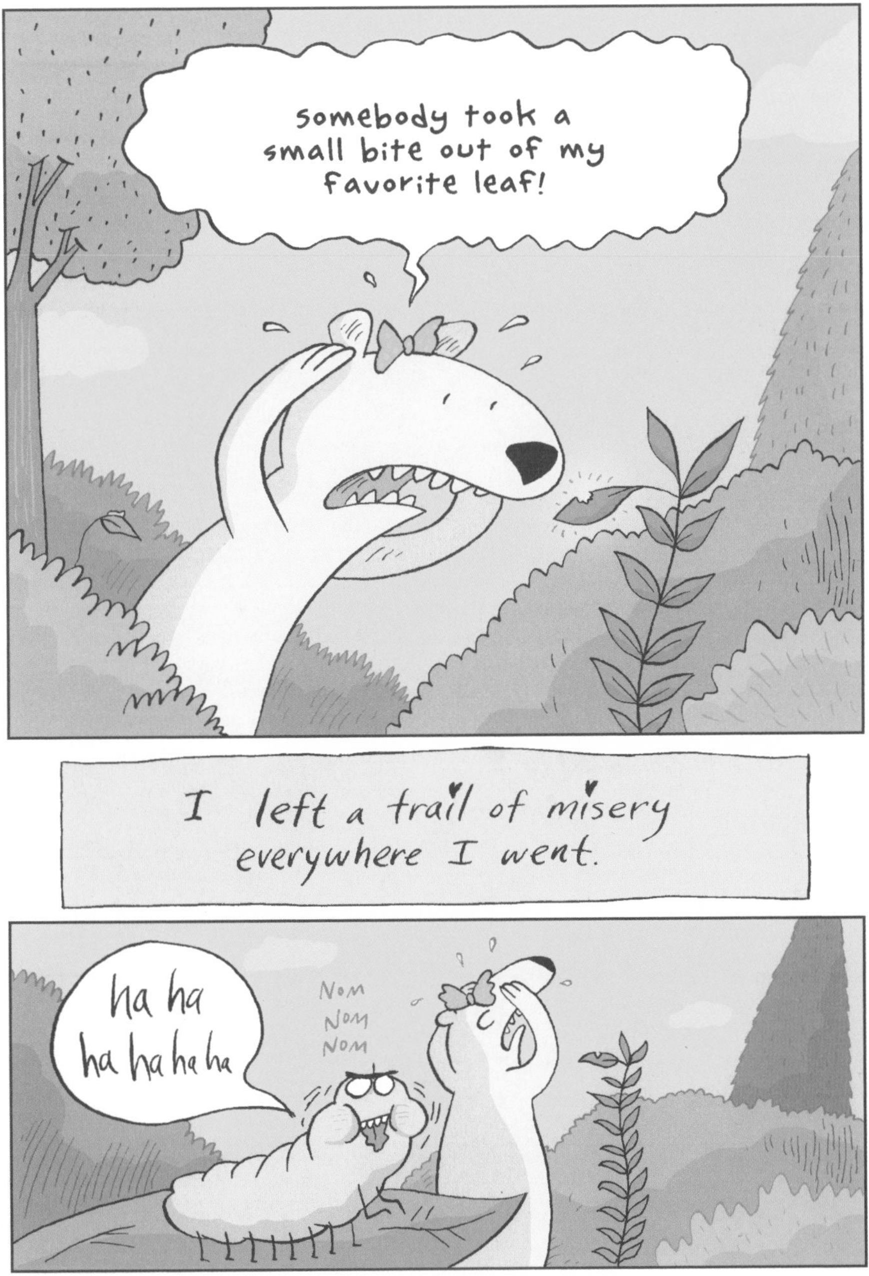
somebody took a small bite out of my favorite leaf!
I left a trail of misery everywhere I went.
ha ha ha ha ha ha
NOM NOM NOM

one night, I decided to go over to CUBVILLE...

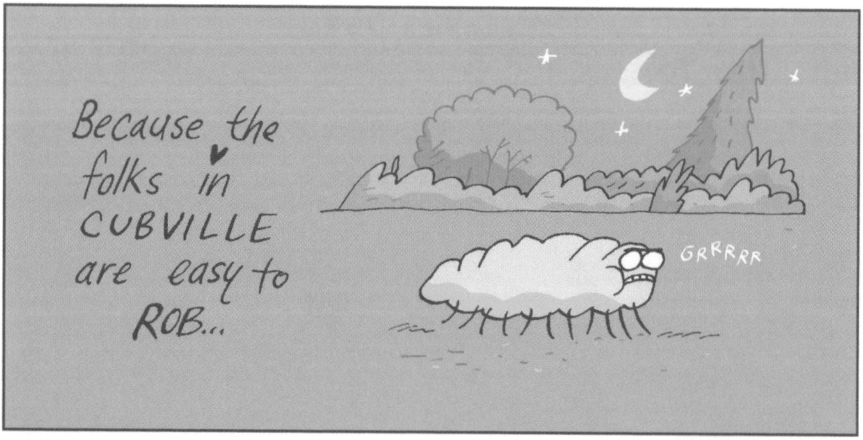
Because the folks in CUBVILLE are easy to ROB...
GRRRRR

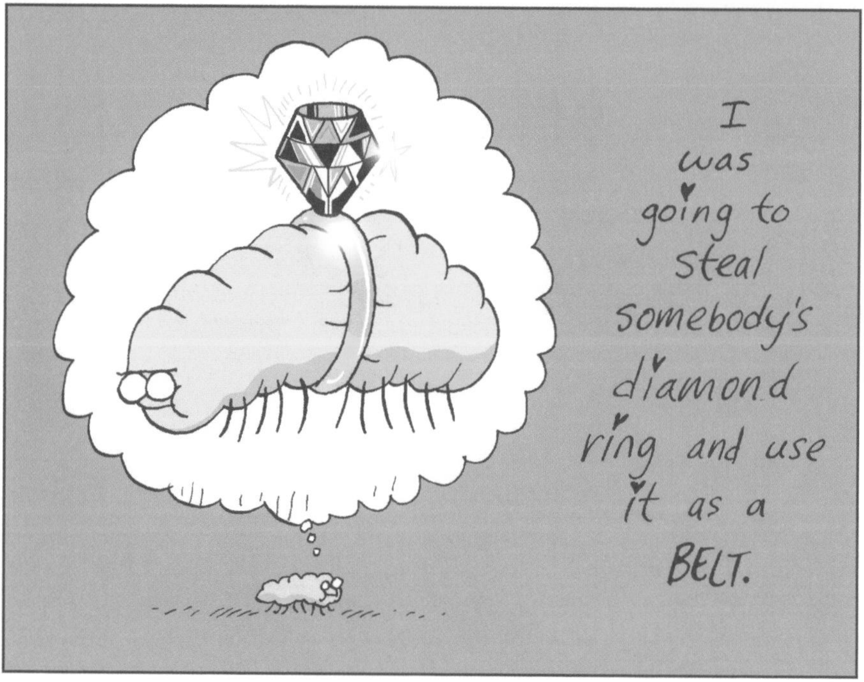
I was going to steal somebody's diamond ring and use it as a BELT.

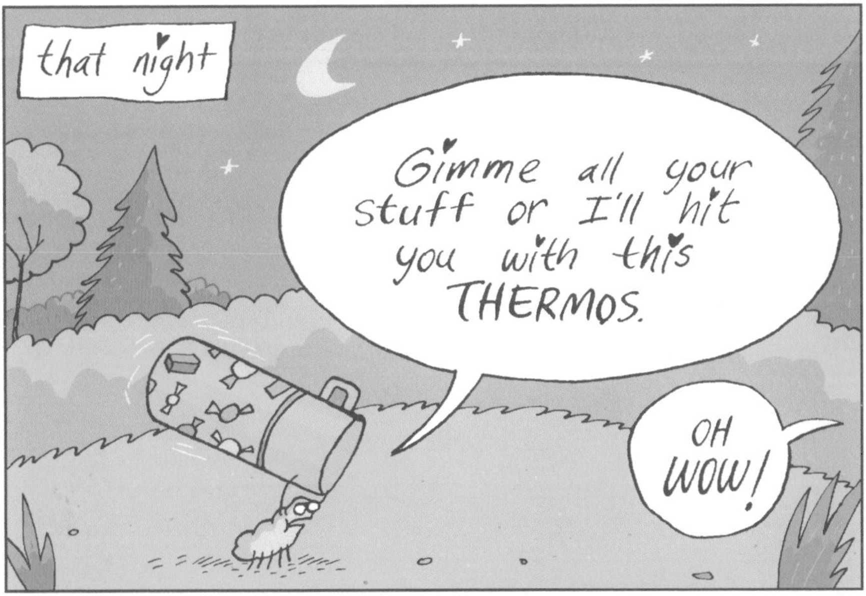
that night
Gimme all your stuff or I'll hit you with this THERMOS.
OH WOW!

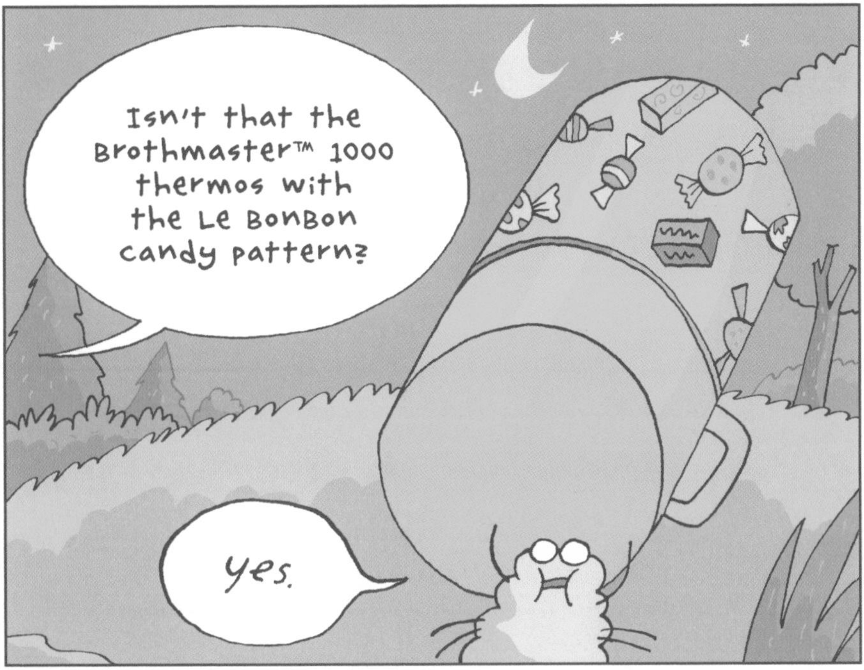
Isn't that the Brothmaster™ 1000 thermos with the Le Bonbon candy pattern?
yes.

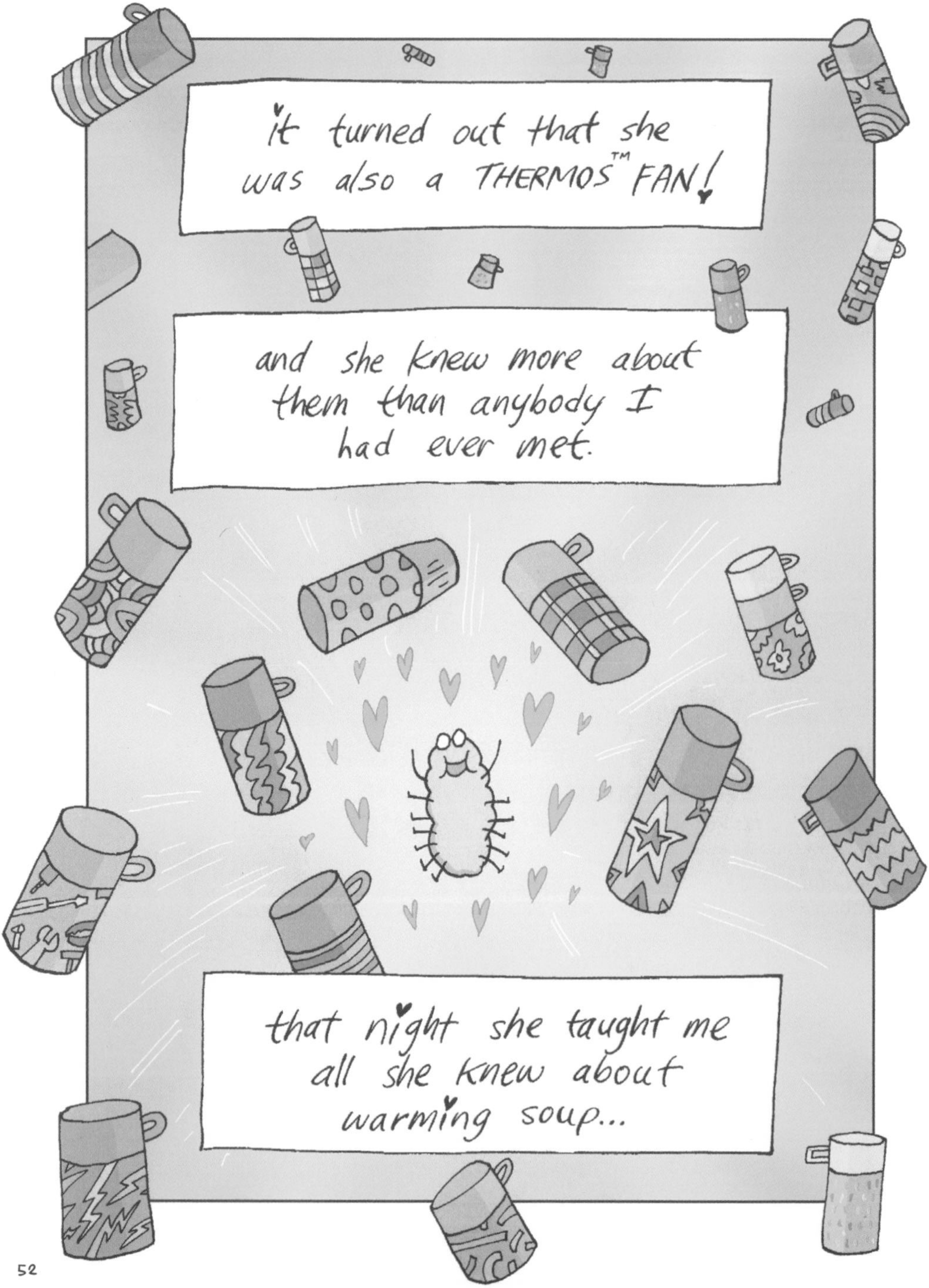

it turned out that she was also a THERMOS™ FAN!
and she knew more about them than anybody I had ever met.
that night she taught me all she knew about warming soup...

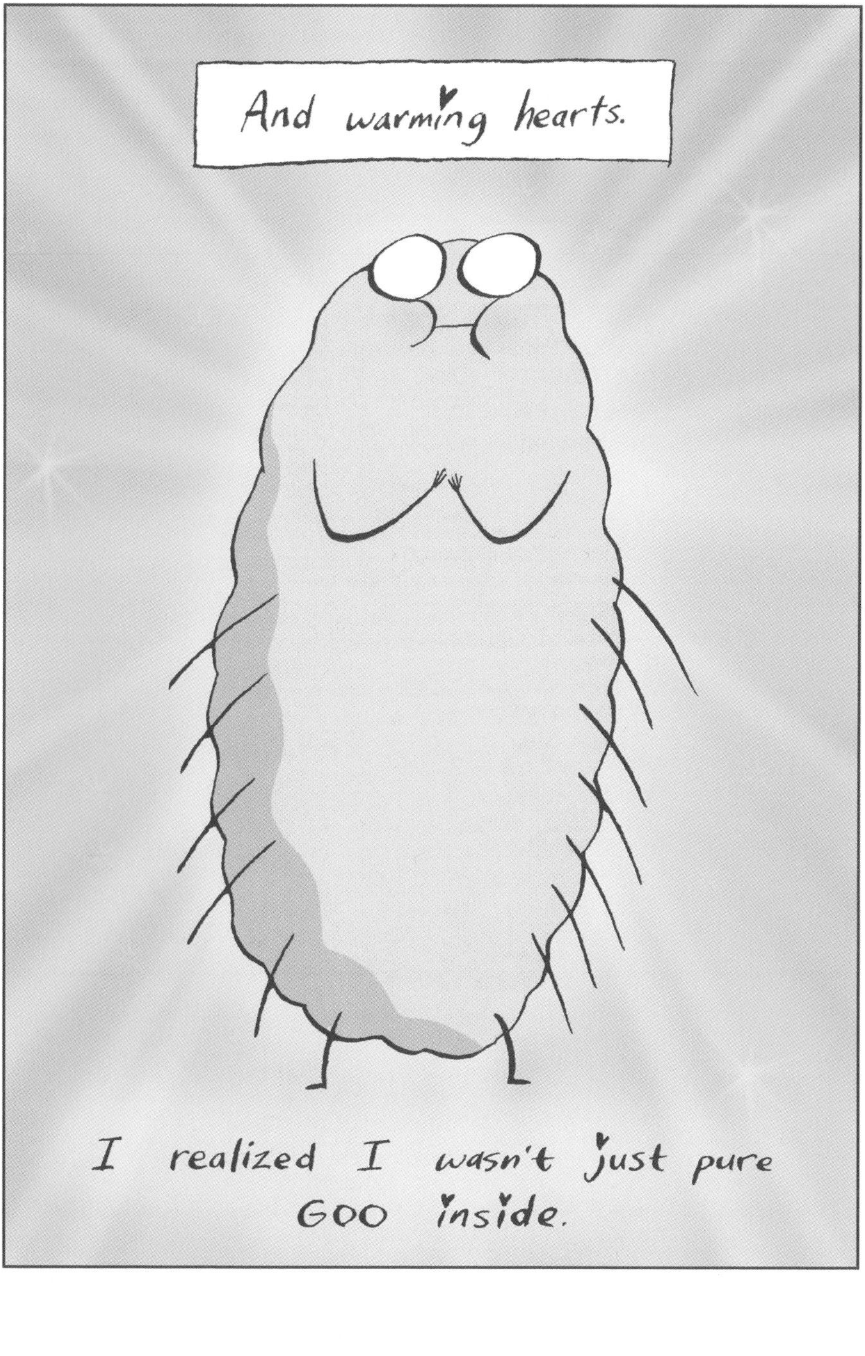
And warming hearts.
I realized I wasn't just pure GOO inside.

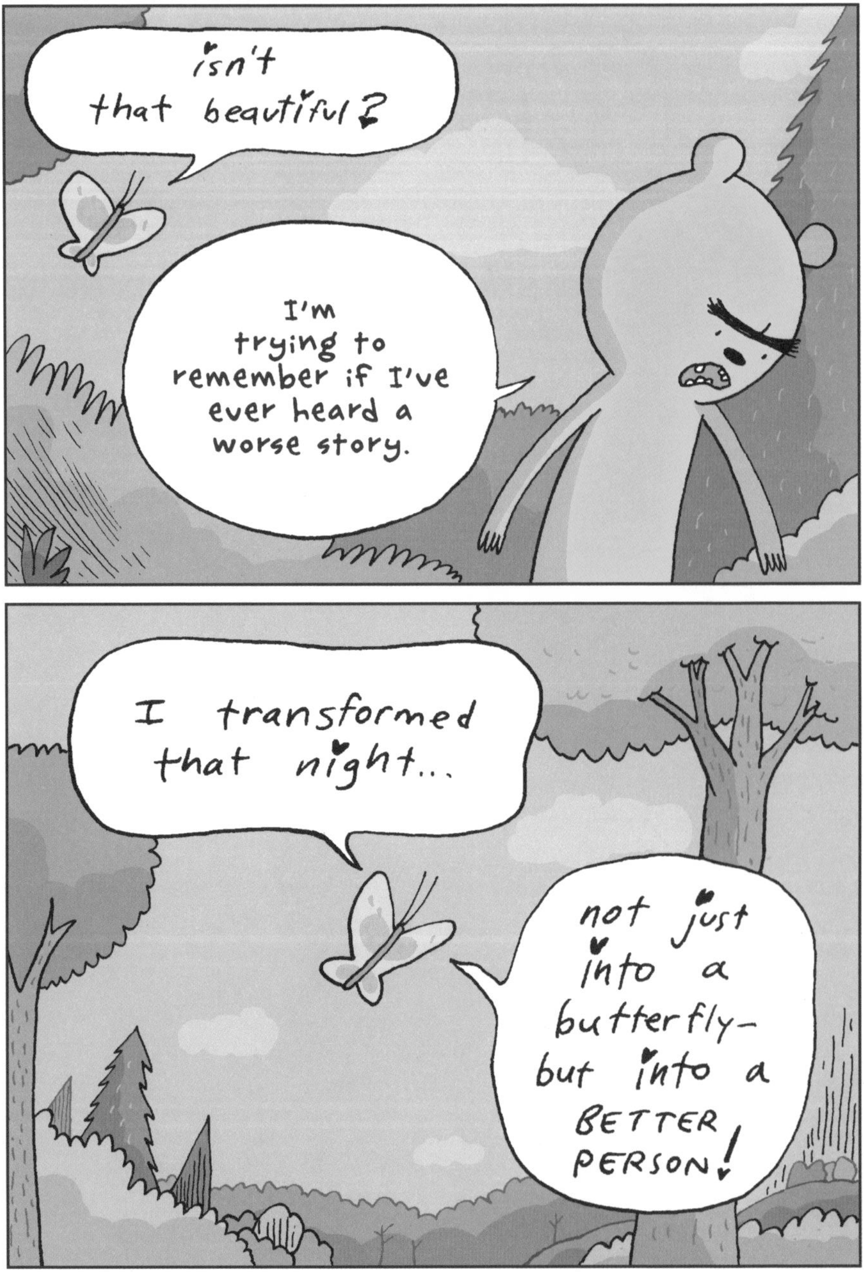
isn't that beautiful?
I'm trying to remember if I've ever heard a worse story.
I transformed that night...
not just into a butterfly- but into a BETTER PERSON!

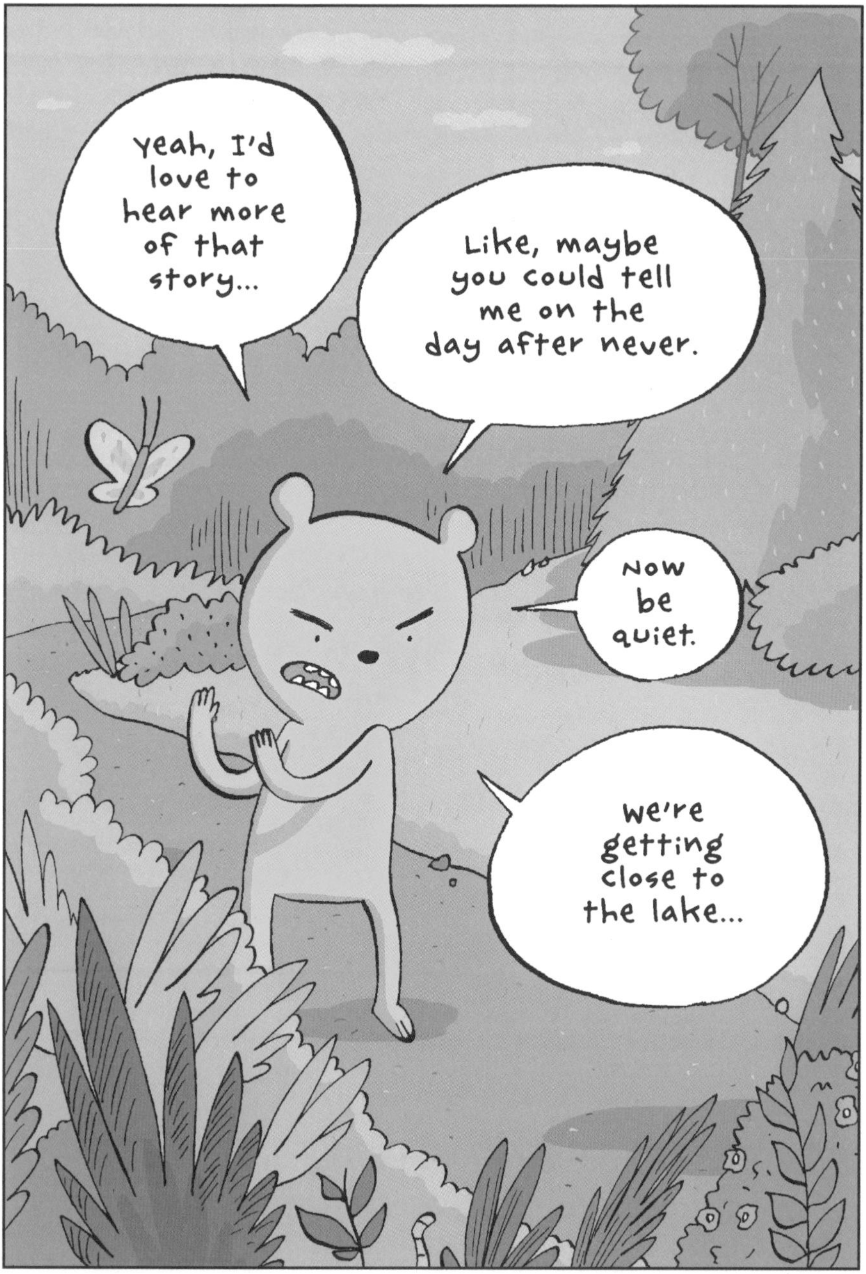
Yeah, I'd love to hear more of that story...
Like, maybe you could tell me on the day after never.
Now be quiet.
We're getting close to the lake...

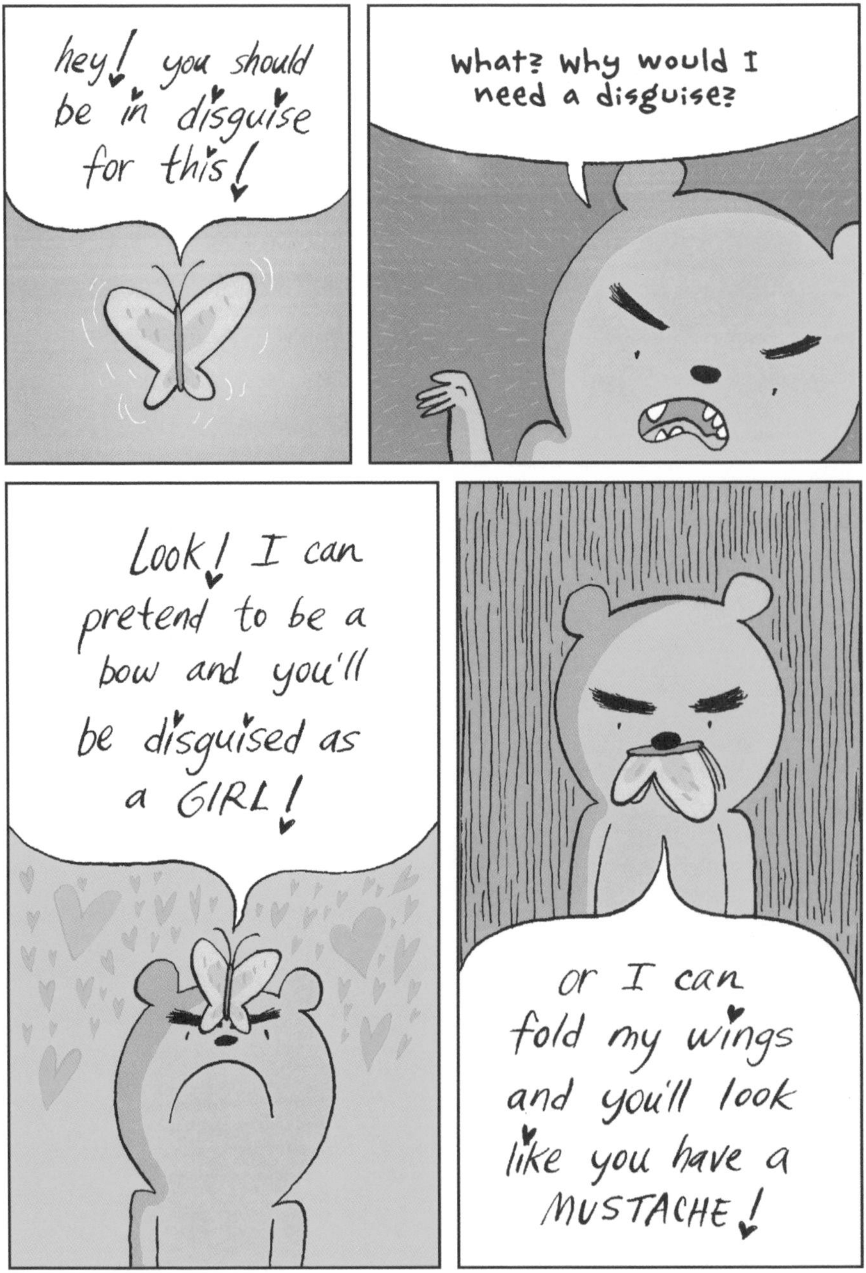
hey! you should be in disguise for this!
what? why would I need a disguise?
Look! I can pretend to be a bow and you'll be disguised as a GIRL!
or I can fold my wings and you'll look like you have a MUSTACHE!

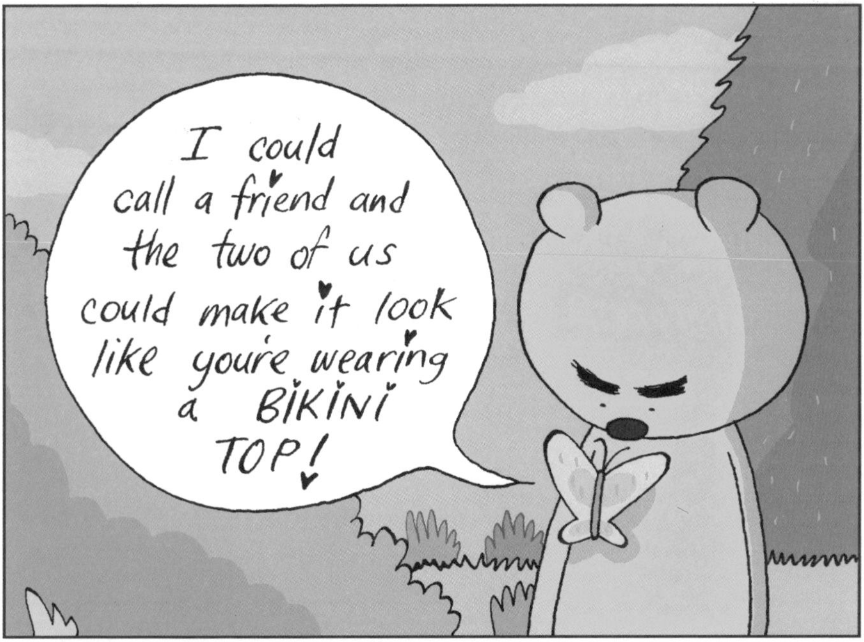
I could call a friend and the two of us could make it look like youre wearing a BIKINI TOP!

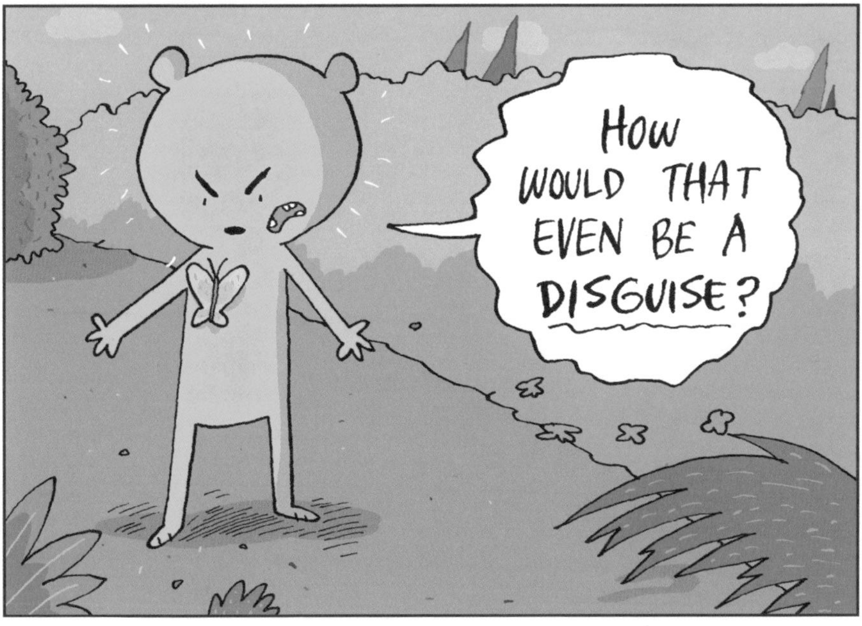
HOW WOULD THAT EVEN BE A DISGUISE?

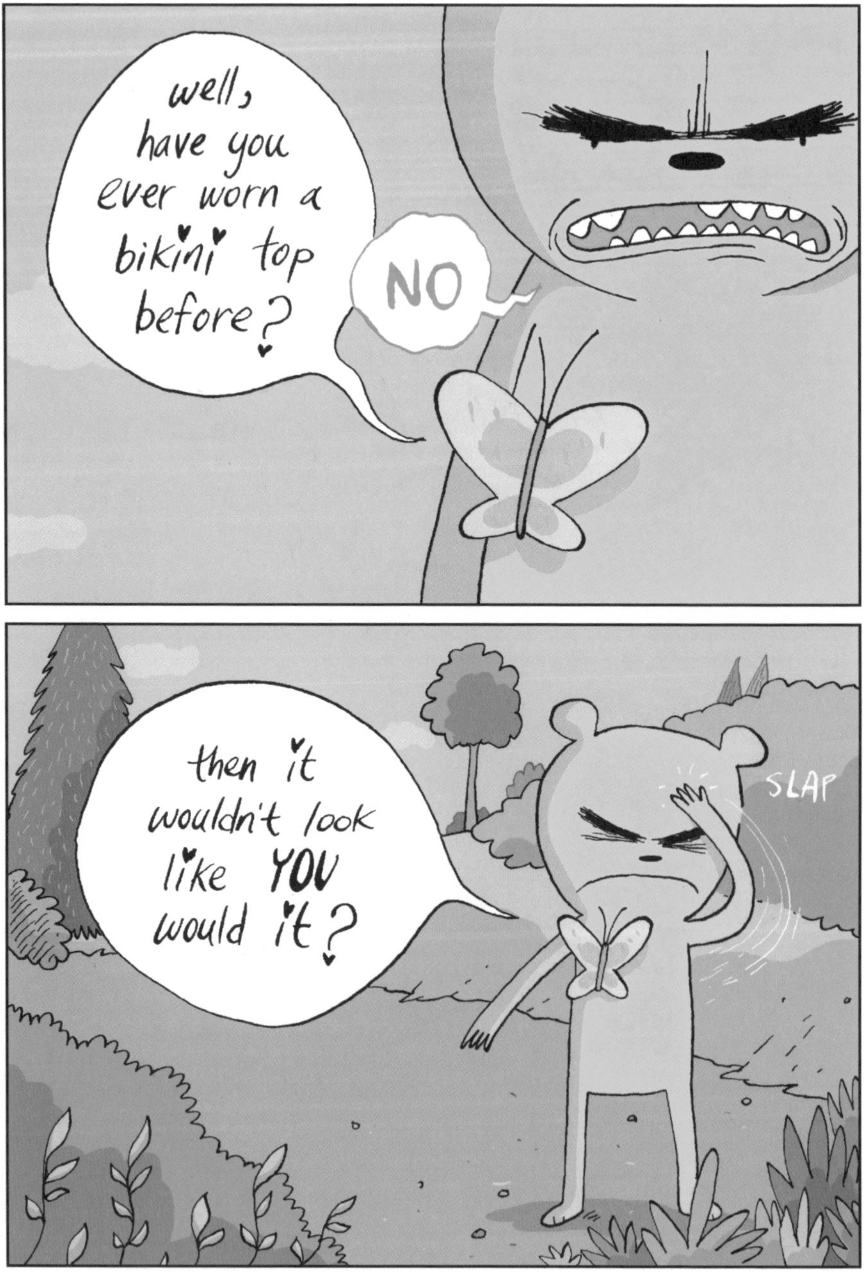

well, have you ever worn a bikini top before?
NO
then it wouldn't look like YOU would it?
SLAP

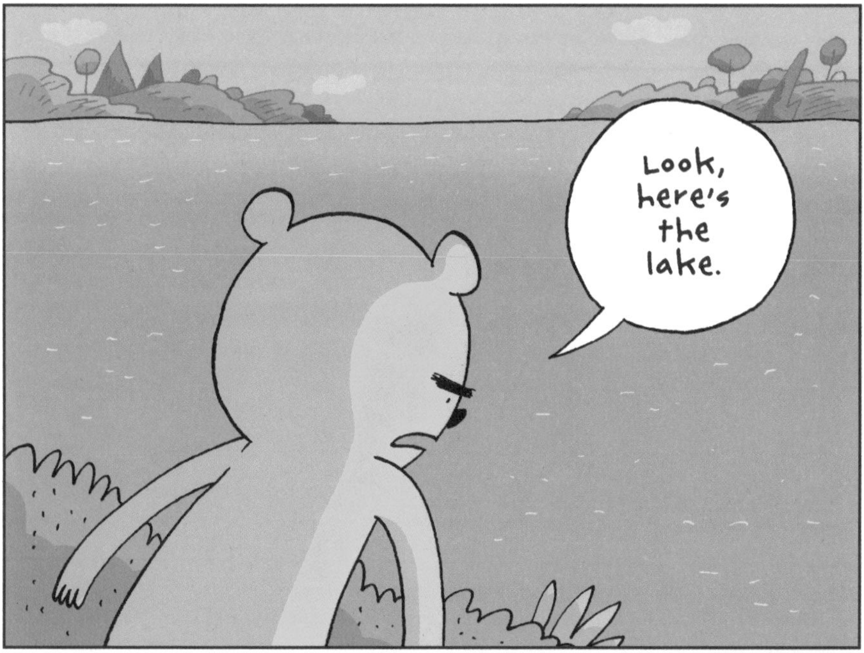
Look, here's the lake.

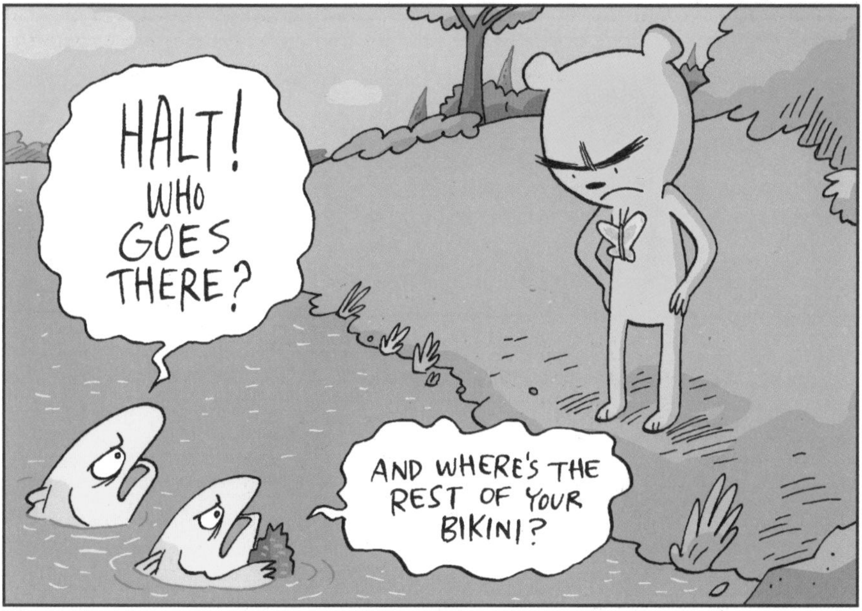
HALT! WHO GOES THERE?
AND WHERE'S THE REST OF YOUR BIKINI?

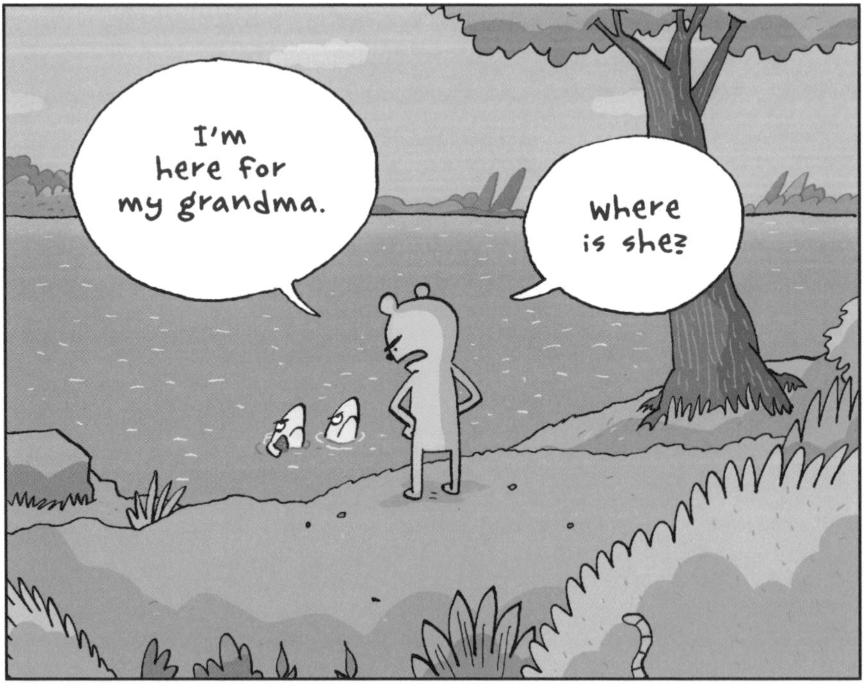
I'm here for my grandma.
Where is she?

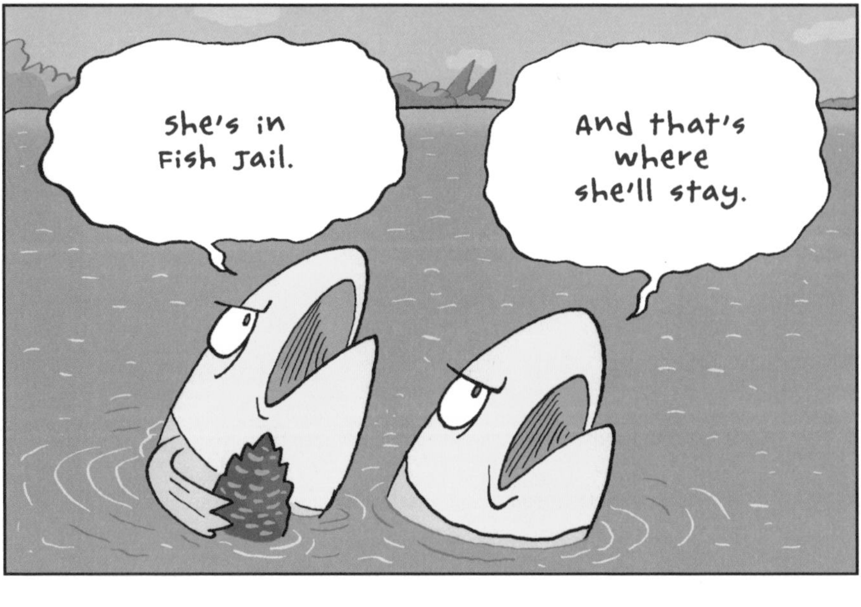
She's in Fish Jail.
And that's where she'll stay.

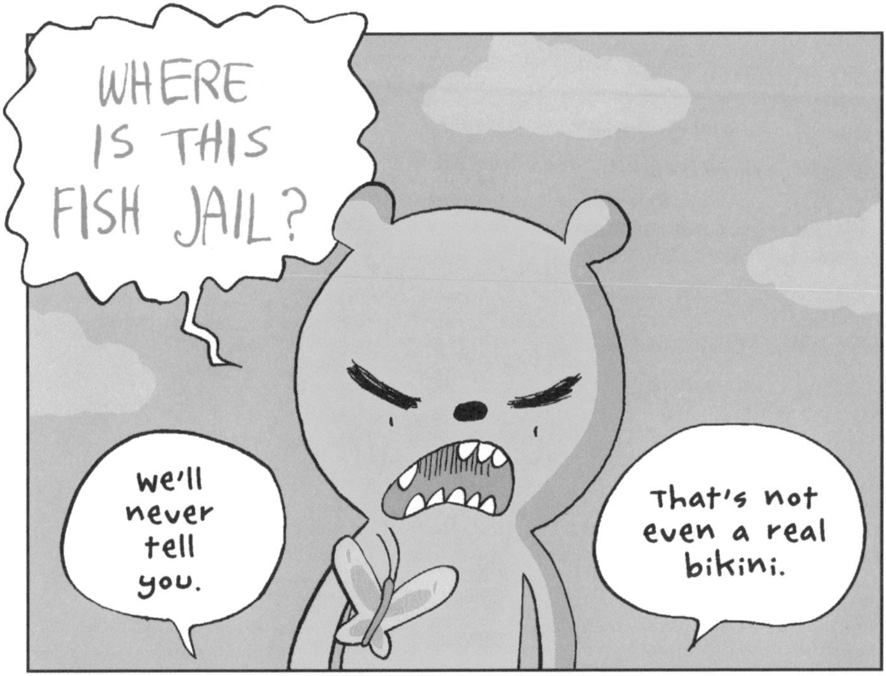
WHERE IS THIS FISH JAIL?
We'll never tell you.
That's not even a real bikini.

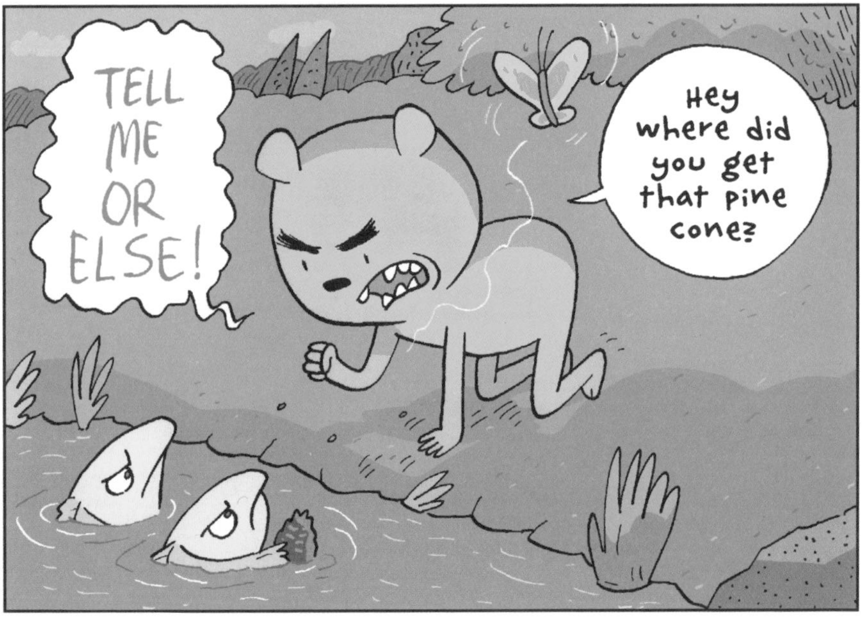
TELL ME OR ELSE!
Hey where did you get that pine cone?

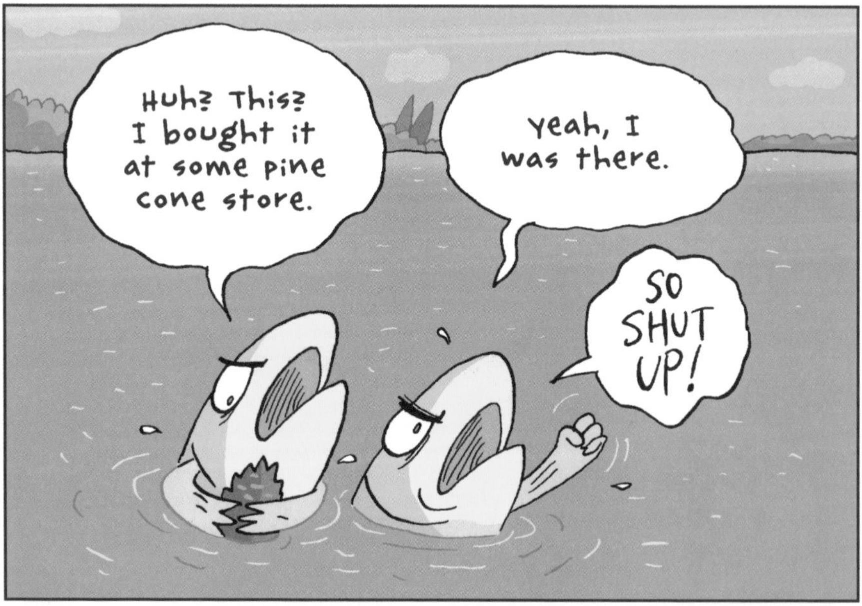
Huh? This? I bought it at some pine cone store.
Yeah, I was there.
SO SHUT UP!

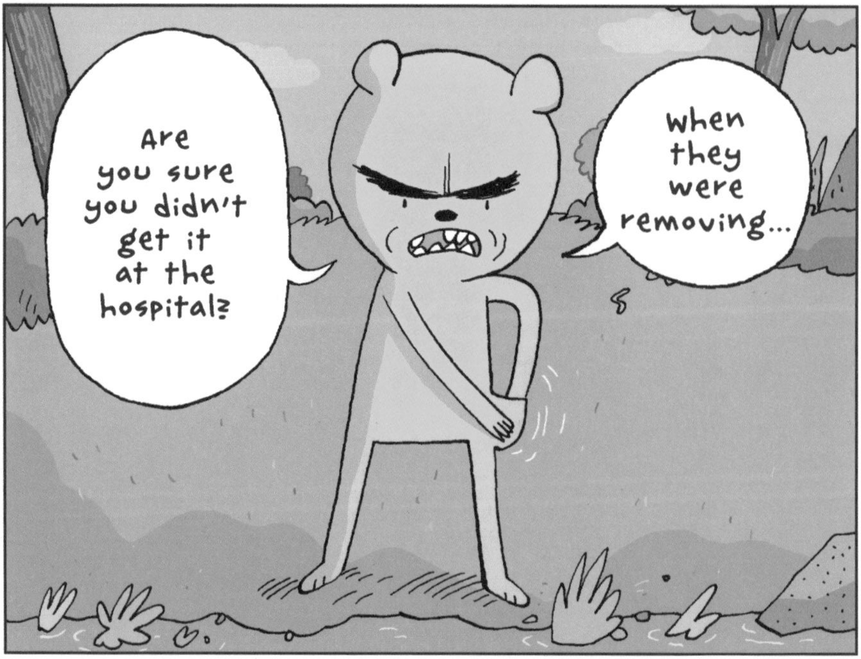
Are you sure you didn't get it at the hospital?
When they were removing...

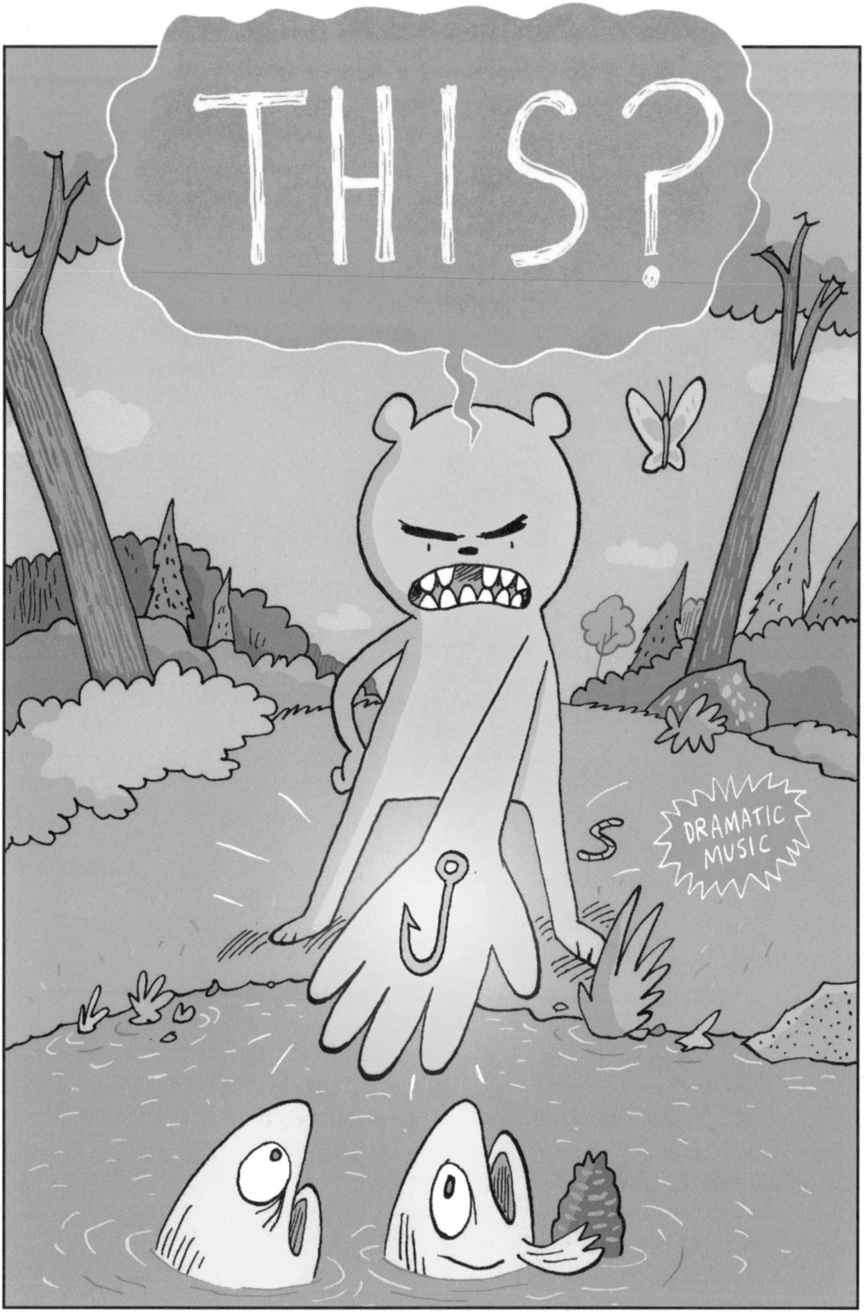
THIS?
DRAMATIC MUSIC

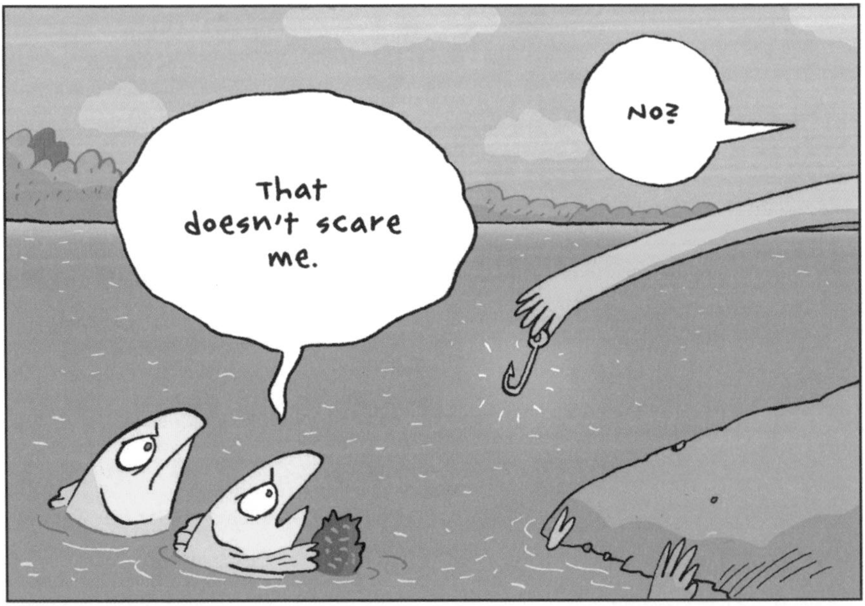
No?
That doesn't scare me.

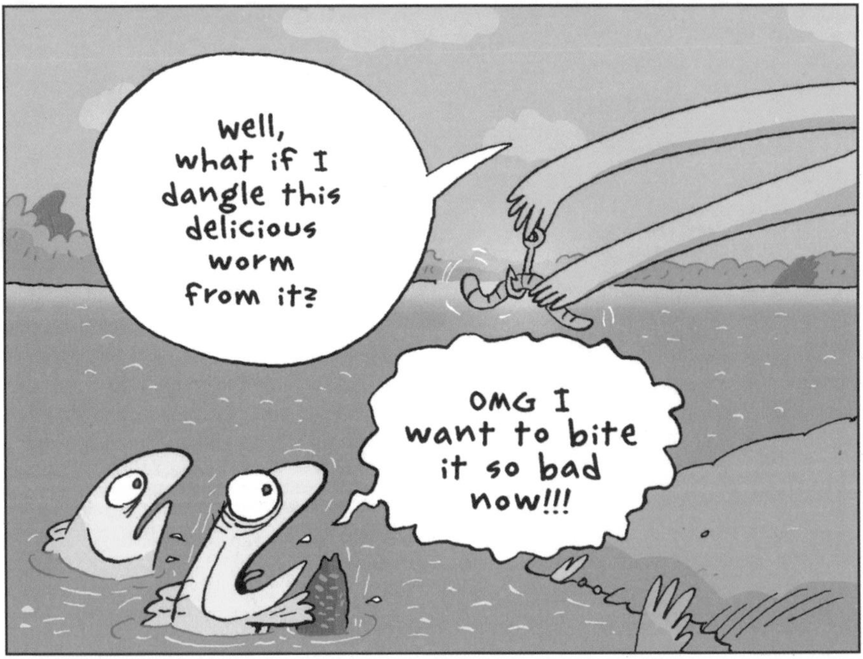
Well, what if I dangle this delicious worm from it?
OMG I want to bite it so bad now!!!

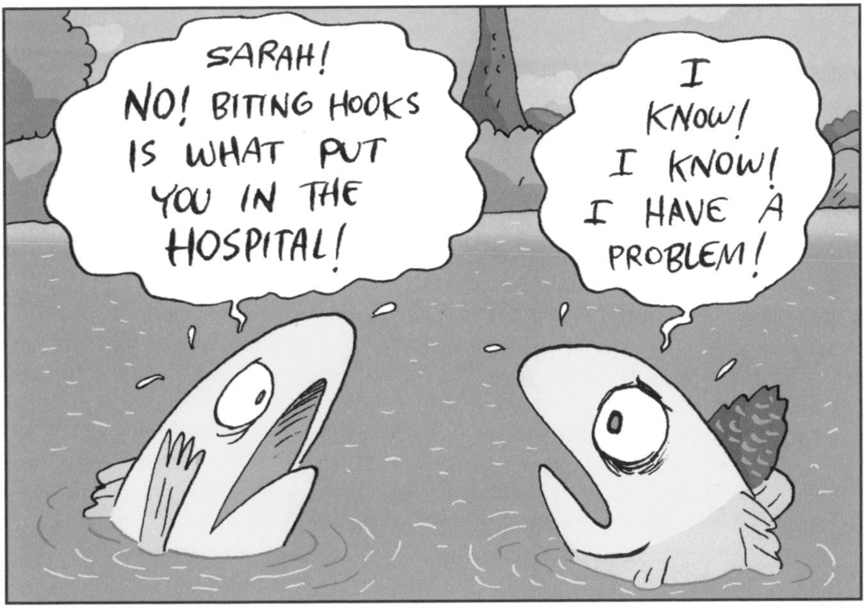
SARAH! NO! BITING HOOKS IS WHAT PUT YOU IN THE HOSPITAL!
I KNOW! I KNOW! I HAVE A PROBLEM!

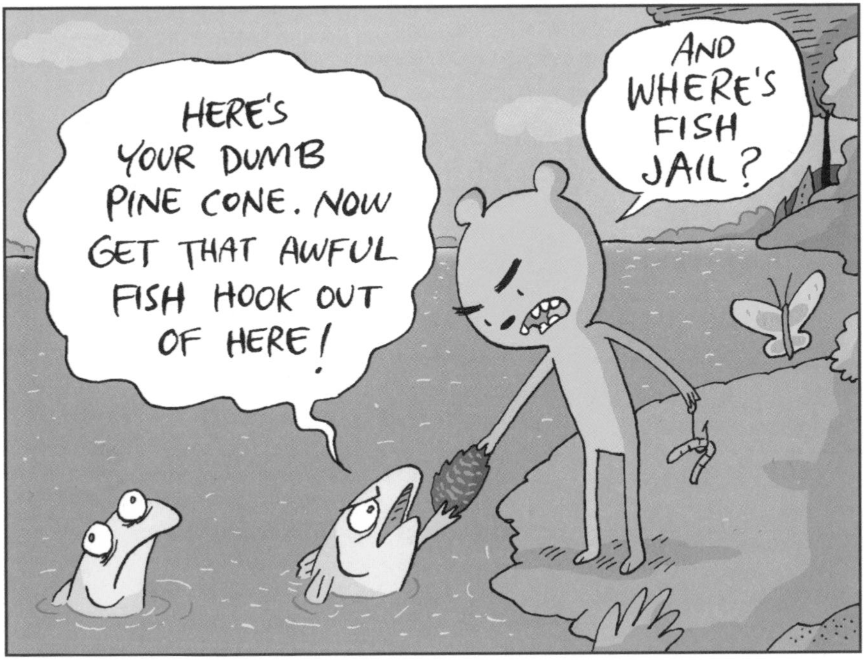
HERE'S YOUR DUMB PINE CONE. NOW GET THAT AWFUL FISH HOOK OUT OF HERE!
AND WHERE'S FISH JAIL?

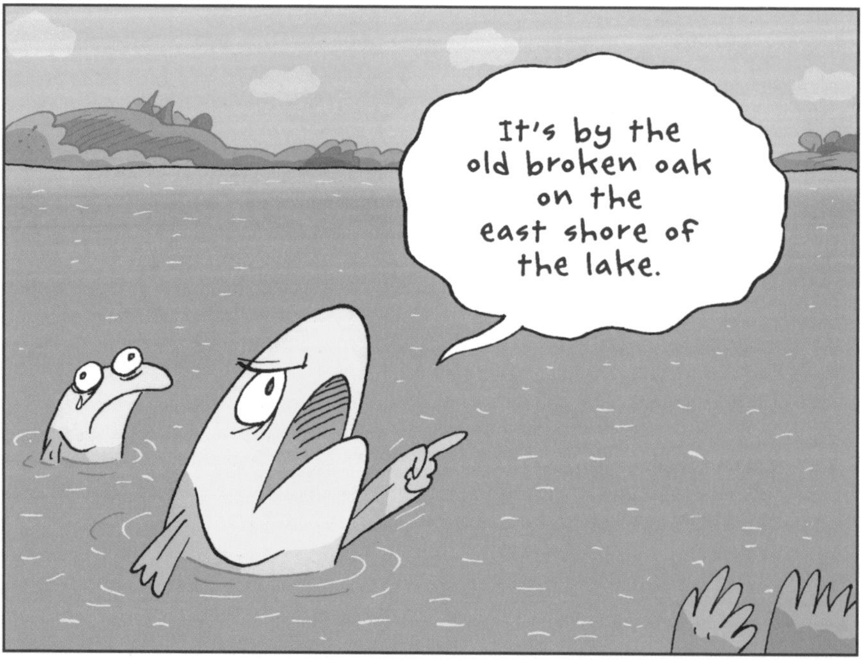
It's by the old broken oak on the east shore of the lake.

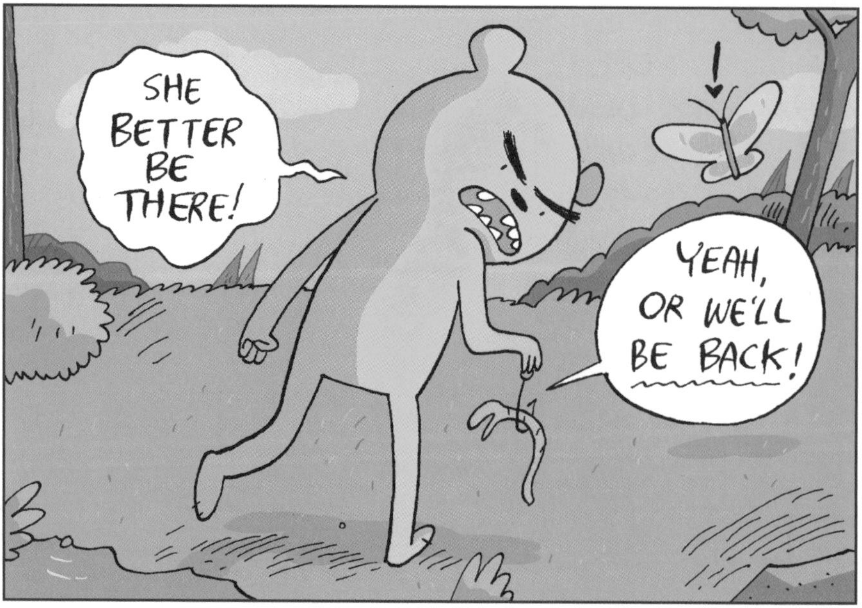
SHE BETTER BE THERE!
!
YEAH, OR WE'LL BE BACK!

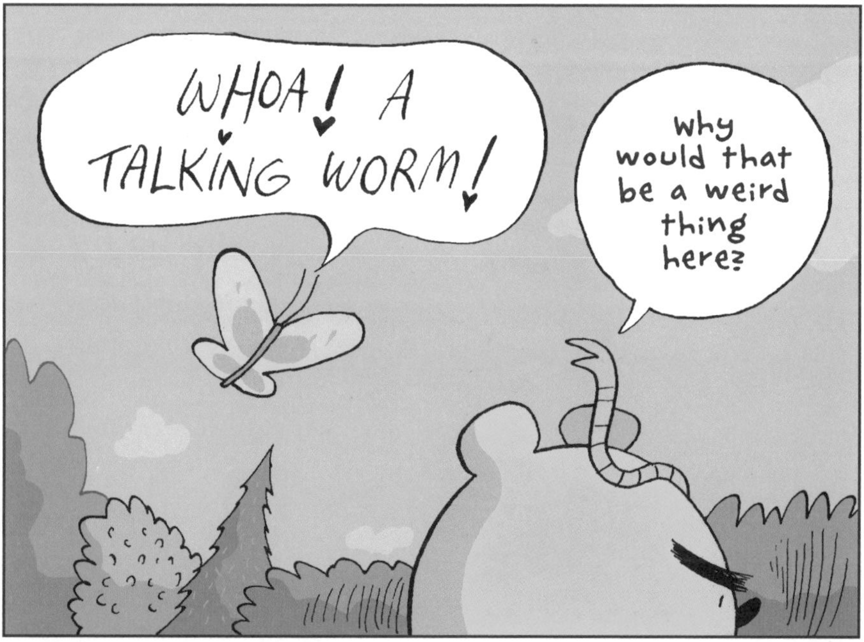
WHOA! A TALKING WORM!
why would that be a weird thing here?

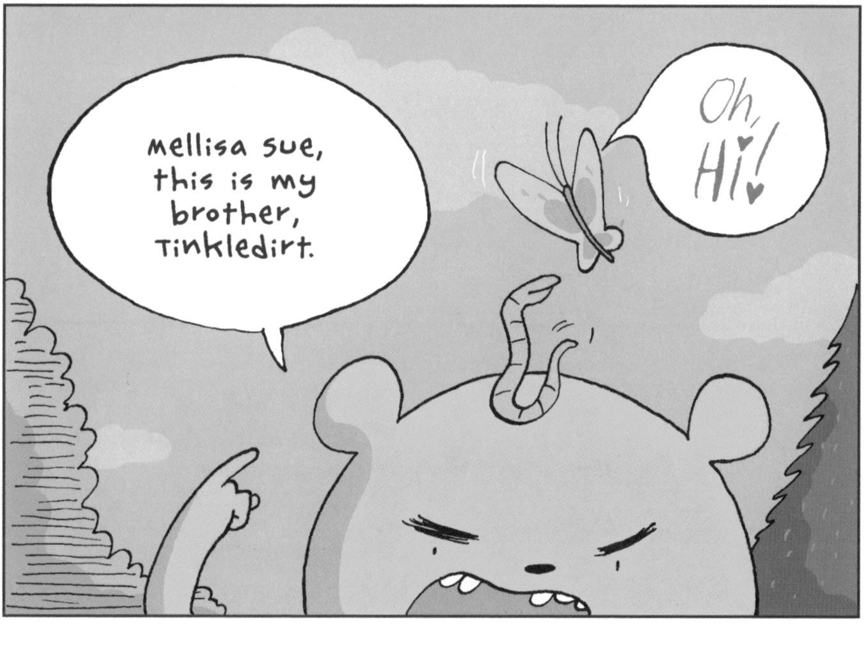
mellisa sue, this is my brother, Tinkledirt.
Oh, Hi!

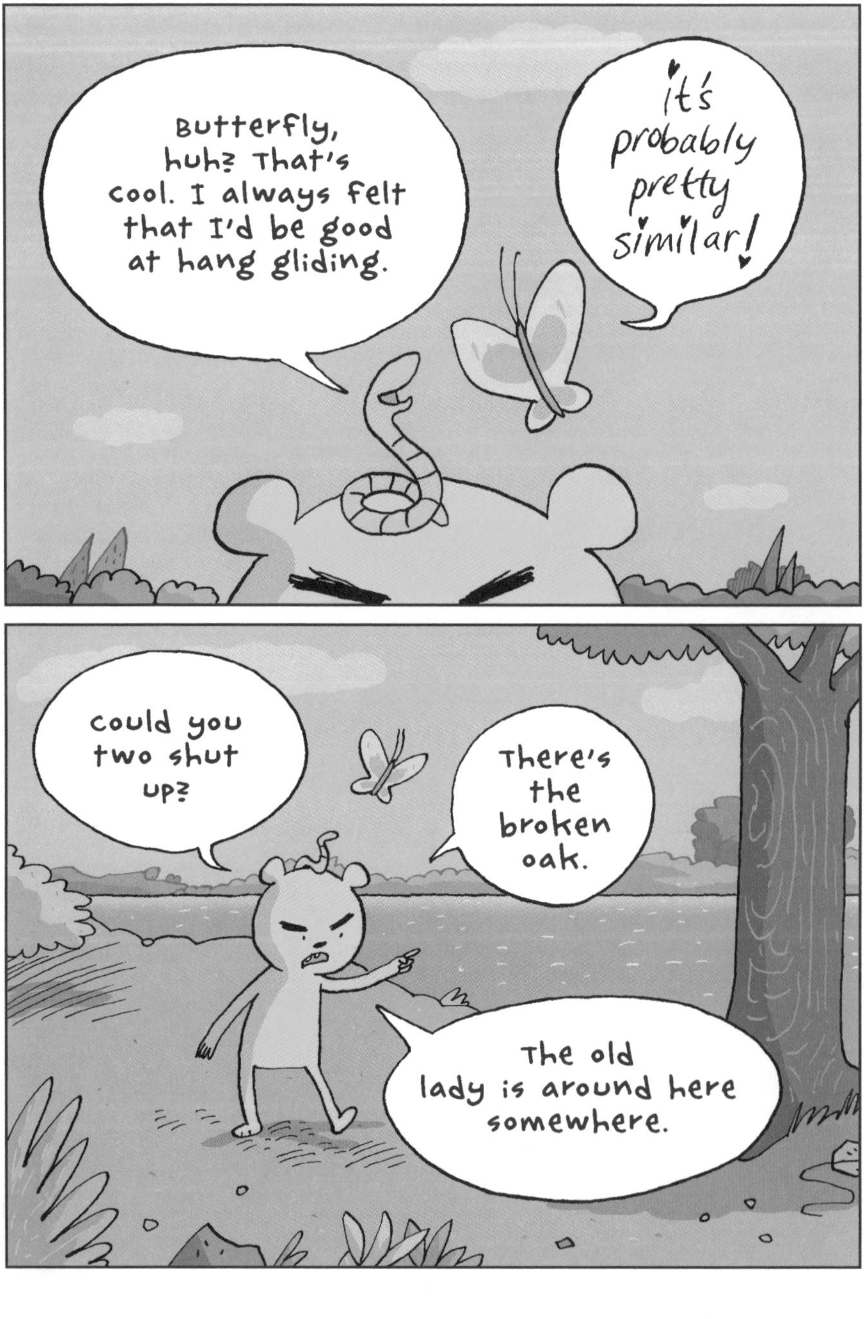
Butterfly, huh? That's cool. I always felt that I'd be good at hang gliding.
It's probably pretty similar!
Could you two shut up?
There's the broken oak.
The old lady is around here somewhere.

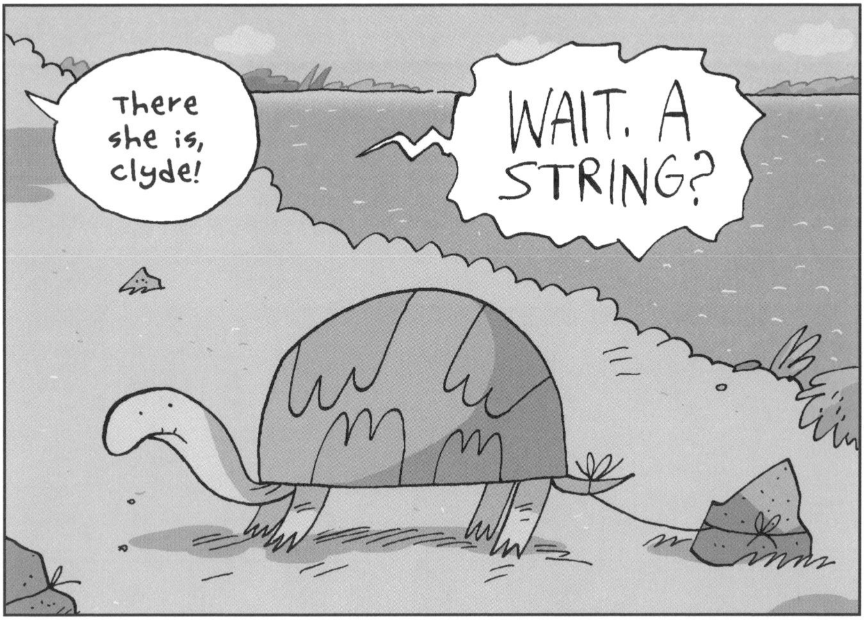
There she is, clyde!
WAIT. A STRING?

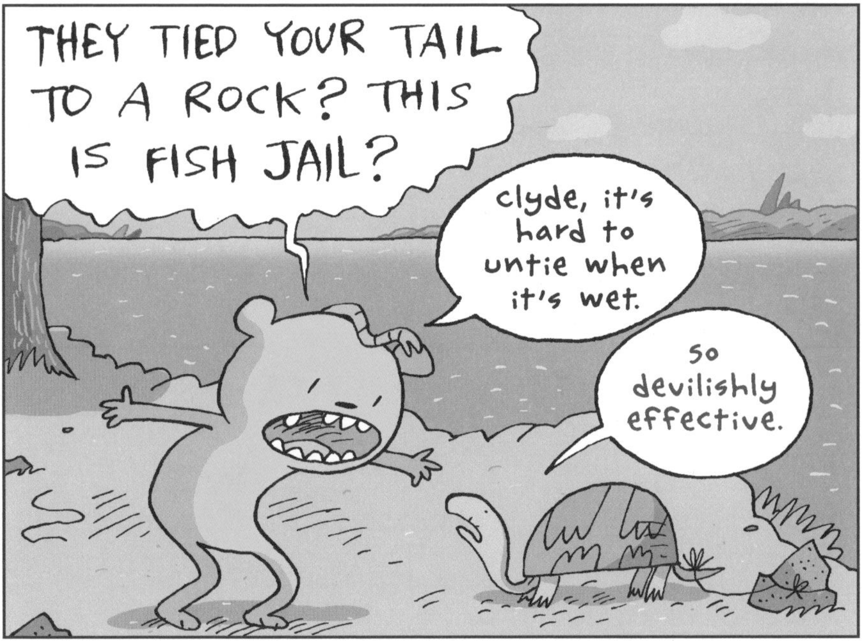
THEY TIED YOUR TAIL TO A ROCK? THIS IS FISH JAIL?
clyde, it's hard to untie when it's wet.
So devilishly effective.

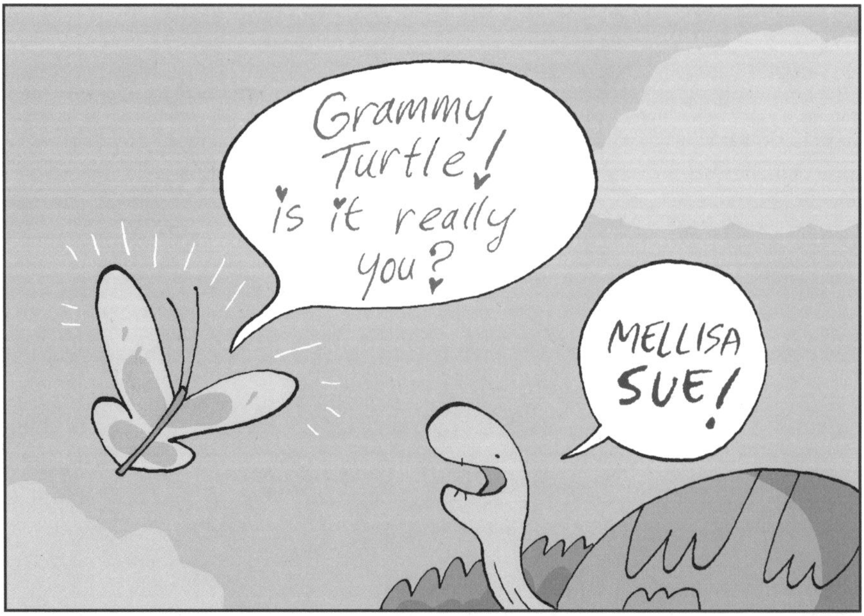
Grammy Turtle! is it really you?
MELLISA SUE!

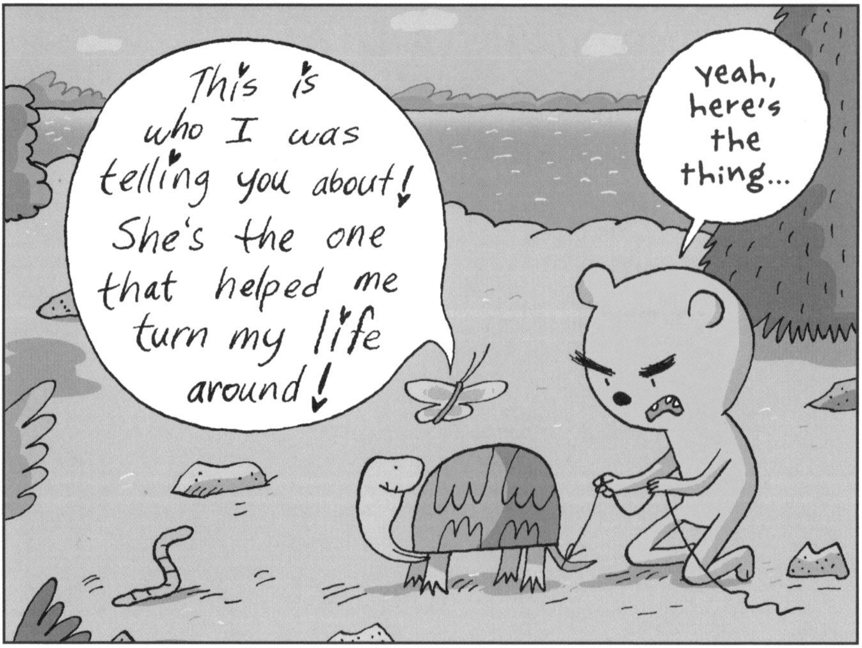
This is who I was telling you about! She's the one that helped me turn my life around!
Yeah, here's the thing...

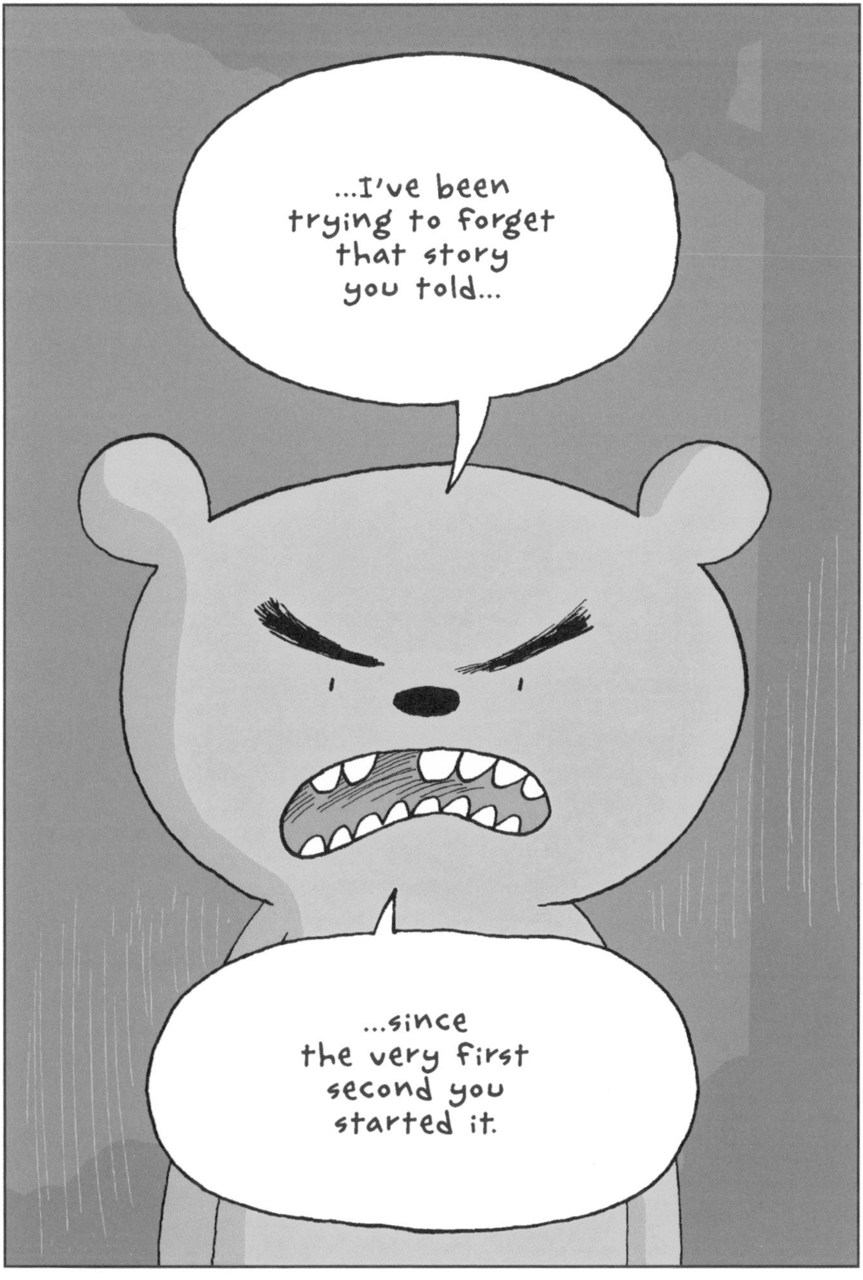
...I've been trying to forget that story you told...
...since the very first second you started it.

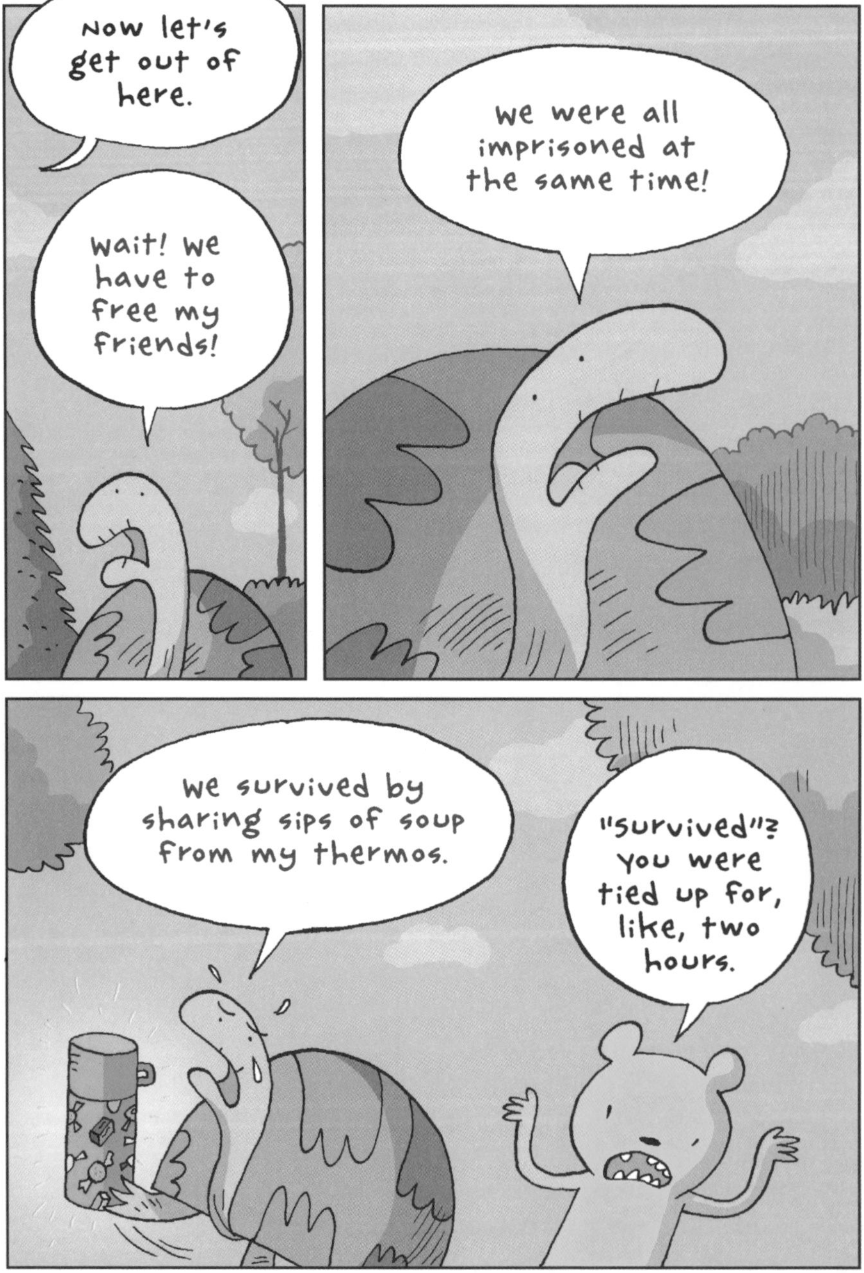
Now let's get out of here.
Wait! We have to free my friends!
We were all imprisoned at the same time!
We survived by sharing sips of soup from my thermos.
"Survived"? You were tied up for, like, two hours.

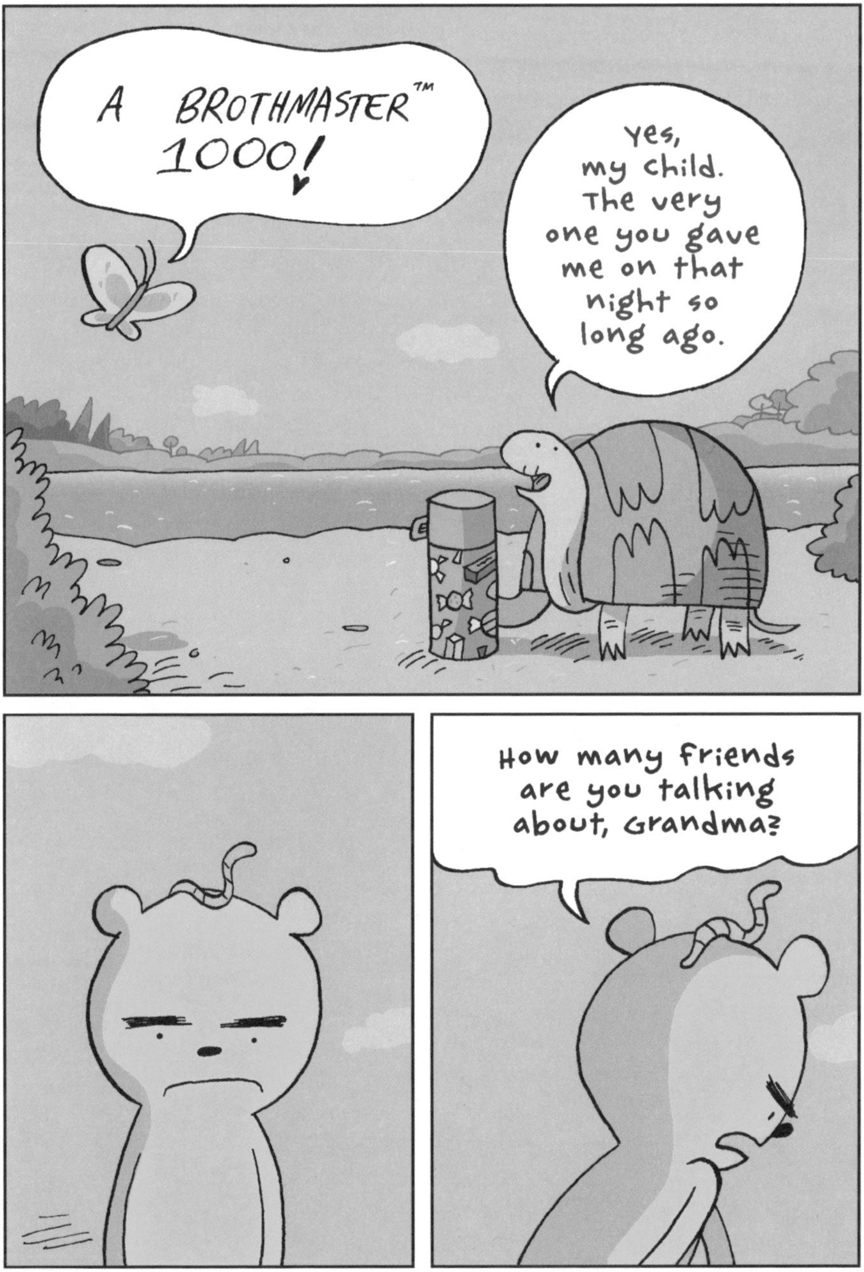
A BROTHMASTER™ 1000!
Yes, my child. The very one you gave me on that night so long ago.
How many friends are you talking about, Grandma?

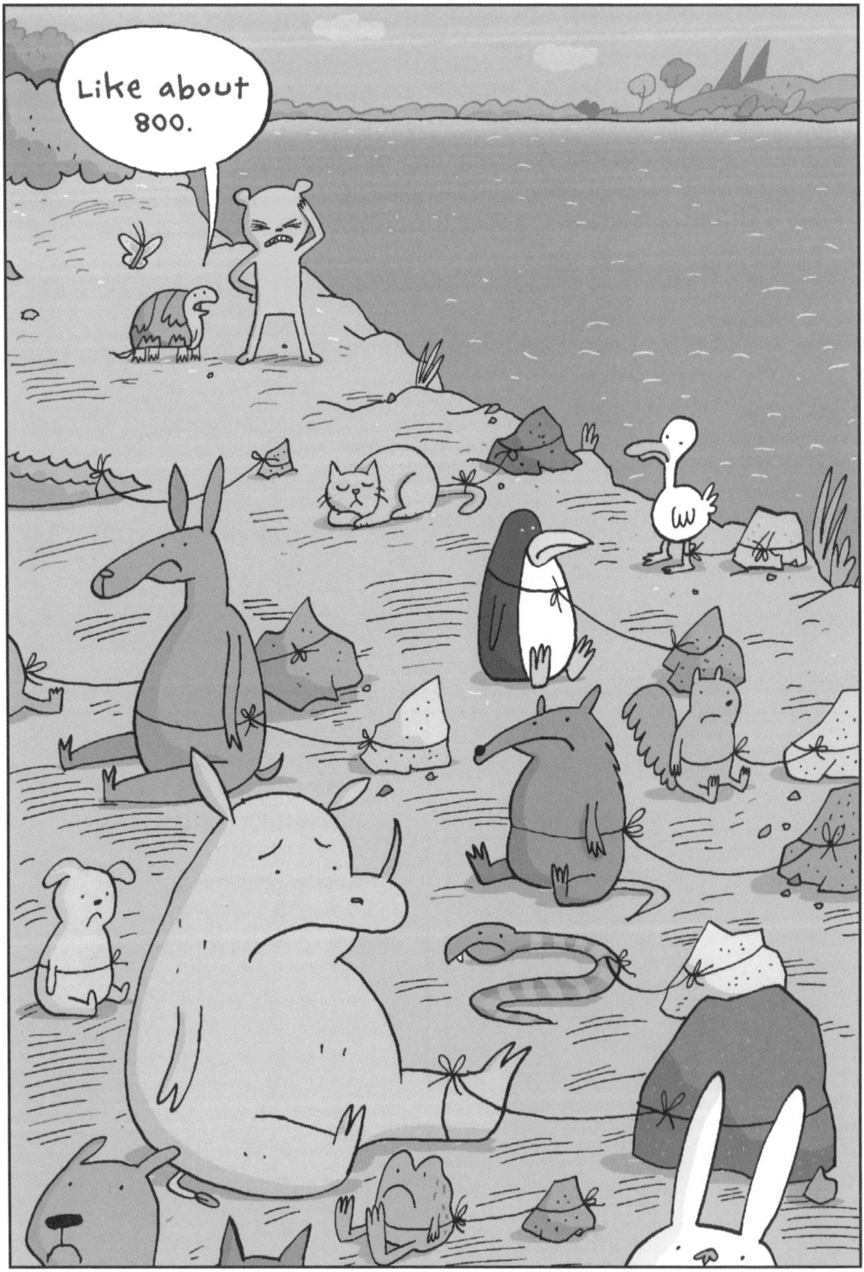
Like about 800.

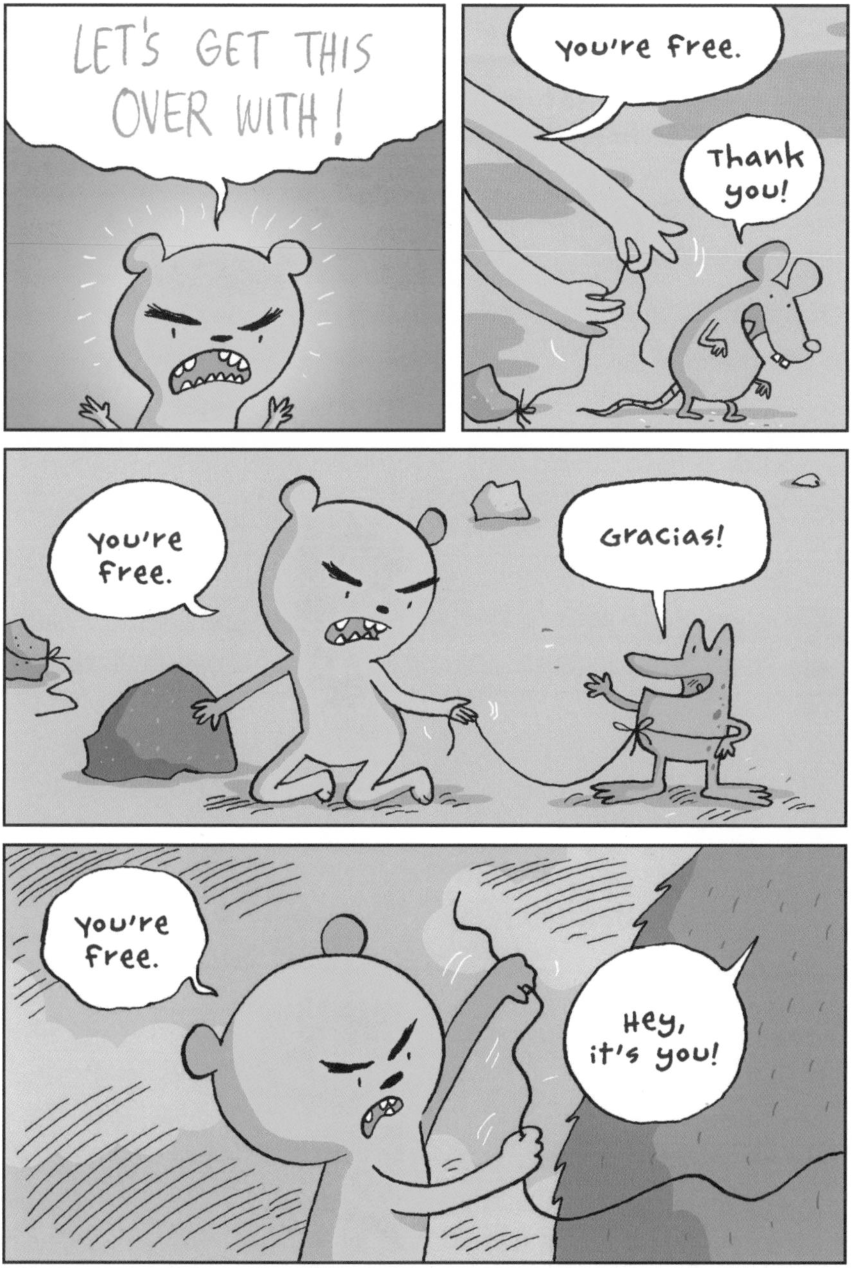
LET'S GET THIS OVER WITH!
You're free.
Thank you!
You're free.
Gracias!
You're free.
Hey, it's you!

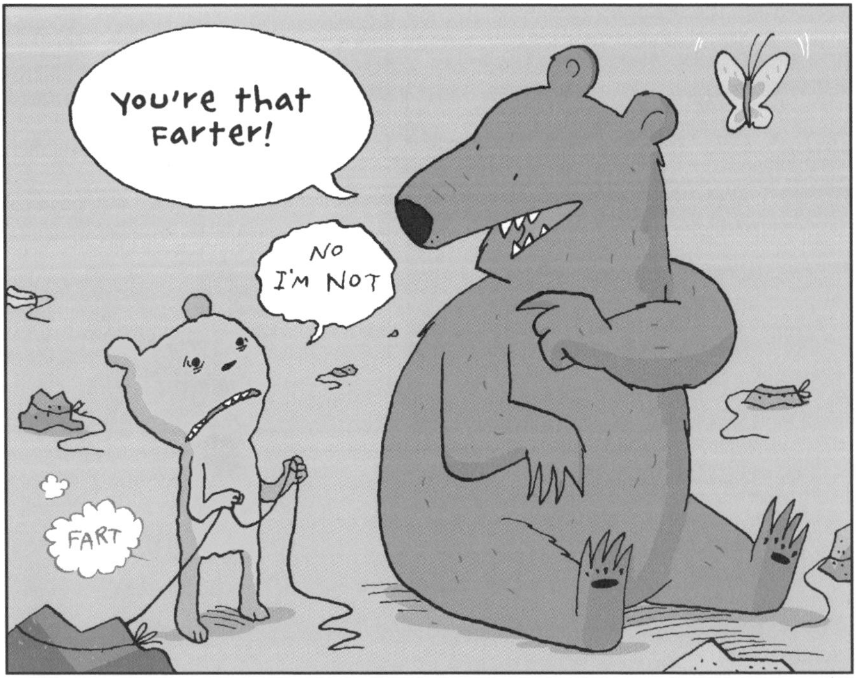
you're that Farter!
NO I'M NOT
FART

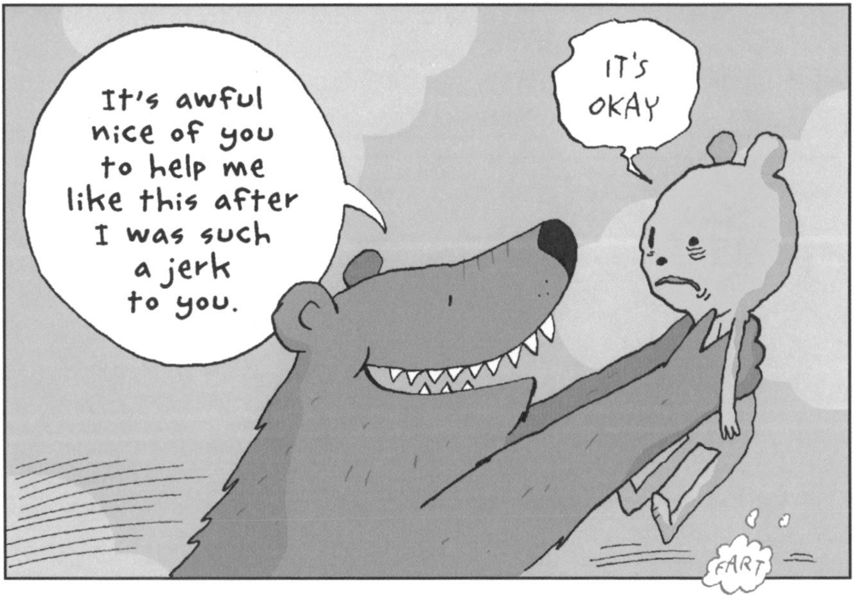
It's awful nice of you to help me like this after I was such a jerk to you.
IT'S OKAY
FART

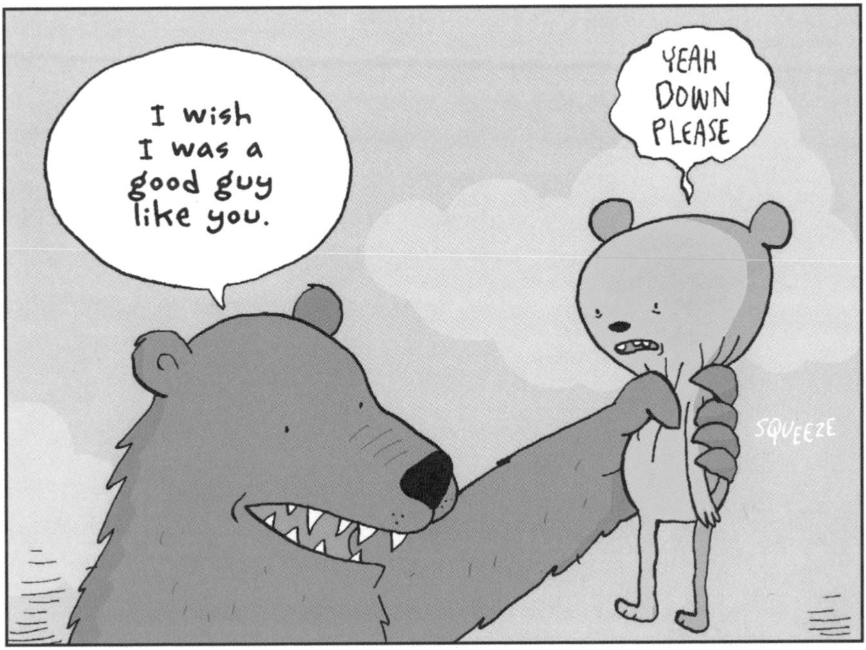
I wish I was a good guy like you.
YEAH DOWN PLEASE
SQUEEZE

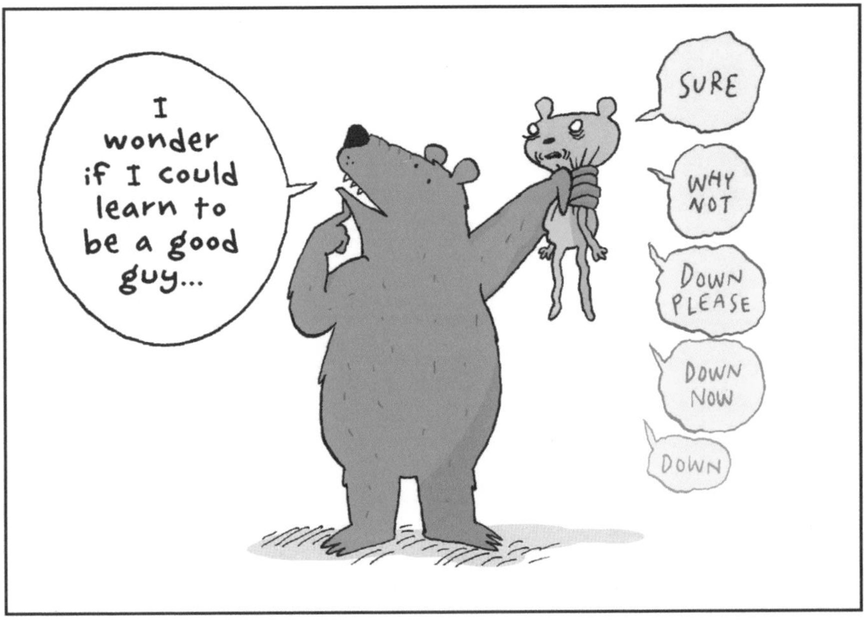
I wonder if I could learn to be a good guy...
SURE
WHY NOT
DOWN PLEASE
DOWN NOW
DOWN

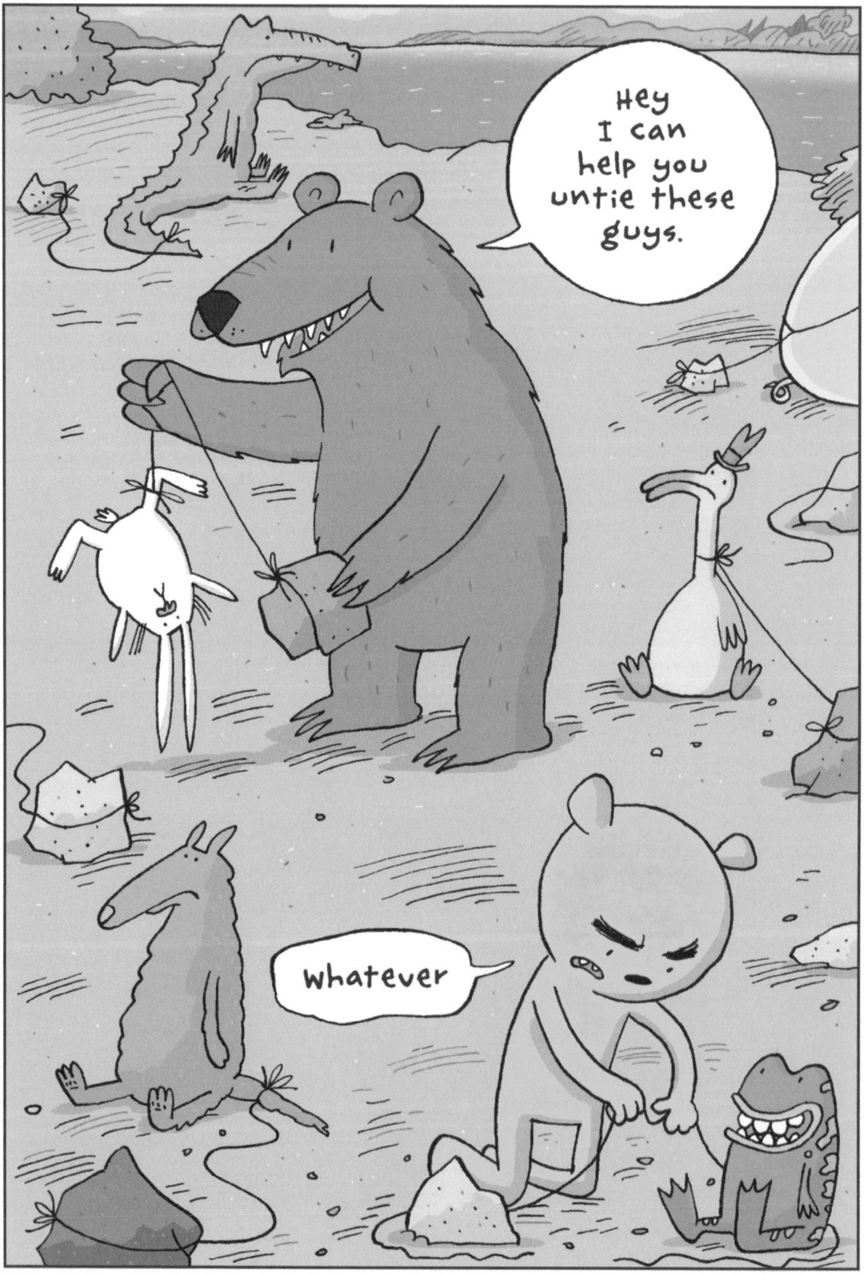
Hey I can help you untie these guys.
whatever

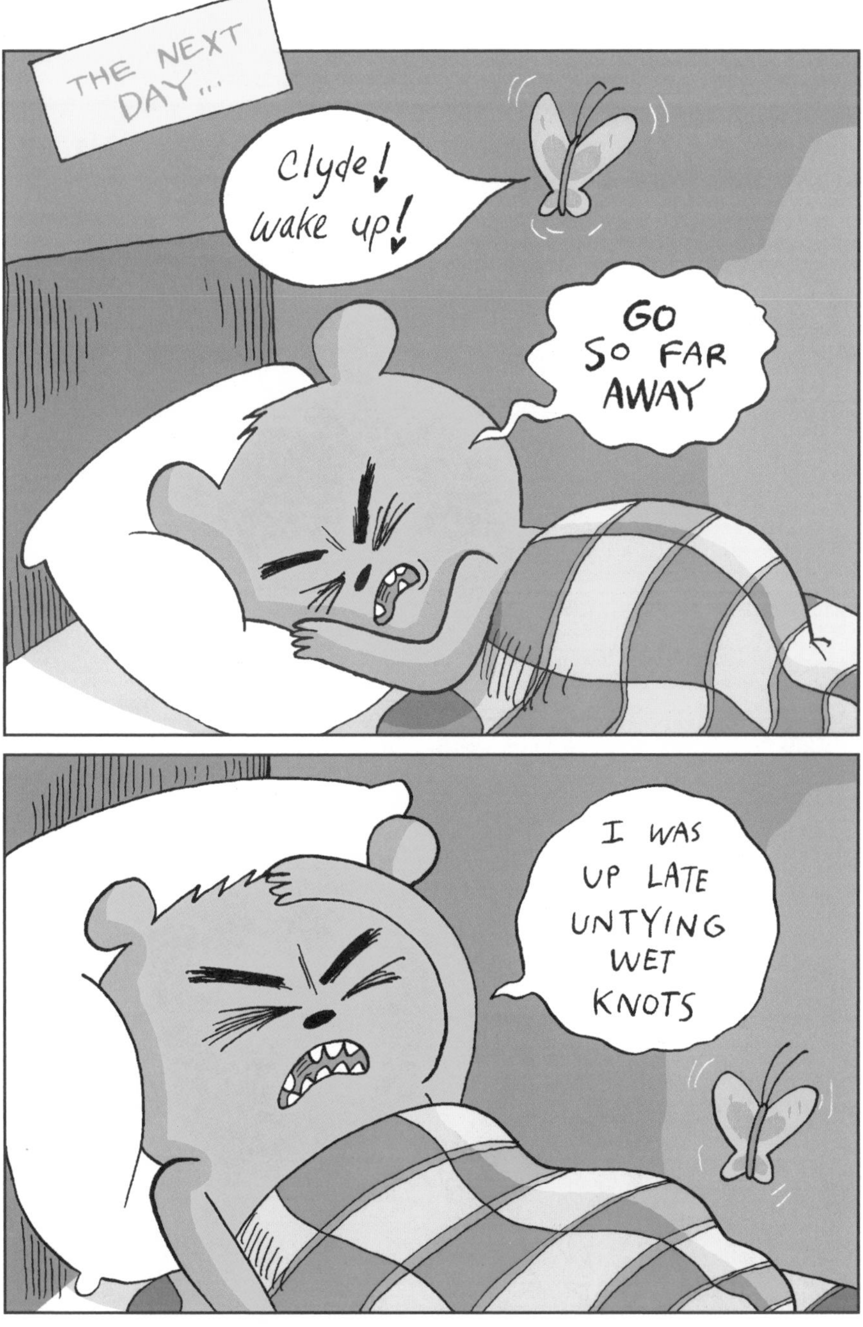
THE NEXT DAY...
Clyde! wake up!
GO SO FAR AWAY
I WAS UP LATE UNTYING WET KNOTS

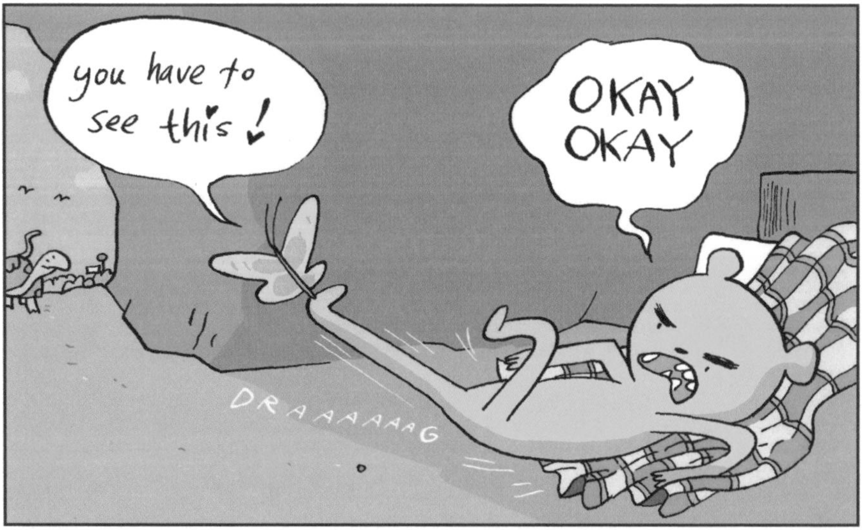
you have to see this!
OKAY OKAY
DRAAAAAAG

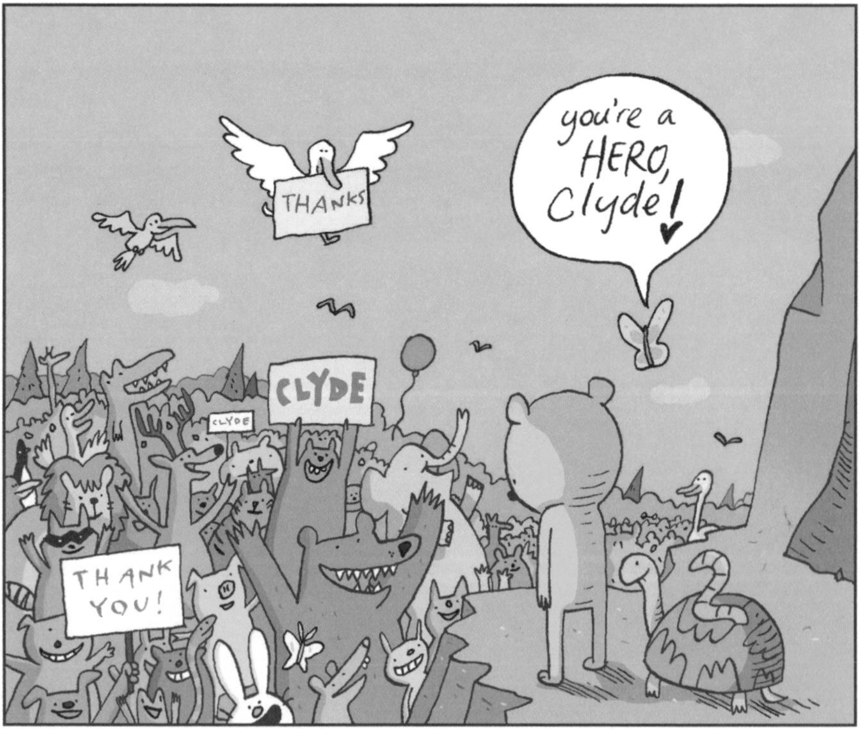
THANKS
you're a HERO, Clyde!
CLYDE
CLYDE
THANK YOU!

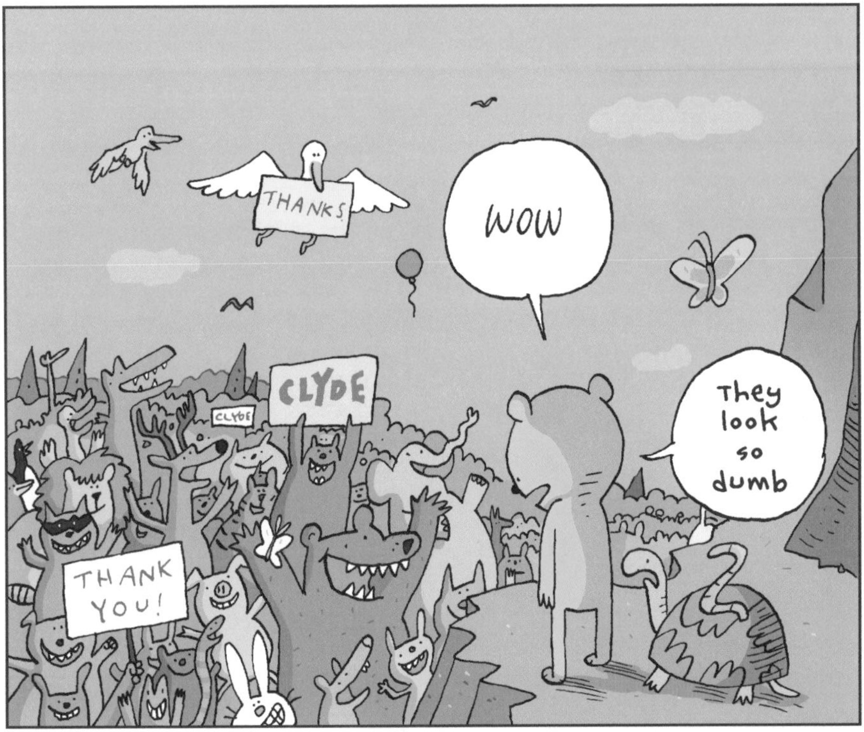
THANKS
WOW
CLYDE
CLYDE
They look so dumb
THANK YOU!

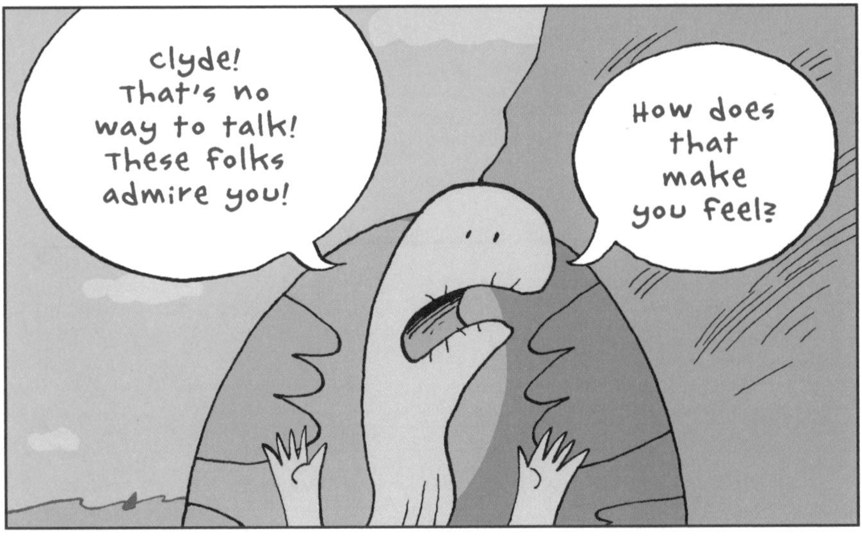
clyde! That's no way to talk! These folks admire you!
How does that make you feel?

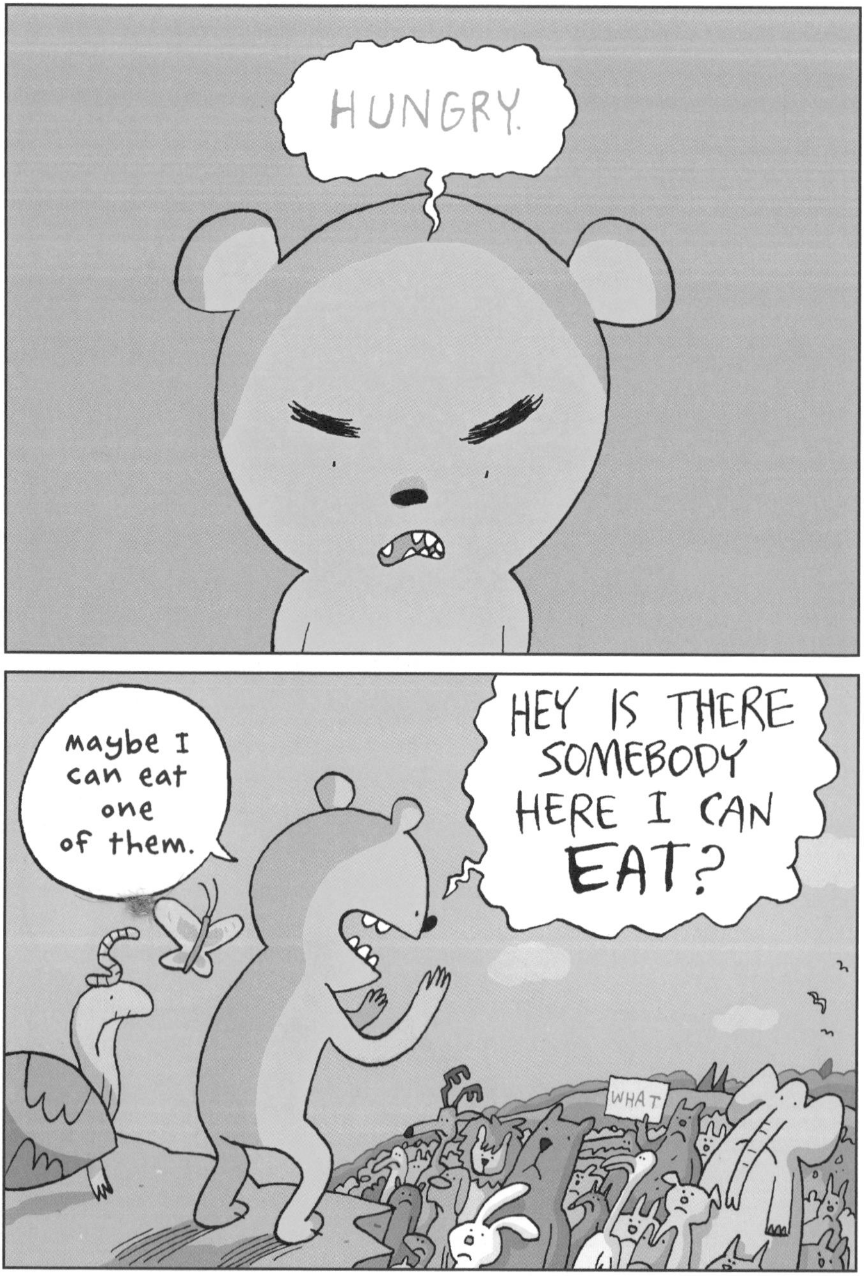
HUNGRY.
maybe I can eat one of them.
HEY IS THERE SOMEBODY HERE I CAN EAT?
WHAT

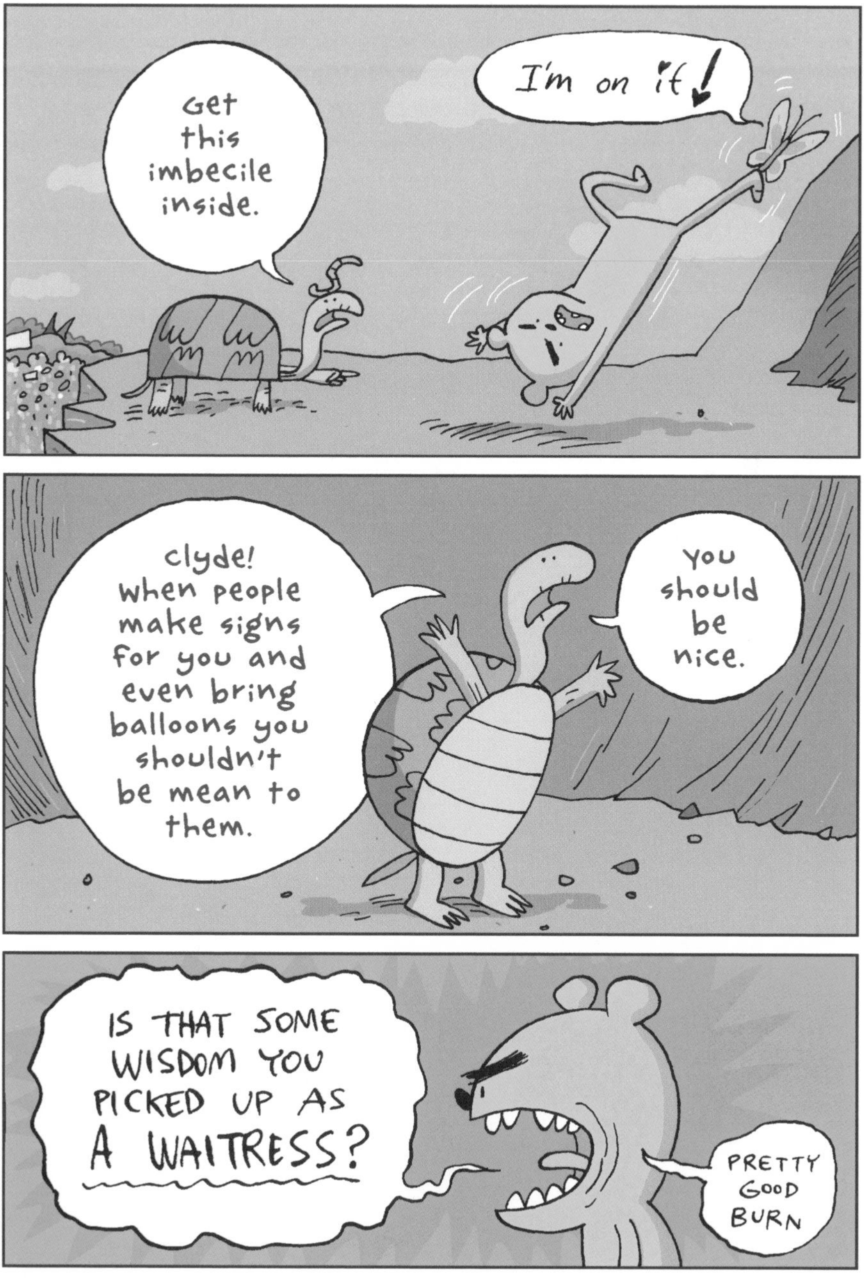
Get this imbecile inside.
I'm on it!
clyde! when people make signs for you and even bring balloons you shouldn't be mean to them.
You should be nice.
IS THAT SOME WISDOM YOU PICKED UP AS A WAITRESS?
PRETTY GOOD BURN

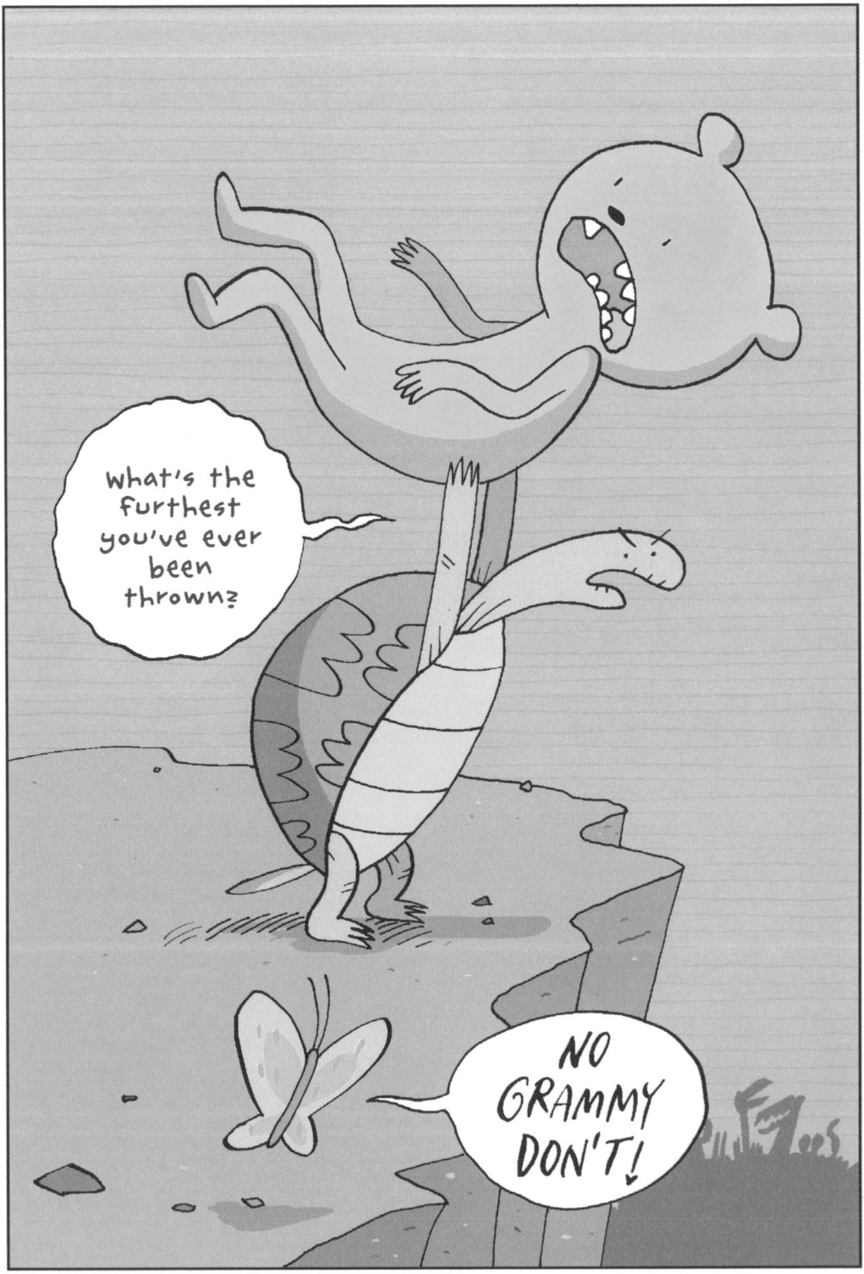
What's the furthest you've ever been thrown?
NO GRAMMY DON'T!

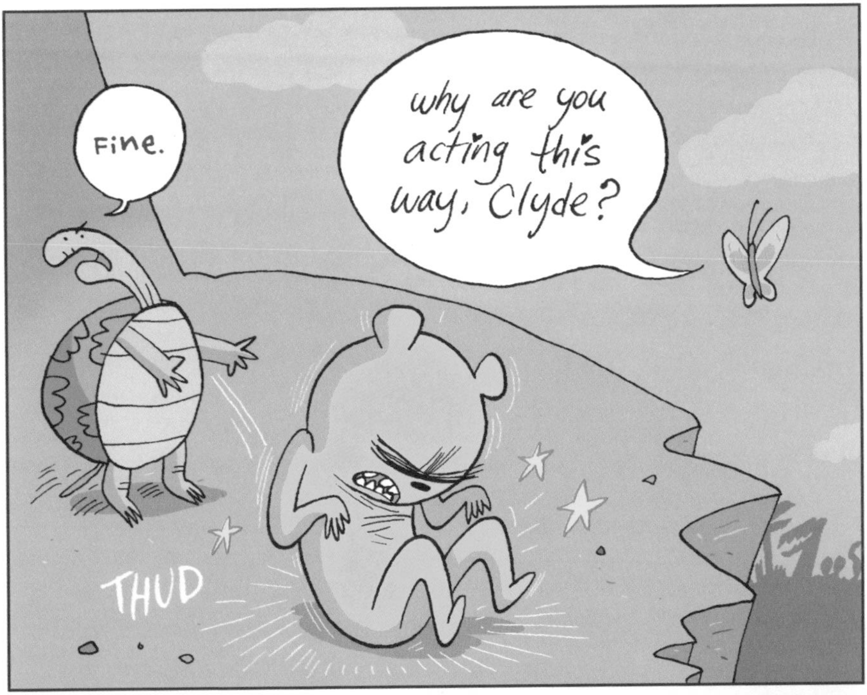
Fine.
why are you acting this way, Clyde?
THUD

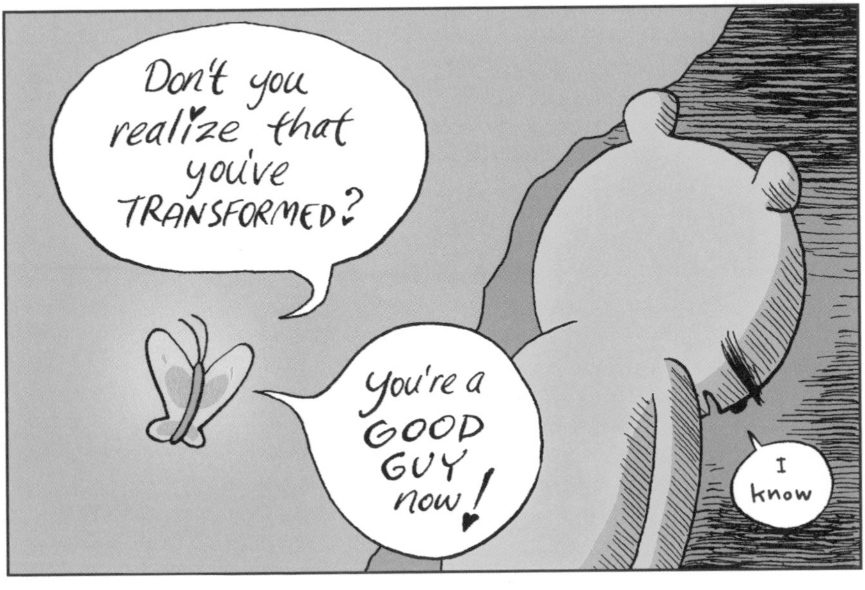
Don't you realize that you've TRANSFORMED?
You're a GOOD GUY now!
I know

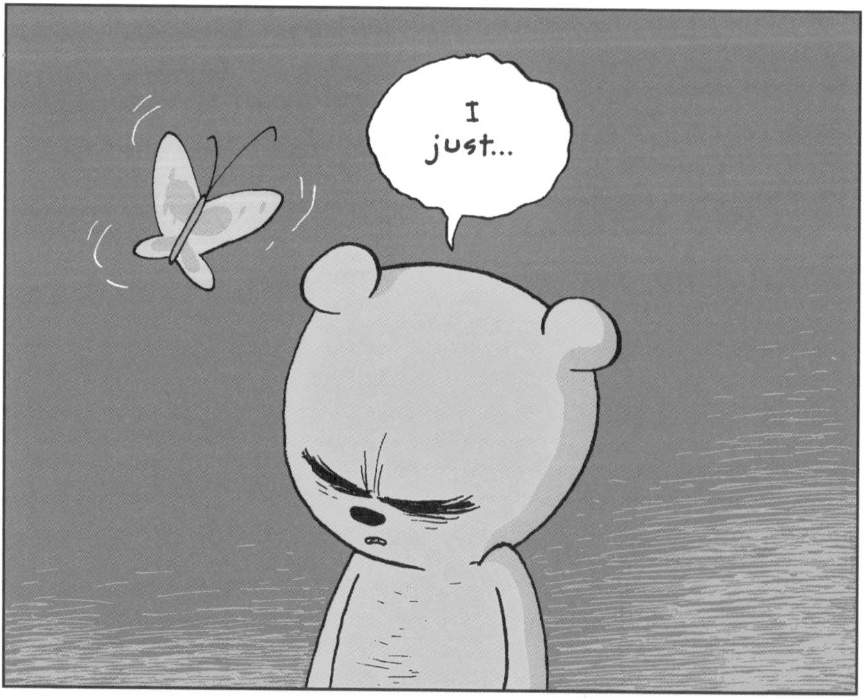
I just...

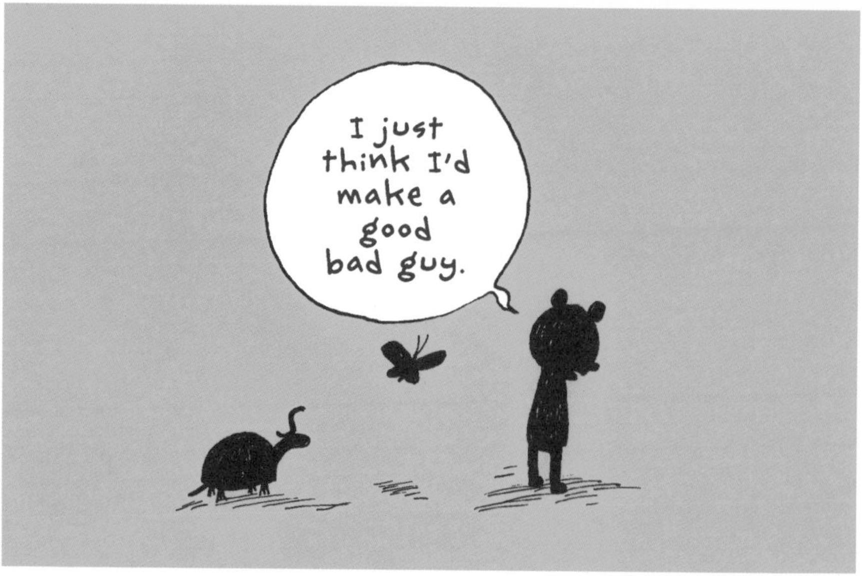
I just think I'd make a good bad guy.

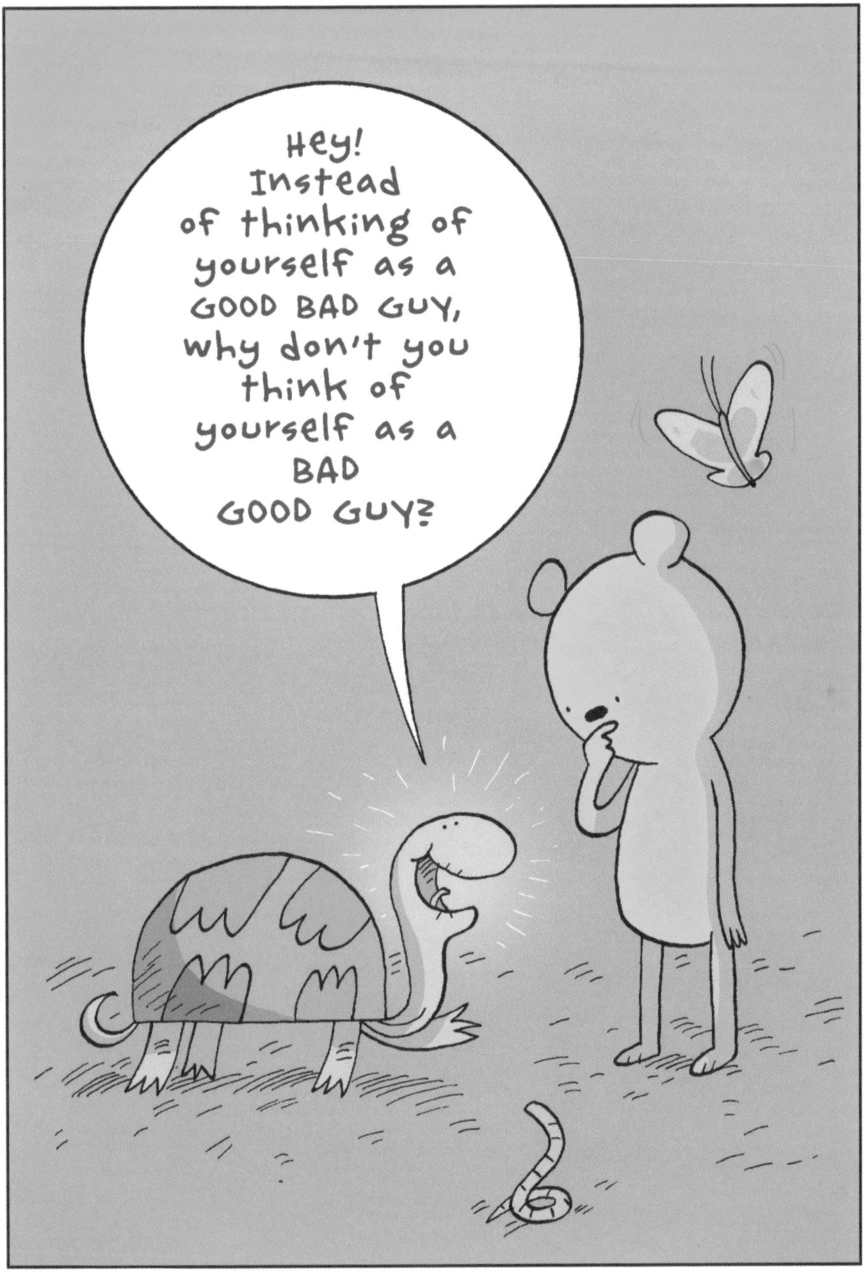
Hey! Instead of thinking of yourself as a GOOD BAD GUY, why don't you think of yourself as a BAD GOOD GUY?

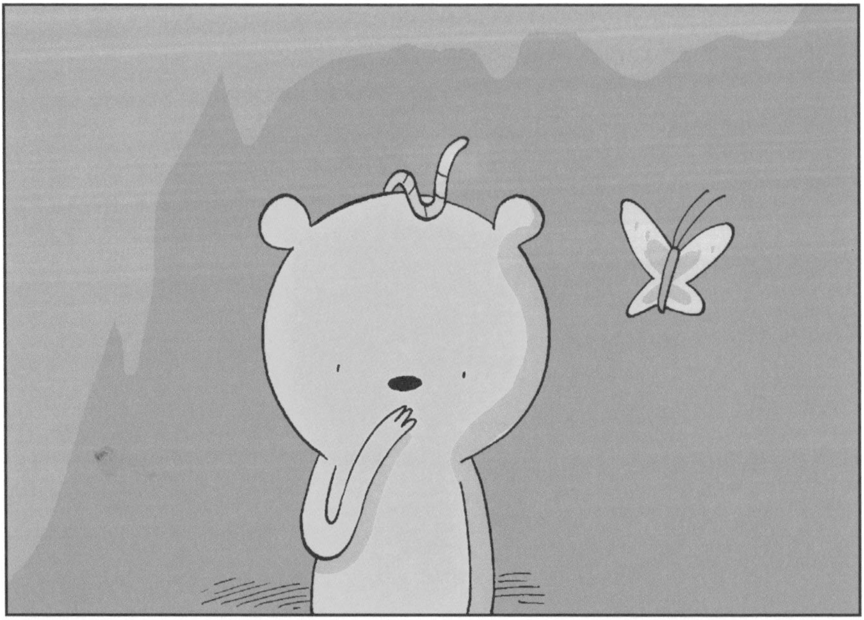

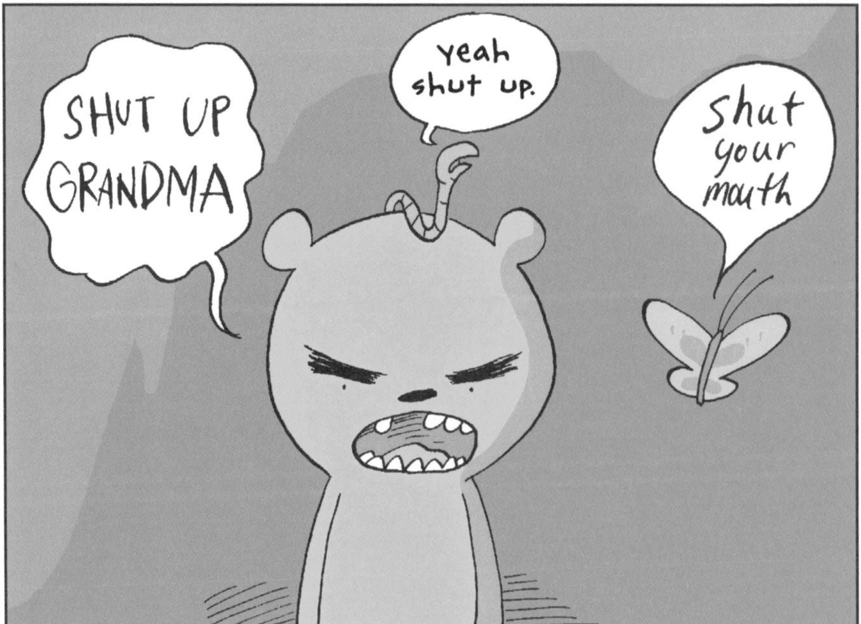
SHUT UP GRANDMA
yeah shut up.
Shut your mouth

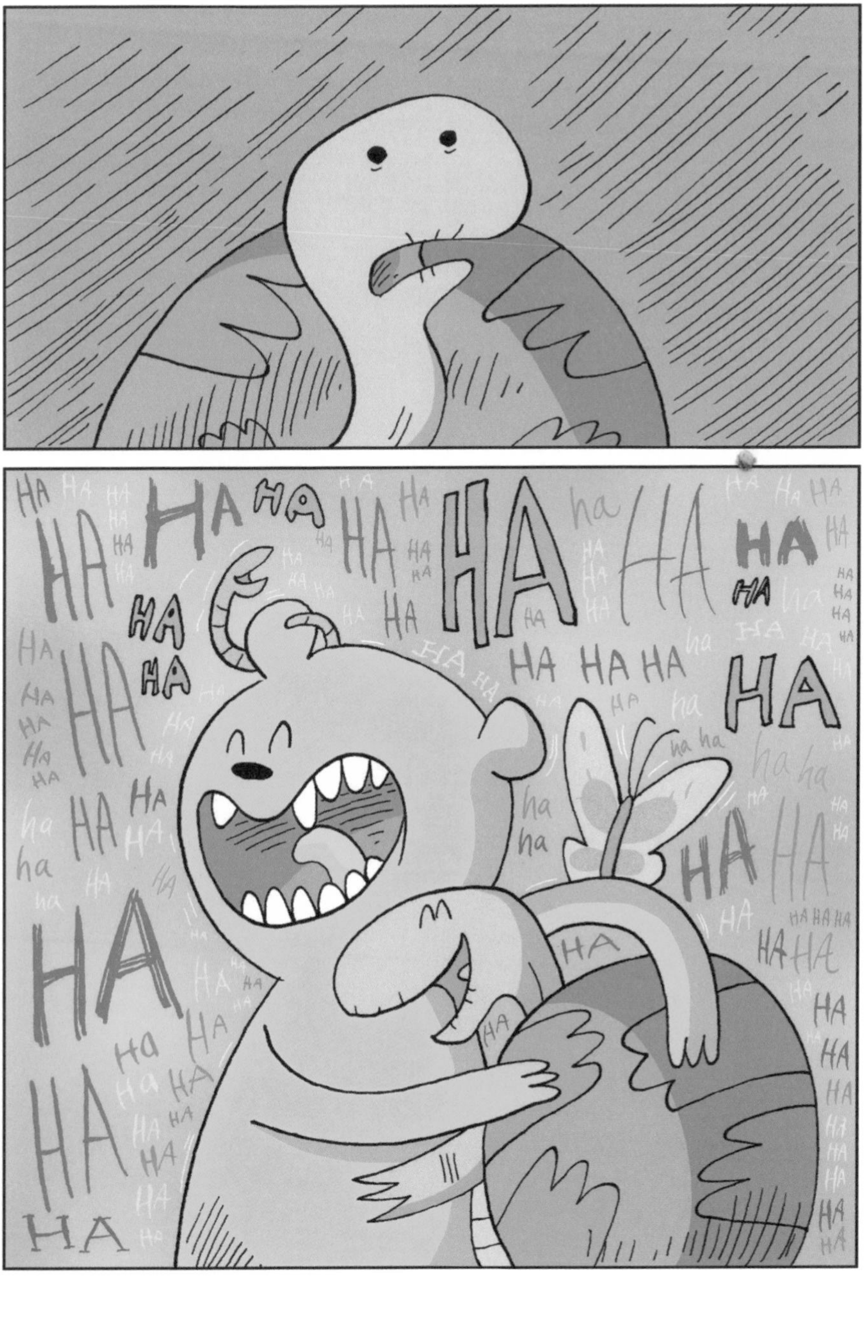
HA HA HA HA HA HA HA HA HA HA ha HA HA HA
HA HA HA HA HA HA HA HA HA HA HA HA
HA HA HA HA HA HA HA
HA HA HA HA HA HA HA
HA HA HA HA HA HA HA ha HA
ha ha ha ha
ha ha HA HA HA HA HA
HA HA HA HA HA HA
ha ha HA HA HA HA HA HA
HA HA HA HA HA HA HA HA HA HA HA
HA HA HA HA HA HA HA HA

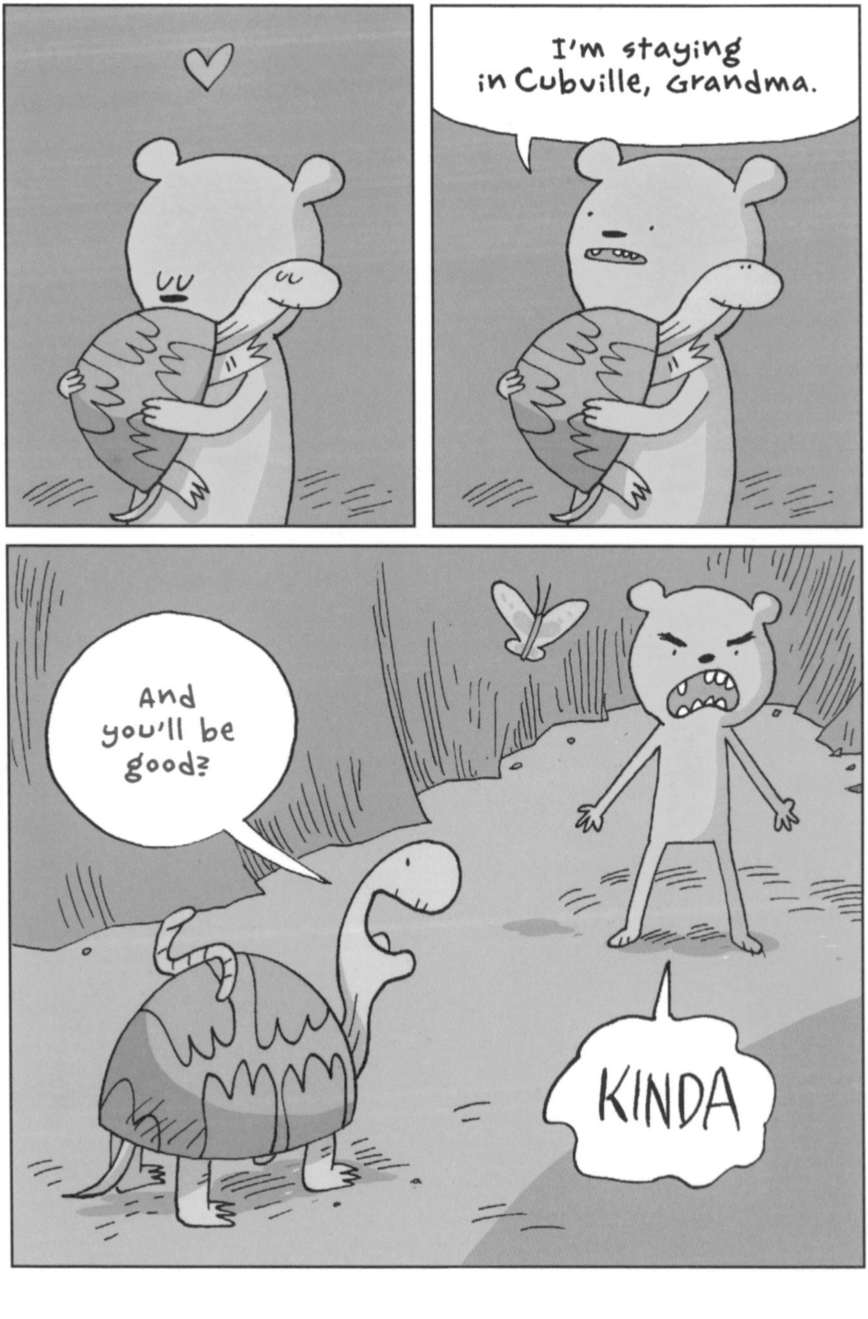
I'm staying in Cubville, Grandma.
And you'll be good?
KINDA

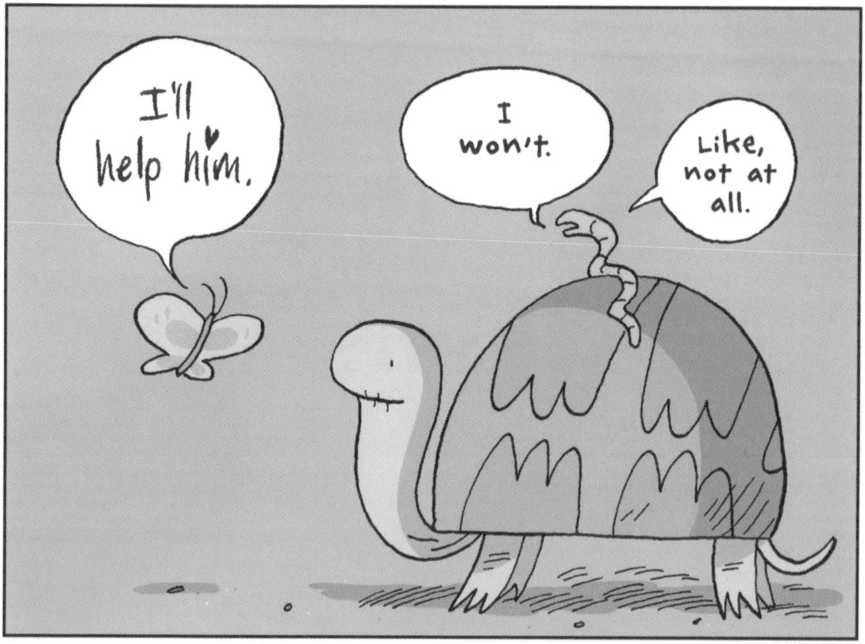
I'll help him.
I won't.
Like, not at all.

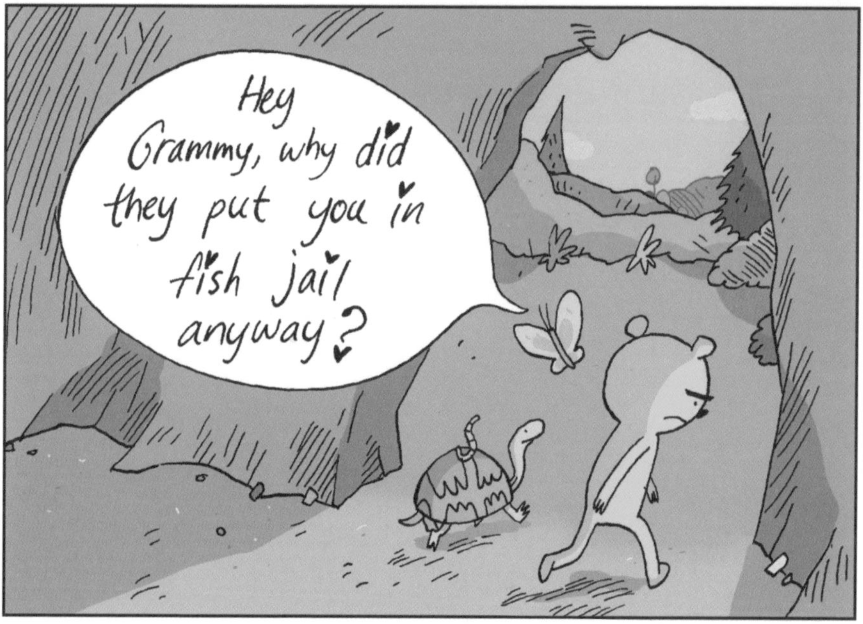
Hey Grammy, why did they put you in fish jail anyway?

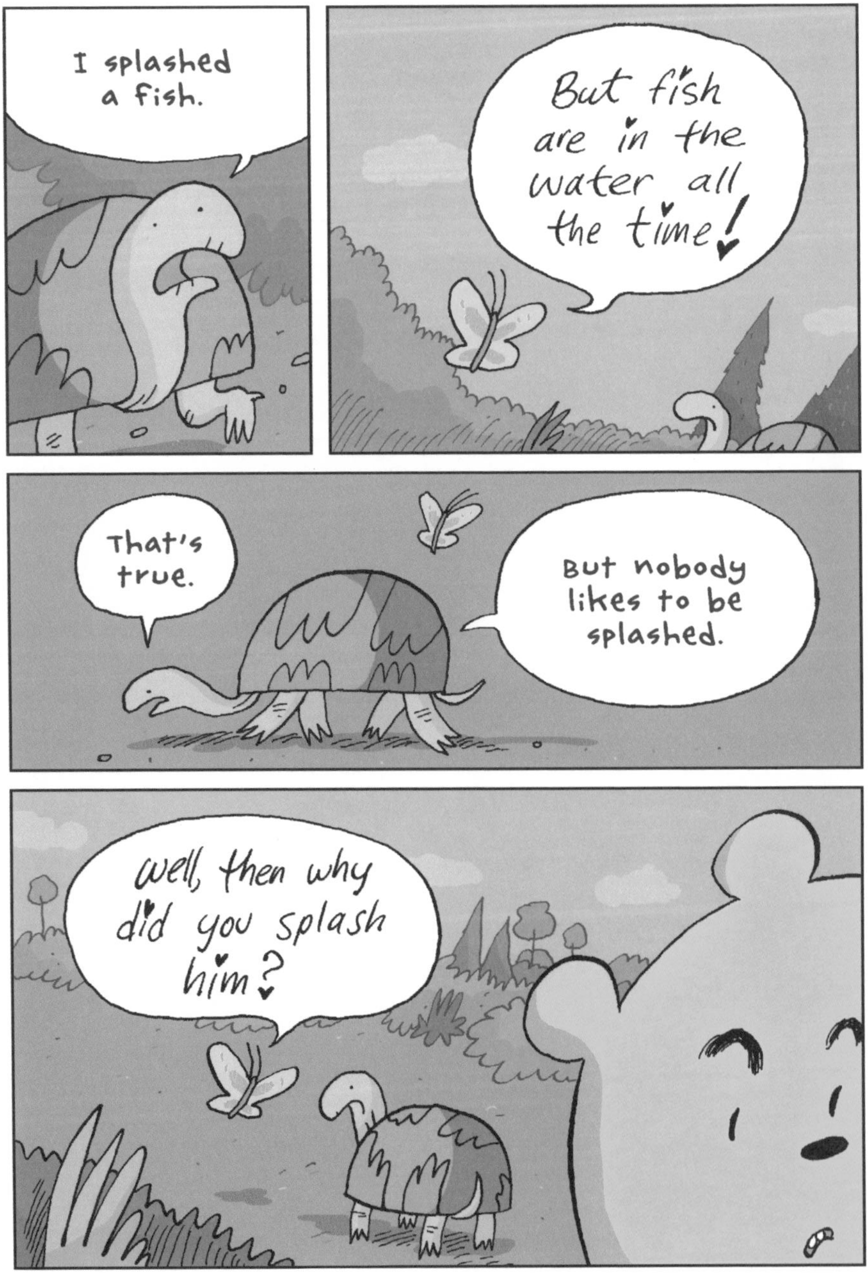
I splashed a fish.
But fish are in the water all the time!
That's true.
But nobody likes to be splashed.
well, then why did you splash him?

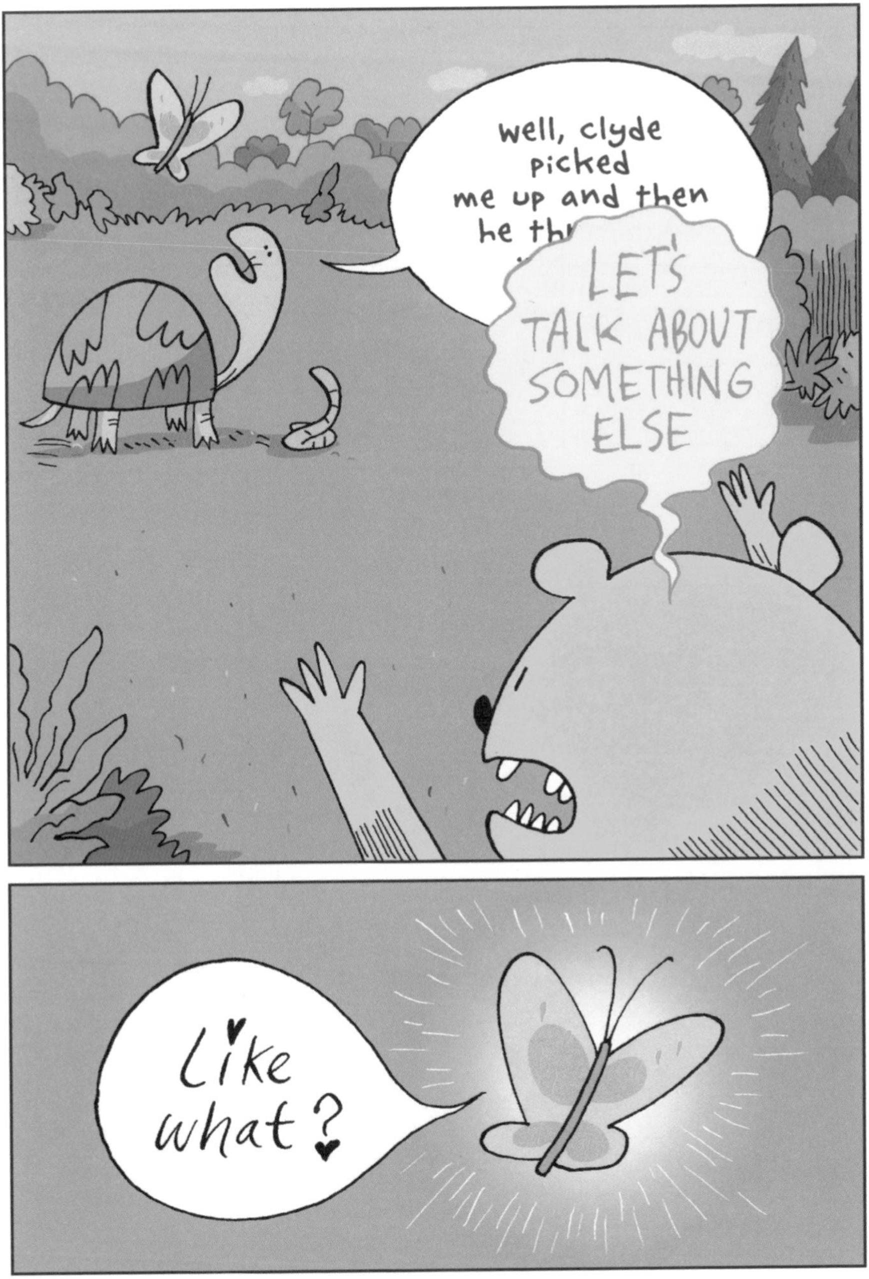
well, clyde picked me up and then he
LET'S TALK ABOUT SOMETHING ELSE
Like what?

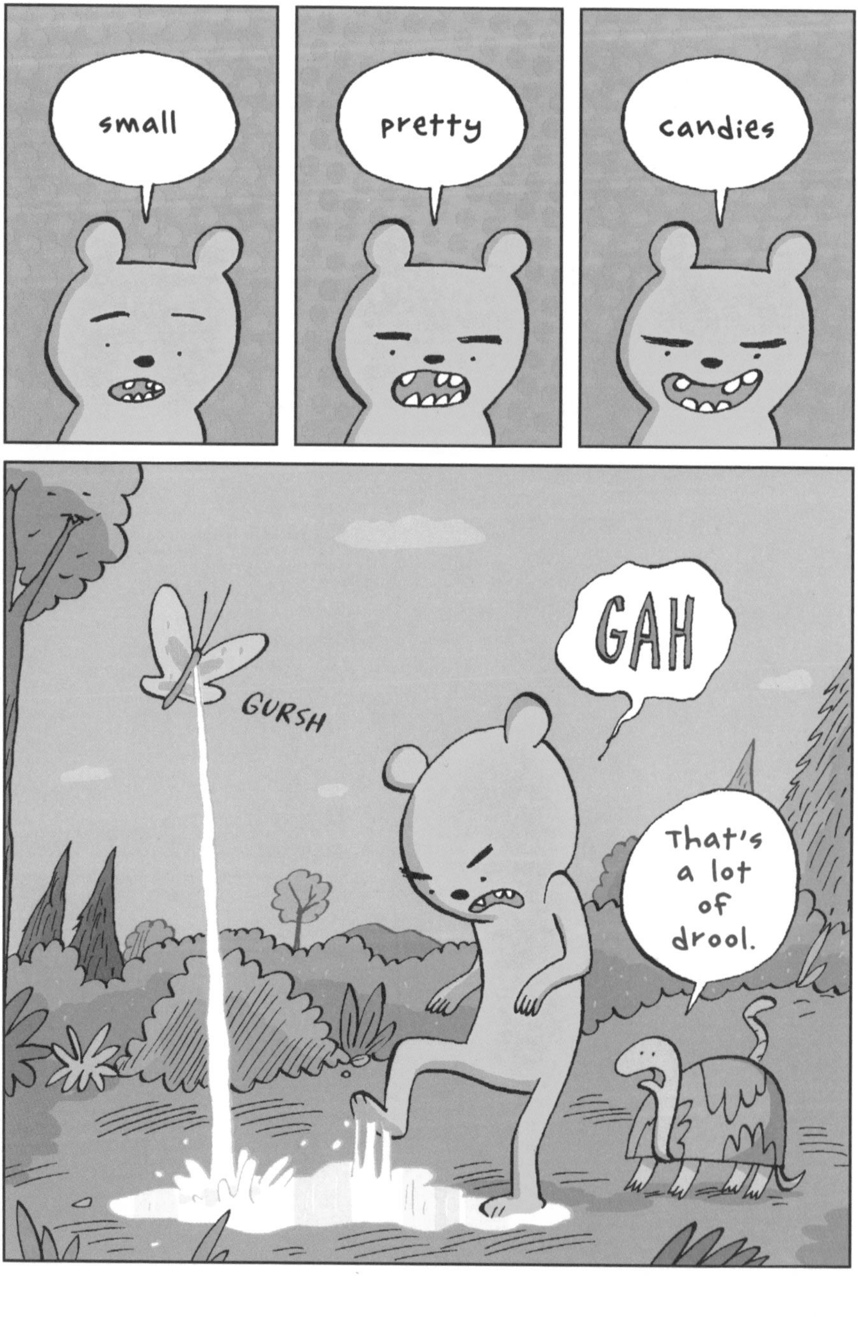
small
pretty
candies
GURSH
GAH
That's a lot of drool.

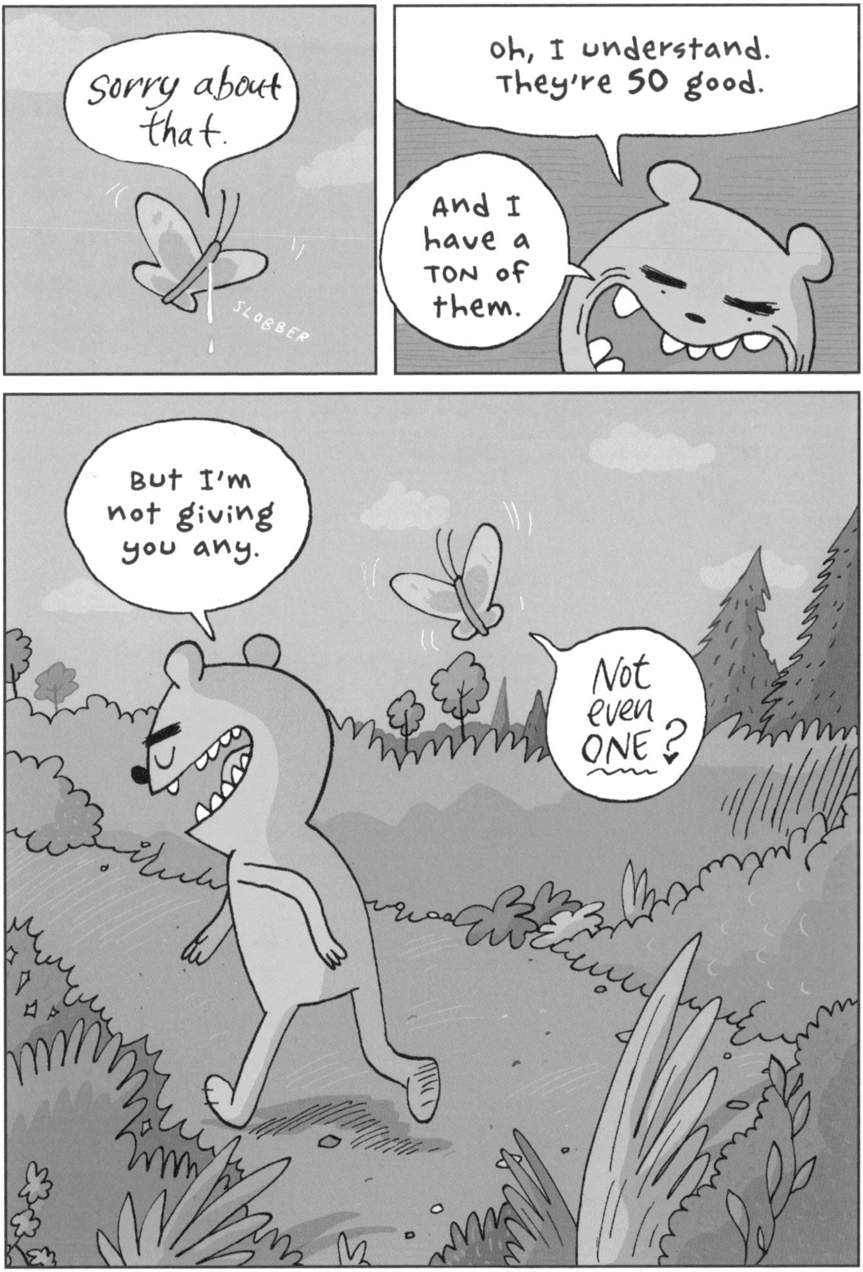
Sorry about that.
SLOBBER
Oh, I understand. They're SO good.
And I have a TON of them.
But I'm not giving you any.
Not even ONE?

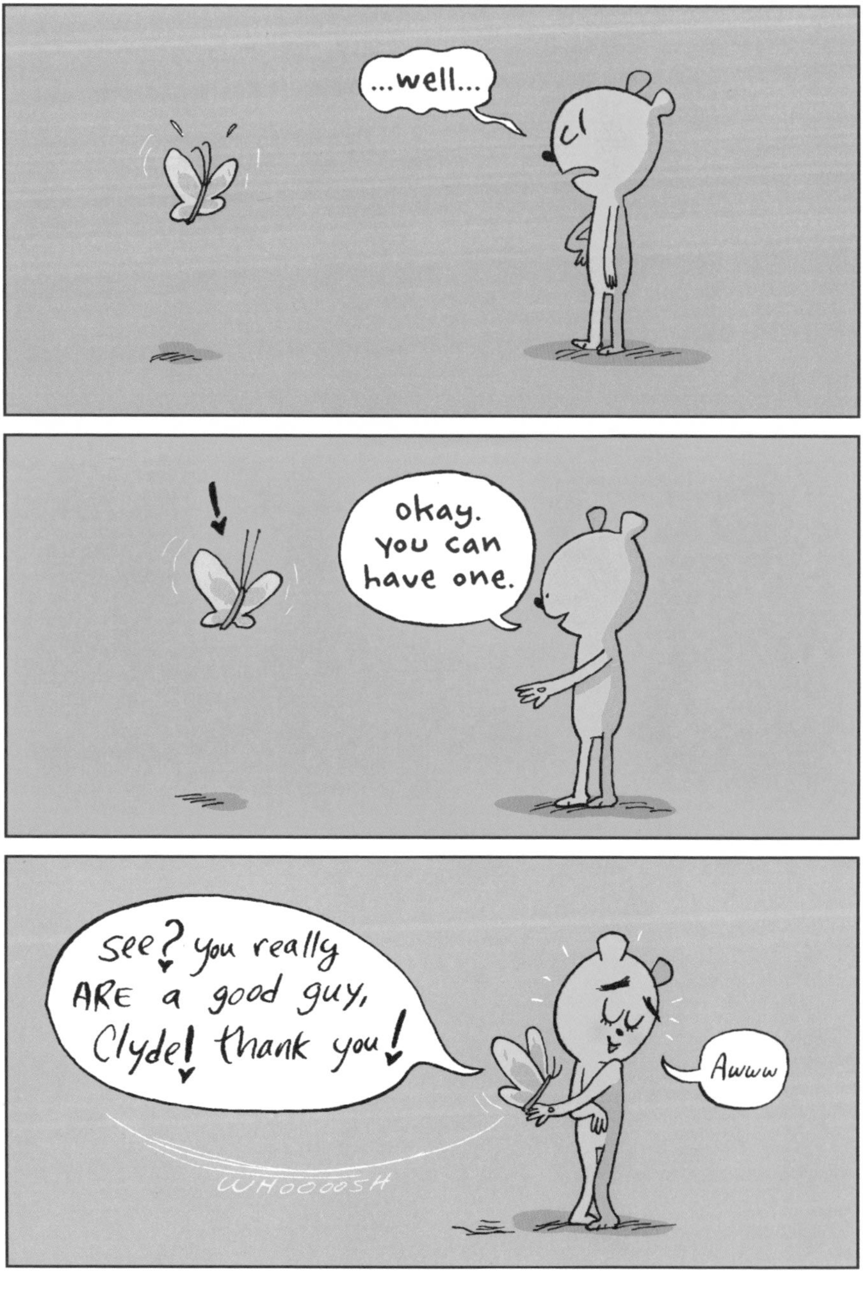
...well...
okay. you can have one.
see? you really ARE a good guy, Clyde! thank you!
Awww
WHOOOOSH

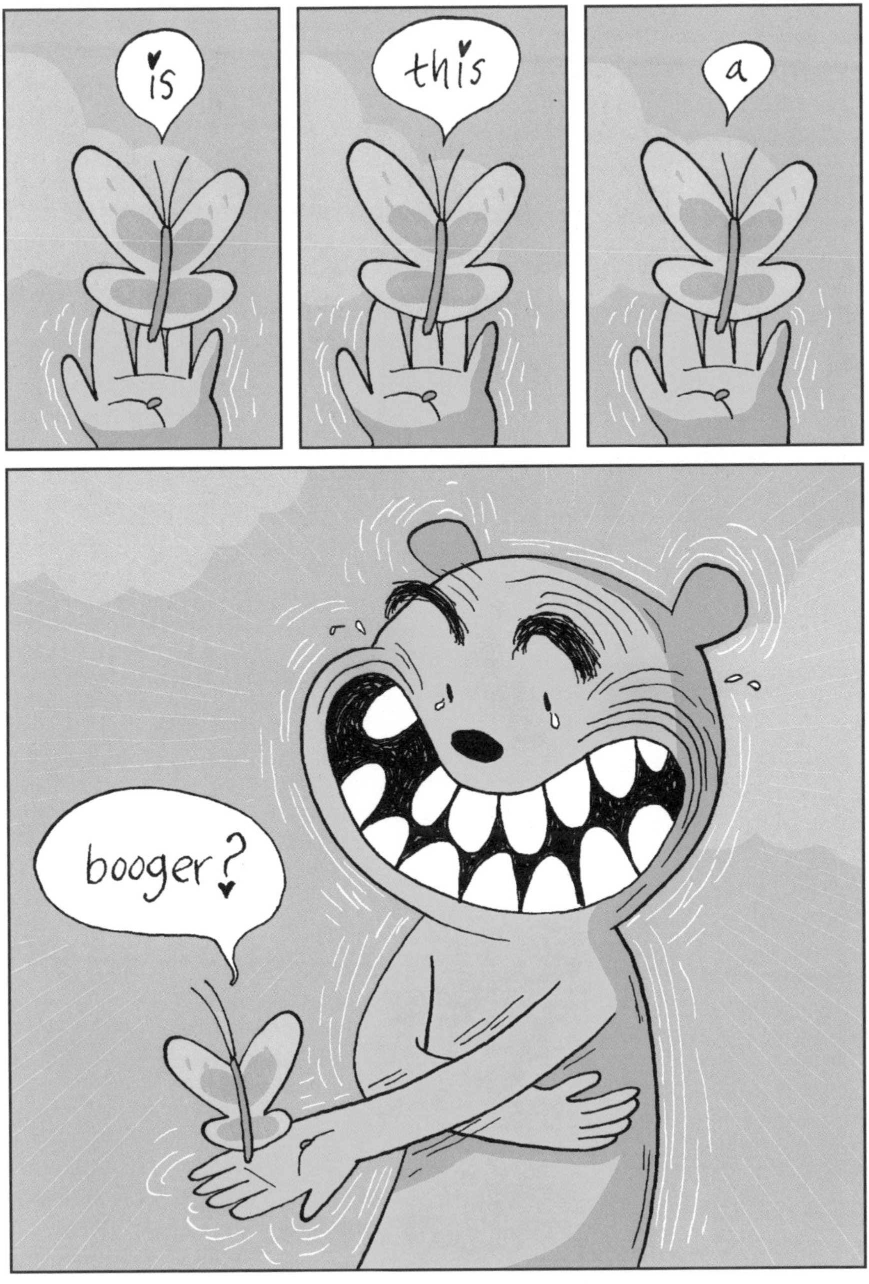
is
this
a
booger?

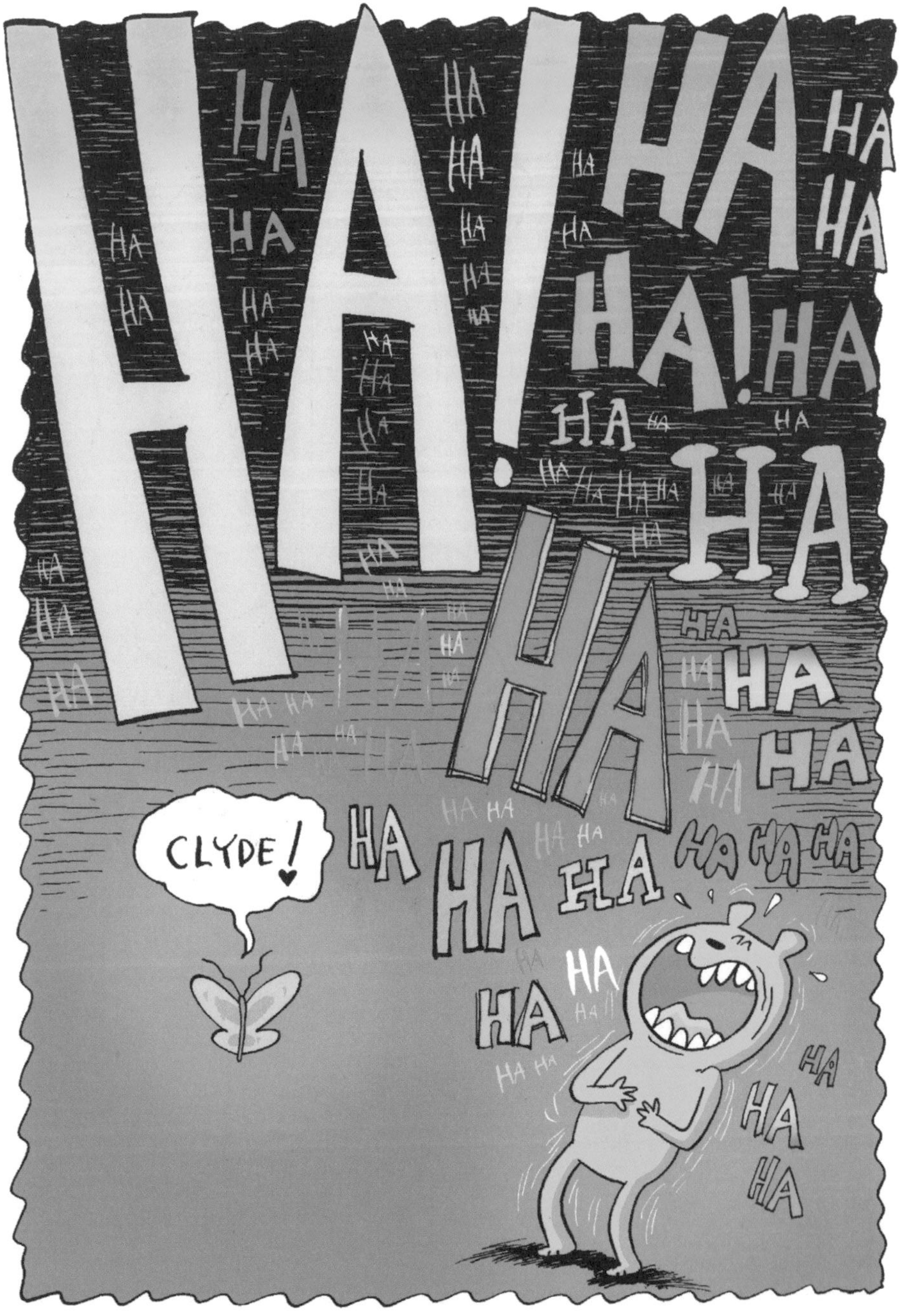
HA!HA!HA!HA
HA HA HA HA HA HA HA
CLYDE!♥
HA HA HA HA HA HA HA

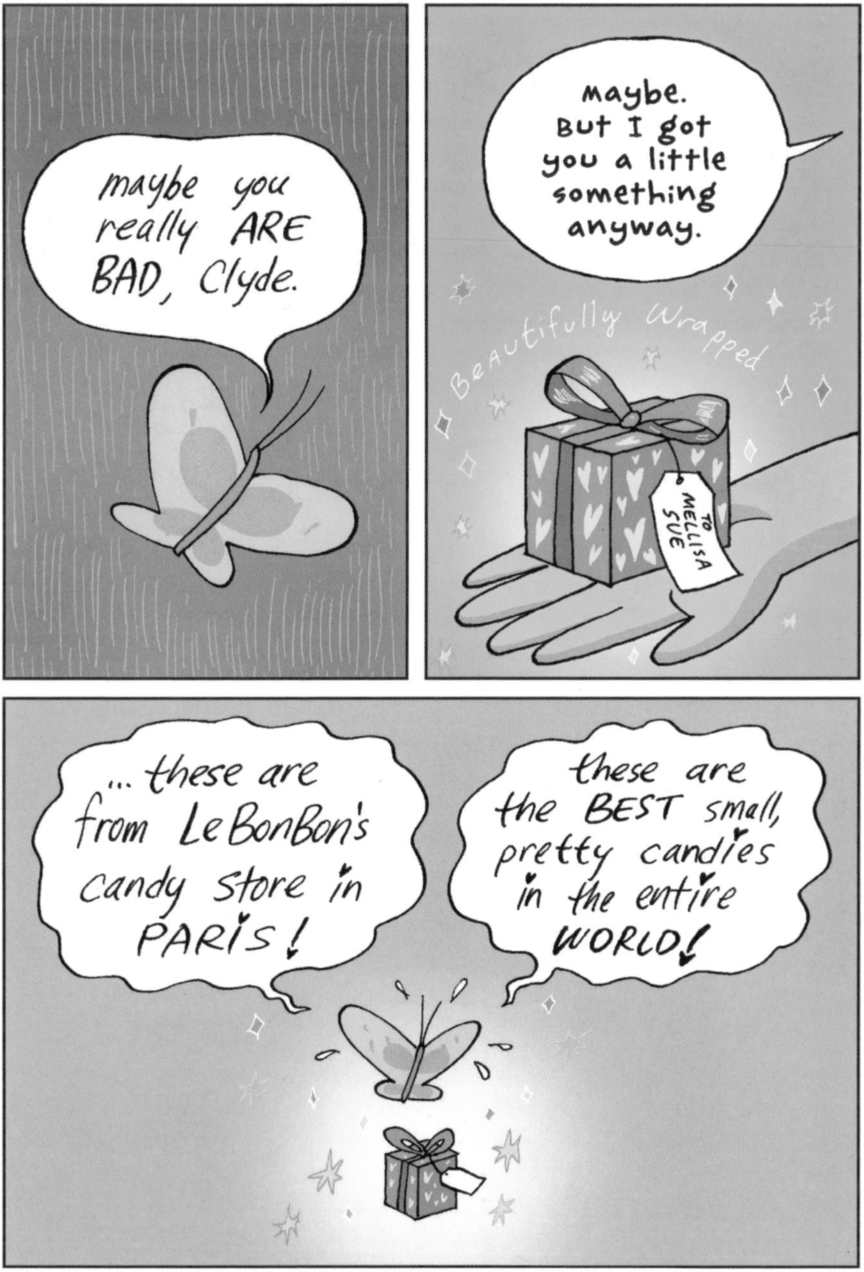
maybe you really ARE BAD, Clyde.
maybe. But I got you a little something anyway.
Beautifully Wrapped
TO MELLISA SUE
... these are from Le BonBon's candy store in PARIS!
these are the BEST small, pretty candies in the entire WORLD!

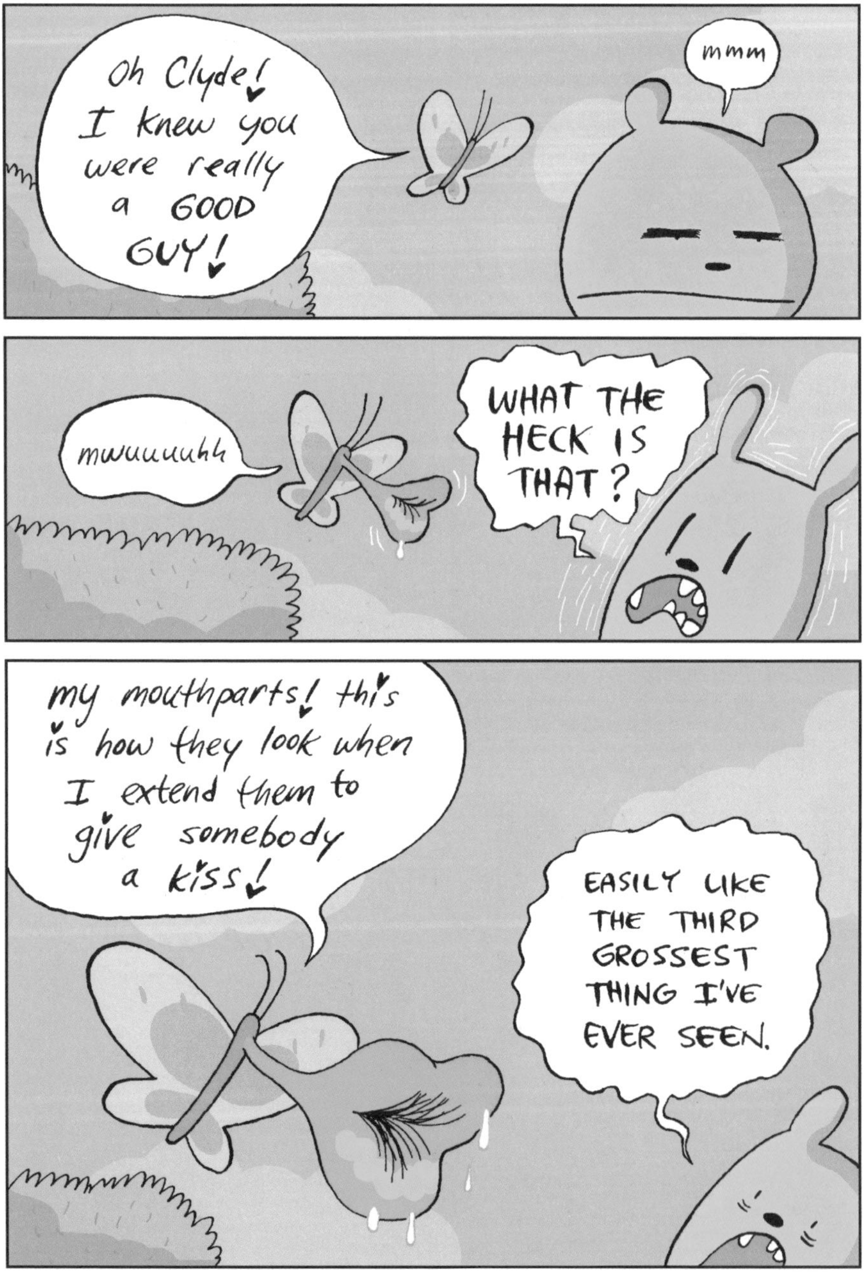
Oh Clyde! I knew you were really a GOOD GUY!
mmm
mwuuuuhh
WHAT THE HECK IS THAT?
my mouthparts! this is how they look when I extend them to give somebody a kiss!
EASILY LIKE THE THIRD GROSSEST THING I'VE EVER SEEN.

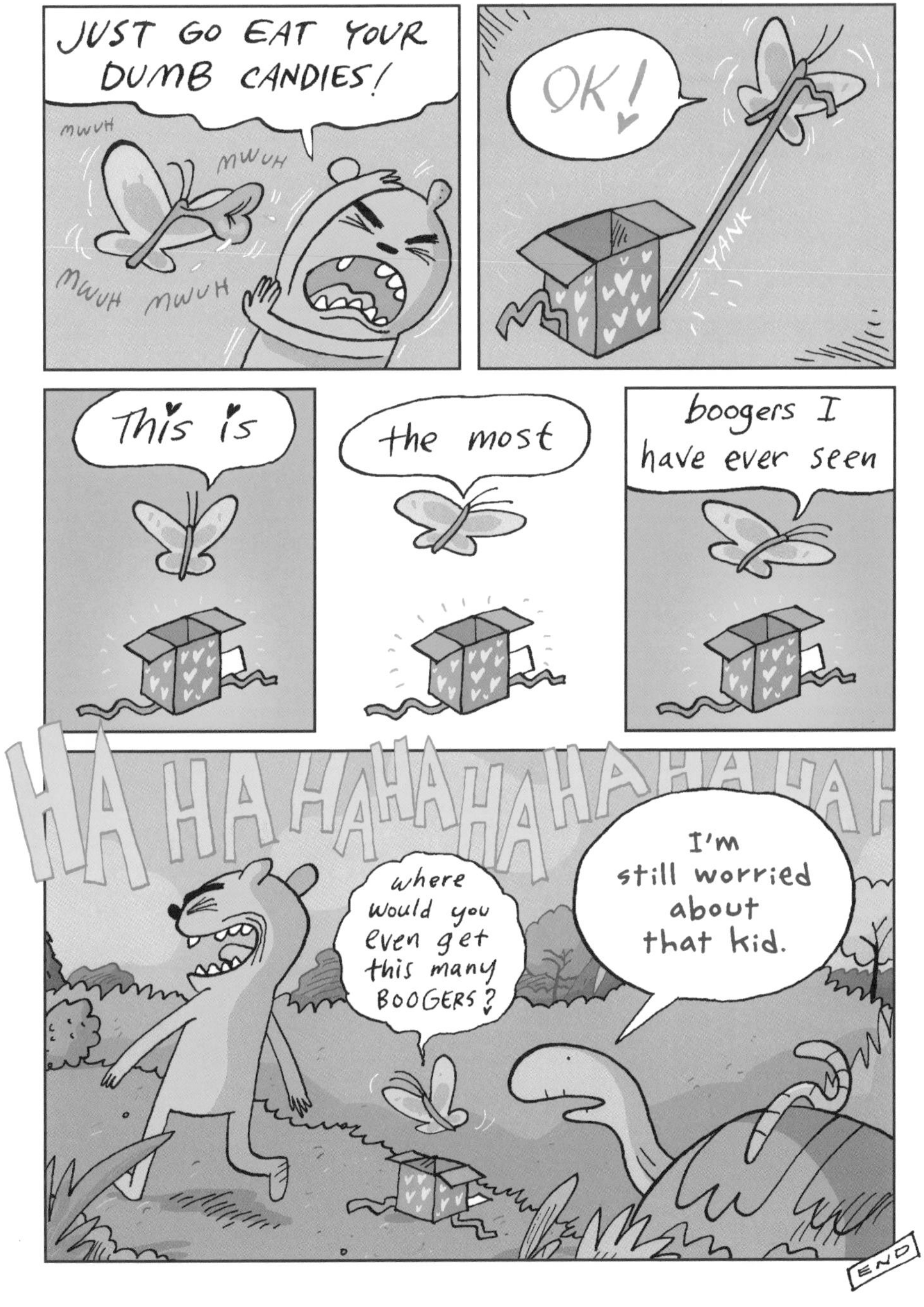
JUST GO EAT YOUR DUMB CANDIES!
MWUH
MWUH
MWUH MWUH
OK!
YANK
This is
the most
boogers I have ever seen
HA HA HAHAHAHAHAHAHA
where would you even get this many BOOGERS?
I'm still worried about that kid.
END